A girl called London

by Clare Lydon

custard
books

First Edition June 2017
Published by Custard Books
Copyright © 2017 Clare Lydon
ISBN: 978-1-912019-56-4

Cover Design: Kevin Pruitt
Editor: Laura Kingsley
Copy Editor: Gill Mullins
Typesetting: Adrian McLaughlin

Find out more at: www.clarelydon.co.uk
Follow me on Twitter: @clarelydon
Follow me on Instagram: @clarefic

Also by Clare

London Romance Series
London Calling (Book 1)
This London Love (Book 2)
The London Of Us (Book 4)
London, Actually (Book 5)
Made In London (Book 6)

Other Novels
The Long Weekend
Nothing To Lose: A Lesbian Romance
Twice In A Lifetime
Once Upon A Princess
You're My Kind

All I Want Series
All I Want For Christmas (Book 1)
All I Want For Valentine's (Book 2)
All I Want For Spring (Book 3)
All I Want For Summer (Book 4)
All I Want For Autumn (Book 5)
All I Want Forever (Book 6)

Boxsets
All I Want Series Boxset, Books 1-3
All I Want Series Boxset, Books 4-6
All I Want Series Boxset, Books 1-6
London Romance Series Boxset, Books 1-3

ACKNOWLEDGEMENTS

And so we come to the end of the third book in the London Romance series — it's only been two years since the last one, but I hope it was worth the wait. I loved going back to visit Jess and Lucy, Kate and Meg, and there will be another book in this series coming soon — so watch this space.

For this book, huge thanks are due to my fabulous friend and dog walker extraordinaire, Sarah Mooney, who patiently let me walk with her for a couple of days and quiz her on the habits of dogs and their owners. I met some fab dogs along the way, and particular thanks are due to Moby, Woody and Ella who all inspired the dogs you meet in this book. Plus, a huge debt of gratitude to my friend Nikki Barnett, who gave me the lowdown on becoming and being a barrister.

Thanks to my first reader Tammara Adams, who gave me a concise and brilliant critique of the book — you're plain brill. Thanks also to my early reading team for your eagle eyes on the final proof — in particular Hilary and Susie — and for all your encouragement along the way.

A fistful of gratitude to the fantastic foursome of my cover designer, Kevin Pruitt; my editor, Laura Kingsley; my copy editor, Gill Mullins; and my typesetter, Adrian McLaughlin. Without the four of you, none of this would be possible. You provide the visuals and the shine to my story, so bravo for you all!

Thanks also to my gorgeous wife Yvonne for her comments and suggestions, and also for putting up with me and my fragile ego. She generally knows a good steak and a bottle of Malbec cures most things, and she's usually right.

Finally, thanks to you for reading — it really does mean so much that you spent some time with my story, and I hope you enjoyed it. Thanks for buying, for reading, and hopefully reviewing it. Do let me know what you think, I love getting all your comments and emails. Look out for another London Romance this year — it turns out, London Romances are like buses: you wait two years, then two come along at once.

Connect with me:
Twitter: @clarelydon
Facebook: clare.lydon
Instagram: @clarefic
Email: mail@clarelydon.co.uk
Join my VIP Readers' Group: www.clarelydon.co.uk/it-had-to-be-you

If your family doesn't accept you for who you truly are,
just know: you're not alone.

Chapter One

"I've got two pieces of advice for you. You got a pencil handy?"

"Sure," Tanya lied, sitting on her sofa. Her gran sounded perky today, more like her old self.

"First, don't grow old gracefully, okay?" Her gran cleared her throat at the other end of the phone.

"No problem, I'll follow your lead," Tanya replied. "And number two?"

"Stop working so much, loosen up, have more sex," her gran continued, deadpan.

"That's more than two pieces of advice."

She could almost feel her gran smiling down the phone. "Okay, have more sex."

"Have more sex it is," Tanya said, her cheeks heating up as she said the word 'sex' down the phone. Even at 83, her gran had a habit of making her stop in her tracks.

"I wish it were that easy," Tanya mumbled under her breath. She didn't want to count on her hands how many months it'd been, but she knew she'd need all her fingers and thumbs, repeat to fade.

"It is — just go out there, find a woman you like the look of and charm her."

Tanya stared at the violet lounge wall of her rented flat: she hated the colour, but she wasn't sticking around long enough to paint it. Perhaps a new address would give her more luck romantically, too? She hadn't been inclined to charm any women of late: the thought of bringing them back here felt unrepresentative of who she really was.

"I'll note it down," she said. "I just need to locate my charm and we're good to go."

"You've got charm by the bucketload — you're my flesh and blood!" Her gran's voice went up at the end, as if she couldn't believe her granddaughter's hesitation. Tanya pictured her propped up in her hospice bed, laughing more than any of her bedfellows, just like always.

Her gran had always taken the starring role in her life and lived it in high-definition.

"Now I've given you my wisdom, next question: have you spent my money yet? I know we discussed a flat, but drugs and hookers would be okay too, if that's what you need." More coughing followed, and Tanya could tell her gran was getting a little over-excited.

Still, she wasn't going to scold her.

Not now.

"I haven't spent it yet," Tanya replied, flexing her toes. "Although I am seeing a place this weekend that looks promising, so I'll report back. It's by the river." She paused. "And if it's good, I promise I'll blow a grand on cocaine and hot women to celebrate." She smiled at her own joke, at the absurdity of it. She was more likely to buy a bottle of decent red, but she didn't want to dampen her gran's spirits.

Her gran rasped down the phone at that, before succumbing to another coughing fit.

Tanya waited for her to recover; she knew it would take a few moments.

"Take photos, please," her gran said, when she had her breath back. "Of the flat, too."

Now it was Tanya's turn to laugh.

How her gran had managed to spawn her humourless mother was a mystery.

"But seriously, I want to know my only granddaughter has somewhere decent to live before I die."

Tanya shook her head: that outcome was too outrageous to consider, so she squashed it down, along with the clamour of emotion it brought with it. "You're not going to die, Gran."

There was a pause before her gran replied. "We're all going to die, sweetheart," she said. "I'm just a little closer than most."

Chapter Two

Tanya Grant was going to be late, and she *hated* being late – it simply wasn't in her DNA.

Tanya hated being late almost as much as she hated her own mother.

Almost.

Somebody on her train had pulled the emergency cord, which meant she'd now been stuck in a tunnel for nearly half an hour. She checked her watch for the third time in five minutes and tapped her black Chelsea boot on the train carriage floor. She couldn't miss this viewing — the flat had looked incredible online.

Beside her sat a young man with beautiful, smooth skin, wearing perfectly ripped jeans. "That's not going to help, you know," he said, raising a styled eyebrow in her direction.

She didn't reply at first, wondering if she'd imagined the words; however, he was looking at her, expecting some response.

She put her index finger to her chest. "Sorry, are you talking to me?"

He nodded. He had a piercing in his bottom lip: Tanya had always found those so off-putting. Didn't they get in the way when you wanted to do things like eat, drink or kiss?

"You're constantly checking your watch and sighing. I'm just saying, it's not going to make the train move any faster." He gave her a smile that disarmed her. People didn't speak to each other on London transport, so why was he breaking the rules? "You're going to be late, accept it. Stop fretting."

Tanya stared at the young man: she knew he was right. Her gran's words on her call the other day rattled in her head: loosen up.

"I know," Tanya replied. "But it makes me feel like I'm doing something."

The young man shrugged. "Just so long as you know it's pointless." He gave her that smile again, glancing around the carriage before his eyelids drooped, shutting out the world completely.

Tanya let out a long breath, just as the carriage's lights flickered and the train began to move, the tunnel's thick brick walls sliding by the windows.

Apologies ladies and gentlemen, but the alarm has now been sorted and we're on the move. We'll be pulling into our next station, Woolwich, in a few minutes time.

True to his word the driver did just that, and Tanya sprang from the train, zipping in between fellow passengers, whizzing past commercials for a popular bourbon brand, another for a bank and one for a book that'd been on her list to read for as long as she cared to remember. But honestly, who had time to read these days? Not a busy person like her.

The grey concrete was hard under the soles of her black boots as she ran to the end of the platform using the full length of her long legs, veering too late from a woman ahead of her. Tanya's shoulder slammed into her, and the woman rocked sideways, her glasses falling from her face and clattering as they hit the floor. "Hey!" the woman said, her eyes watery, her face a frown.

Tanya skidded to a halt. She bent down to pick up the woman's glasses from the cold floor and pressed them back into her warm hand. "Sorry, I've got to run," she said, throwing the woman an apologetic glance. She then set off once more, passing her Oyster card over the metallic ticket barrier before sprinting towards the stairs, every step bringing her closer to the block of flats on the river that might just be her future home.

Her plan to make a fast exit might have worked, too, had Tanya not slipped on the penultimate step of the stairs, which knocked her off balance. As her other foot missed the top step, her ankle gave way beneath her in a flash of pain, and she fell forward. Her shins hit the concrete steps with a sharp thud, followed by her knees, then her hands.

Tanya squeezed her eyes shut as she came to a halt in a crumpled heap, sprawled face-down at the top of the stairs, pain rippling through her body. When she opened her eyes, her cheek was pressed into the station floor, with shoes walking by sideways as her vision adjusted.

Summoning all her strength, she dragged herself up and onto the station concourse. Then she got onto her knees and gingerly pushed herself up, the heels of her palms stinging. People thronged by her, left and right, nobody stopping to see if she was okay. Would she have stopped if the shoe were on the other foot? Probably not. Outside, she could see it had started to rain, with umbrellas being shaken and unfurled all around.

"Do you need any help?" asked a kind woman, pushing her thick black hipster glasses up her nose. She was around Tanya's age, her short, blonde hair already tussled from the day. She wore skin-tight blue jeans, ripped at the knee, a white shirt and a green army jacket that Tanya would never have attempted, yet she pulled off with aplomb.

Tanya squinted, still dazed, her heart thumping in her chest. With pain still stamping round her body, she couldn't compute sentences yet. However, she couldn't help noticing the woman's eyes, which were simply stunning. Cornflower blue and surrounded by long dark lashes, they weren't a colour Tanya had seen often, and she was momentarily mesmerised. Whoever this woman was, her nose delicate, her lips full, she was brightening up a shitty day. Tanya had to tear her eyes away to stop herself staring.

"I'm fine," she replied, far more abruptly than she'd

intended, before wincing at her tone. Damn it, she hadn't meant that the way it came out. It was her pride that was hurt more than body.

And this woman was only trying to help.

This incredibly hot woman.

The incredibly hot woman gave her a confused frown, her blue eyes rippling again, making Tanya blink rapidly. Was that her natural eye colour or was she wearing contacts? Whatever, the effect was astonishing.

"I just thought I'd ask. Only, it looked like it hurt." She gave Tanya a once-over, along with a concerned smile. "I've got a tissue if you need one."

Tanya shook her head. "I have some," she said. Still curt. She really needed to work on her delivery, as her friend Alice kept telling her.

The woman, giving up, flashed her a thin-lipped smile. "Suit yourself, I was just trying to be nice," she said, before rummaging in her bag and pulling out a packet of cigarettes, along with an umbrella. She didn't look at Tanya again, just put a cigarette between her lips, before shaking out her umbrella and walking away.

Tanya thought about shouting after her, telling her she was sorry for being so abrupt, thanking her for stopping. But she didn't, and this was London — she'd never see her again.

She shrugged, drew a line under her morning so far and regrouped.

She assessed the damage: her jeans were still intact,

as were her hands, and she wasn't bleeding. She was a bit bruised, but other than that, fine. And she really needed to get a move on now.

Tanya checked her watch. If she ran down the main road as best she could, she'd probably only be ten minutes late, and hopefully the estate agent would hang on for her. From what she'd told her, Tanya was the first of many viewings, so she guessed she might even be staying put all day.

She rummaged in her bag to locate her blue umbrella and her phone, checking Google Maps to confirm directions.

Then Tanya took a deep breath, swung her bag over her shoulder and hobbled down the road as fast as she could, wincing as she walked straight into a puddle, dirty water shooting up the inside of her freshly laundered dark blue jeans.

So far, it wasn't her day.

Chapter Three

Wow, people could be rude.

First, Sophie had seen the tall woman knock someone's glasses off because she was in such a rush. But when she saw the same woman fall at the top of the stairs moments later, she'd felt sorry for her. She'd heard the crack when the woman landed and knew it must have hurt.

But when Sophie had asked her if she needed any help, the brunette had brushed her off without so much as a thank you. Sure, she had those cheekbones people would forgive a great deal for, along with a figure to match. And yes, her angular face and rich green eyes had made Sophie look twice, but no amount of good looks made up for rudeness. Good manners cost nothing, but some Londoners didn't seem to be aware of that. Some days, Sophie London hated sharing a name with them.

Sophie shook her head as she turned right into the shortcut to her flat. She shouldn't let it get to her this morning — not after the day she'd already had. It was only just gone 9am, and here she was, slinking home from her lover's house.

Again.

Sophie knew it couldn't continue — of course she did. She'd known it when it started, and she knew it even more so now. After all, she was in her third decade, and there were only so many more nights she could slink home early from a night with her lover, turfed out of the flat because her lover had "things to do". Things to do that weren't being intimate with Sophie. She wasn't sure how she'd fallen into the role of being a fuck buddy to her boss, Helen, but that's where her life was at.

And while she continually told herself she was happy with her lot, that she *liked* having sex with Helen and didn't *need* anything else, she knew deep down it wasn't true. But this morning wasn't the time to face that reality, seeing as she'd only had five hours' sleep and had yet to even brush her hair.

She winced as her right trainer hit a broken paving slab and an inordinate amount of black water sloshed up her inside leg, soaking her sock and her green-and-yellow trainer in the process. Sophie stopped, shook her foot then her head, before turning the corner into the concrete courtyard outside her block of flats.

She took a final drag on her cigarette before crushing the butt underfoot, rain cascading off her umbrella and drumming on the pavement. She'd like another cigarette, but this weather wasn't making it appealing. Instead, she pushed open the giant glass door of her building, shaking out her umbrella and smiling at Roger the concierge.

"Morning Sophie, lovely day for it!" Roger said, a smile creasing his ruddy-cheeked face, his hand raised in a wave.

Sophie had a lot of time for Roger: no matter what, he was always in a good mood which she appreciated.

"Take my advice — stay inside," she said, letting the glass door slam behind her. "How's your morning been?" she asked, walking over to the stack of metal post boxes in the foyer to check if she had any mail. When she saw she didn't, she relocked her post box and walked back to Roger's desk. She could see a copy of *The Sun* newspaper open in front of him.

"Quiet so far — I think everyone's staying in because of the weather," he replied.

"I don't blame them."

"You out all night?" Roger asked, his smile never faltering.

Sophie nodded, replaying her night of no-strings sex in her mind, followed by Helen waking her up and ushering her out. A smile ghosted across her face, but her emotions slumped.

"Stayed at a friend's," she replied, desolation washing over her. The situation was in her hands and only she could change it. She just had to prioritise her mental health over her libido. Easier said than done.

"Anyway, I've got to run. Have a good day," she said, turning towards the lift.

"You too, Sophie!"

She pressed the lift button and saw the down arrow

light up. She tapped her foot as she waited, her soggy trainer making high-pitched squelching sounds on the polished white floor. Ten seconds later the lift arrived, the doors sliding open.

Sophie got in and was just about to hit her floor button when she saw a tall brunette in a long, stone-coloured coat yank open the front doors of her building — if she wasn't mistaken, it was the very same woman who'd just brushed her off at the tube station.

Was she following her? What on earth was she doing in her building?

Sophie squinted as the woman sprinted towards her, a mass of long lines, waving her right arm in the air and shouting: "Hold the lift!"

Sophie did as instructed, hitting the button to keep the doors open: she wasn't looking forward to a second more of this woman's company, but she always held the lift when asked.

The woman's black boots slammed on the polished floor as she approached, before she hurled herself through the metal lift doors way too fast, her tall frame now seeming far too big for such a confined space.

Alarm slithered through Sophie as the new arrival sailed into the lift, heading straight for her. Unable to stop in time, the woman stuck out her hands to break her momentum, but only succeeded in grabbing Sophie's left breast and her right shoulder, slamming into her like a one-woman tornado.

There was a thud as she came to a standstill, and then, due to inactivity, the lift doors slid slowly shut, leaving Sophie and the woman pressed together, with the rest of the world completely sealed out.

Sophie let out an "oomph!" as her back crunched into the mirrored wall, her body pressed into the glass — and all because this woman was in a hurry. Her ribs shuddered and she gasped for breath. The brunette's blue umbrella dripped silently down her trousers and onto her foot.

Pain sizzled through Sophie, quickly followed by incredulity at the gall of this woman: she'd been holding the lift, there had been no need for her to run so fast. But clearly, life ran to this woman's agenda and her agenda alone.

And then, barrelling straight into the back of Sophie's annoyance was a duelling emotion: lust. An attractive woman was pressed into her, one hand on her breast, and no matter what a massive idiot the woman was, Sophie still had eyes and her body still responded. And right now, a zap of desire hit the bull's eye between Sophie's legs, just as the woman eased herself off Sophie, untangling her hands from Sophie's breast and shoulder, and then not quite knowing what to do with them.

She took a step back and eventually let her gaze drift up to Sophie's eyes, biting her lip and wincing.

Sophie stared into her deep green eyes, marbled with blues and greys.

And then her annoyance rose to the surface as she realised the woman was yet to apologise.

In the same way she failed to say thank you earlier.

"What the fuck are you doing?" Sophie asked eventually, pushing herself off the wall with a giant heave, forcing the woman to take a step back as she did so. "I was holding the lift, and then you barrel in, nearly crushing me in the process." The bit of Sophie's brain that lodged attraction was jumping up and down and waving its arms, but she steadfastly ignored it.

The woman, who was a touch taller than Sophie, shrugged, before seeming to realise that wasn't an appropriate response. She followed it up quickly by raising both hands to her chest, palms facing out, and lifting her eyes to meet Sophie's.

"I'm so sorry, I just really wanted to get this lift. Are you okay?" she asked finally. The woman was grimacing as she spoke, and Sophie wasn't surprised: Sophie was winded and she was sure the woman was, too.

"Would it matter what I answered?" Sophie asked. Their faces were still inches apart and up close, the woman's cheekbones were even more chiselled than Sophie recalled, her skin flawless, even after everything that had happened this morning.

Which only angered Sophie that little bit more, seeing as she knew what a state she must look. "You were rude to me at the station, and then you turn up in my lift, landing on me. And why are you in my lift — you're not following me, are you?"

The woman brushed herself down, before rolling her

shoulders, gripping one and wincing before she replied. "Of course I'm not following you, I'm just having a *really* bad morning and I keep running into you."

"You can say that again," Sophie replied, pointing a finger to her chest. "You might want to try looking where you're going and slowing the fuck down before injuring anyone else, particularly me." She paused, shaking her head. "Honestly, wherever you're going will still be there in five minutes."

The woman grimaced, her hand cradling the back of her neck. "Sorry, that came out wrong. A bit like when you asked if I was okay earlier at the station after I fell over." She blew out a long breath, avoiding Sophie's gaze.

"Just slow down for a start," Sophie replied, still bristling, pushing her glasses up her nose. She'd had bad mornings, too, but it didn't mean she steamrollered everyone in her path. "And try being a little nicer when people try to help you — it goes a long way." She paused, before leaning over and hitting floor 20. The lift began its ascent, making a whizzing noise as it did.

The woman's gaze drifted back up to Sophie's, and held it for a few beats.

Looking into her eyes, Sophie's skin prickled and her mouth went dry. This woman's gaze was making her feel hot and exposed, and she wasn't sure she liked the reason why. She should be mad at her, but Sophie could already feel her annoyance fading, being replaced by curiosity about who she was and why she was in such a hurry.

The lift glided to a halt, announcing it was at floor 20, and Sophie pried her gaze away, catching sight of her reflection in the mirror. Her cheeks were flaming red and her face could do with some make-up. She decided it was best to look away and ignore her appearance next to this woman: she might be rude and obnoxious, but she still looked like she'd just stepped off a shoot for designer jeans.

Instead, Sophie pressed the door open button for the second time in as many minutes to hold it there. "Which floor do you need?" she said, indicating with her head towards the lift panel.

The woman licked her lips, her flecked brown hair falling in front of her eyes, her face crinkling as she stepped backwards and took a deep breath. "Floor 30," she said, stuttering slightly, before reaching out with her hand and cradling Sophie's elbow.

At her touch, Sophie drew a deep breath, staring at her elbow which felt like it was glowing red.

"And I am sorry, it was totally my fault. I hope you're not too hurt." The woman's face spelt apology now, and Sophie tried to regulate her breathing, shrugging it off as if she nearly got flattened in her lift every day.

"If I need a new set of ribs, I'll know to come to floor 30 with the bill," Sophie said, before her curiosity got the better of her. "Are you visiting friends or have you moved in?"

The woman shook her head, standing up straight. "Viewing a flat this morning," she replied.

So this could be her new neighbour? Sophie still wasn't sure what to make of that. "Floor 30 is almost the top, great if you've got a river view, which we don't," she said.

"It looked promising online, so I hope it lives up to the hype," the woman replied. "And if I take it, I promise to be more careful in the lift in future, okay?"

Sophie smiled. "Make sure you do," she said, getting out of the lift before looking over her shoulder.

The woman gave Sophie a shy smile, then stuffed her hands in her pockets and cast her gaze to the floor, then back up again. Hands in her pockets: Sophie's gaydar twitched. It was just a shame the woman was such a hot mess.

"Good luck with the viewing," Sophie said, as the lift doors slid shut.

"Thanks," said the woman, giving her a pained smile.

Chapter Four

Tanya didn't recall getting 'the feeling' before — but that was exactly what was happening as she stood in the open-plan living room of this Woolwich flat, staring out at the River Thames below. It wasn't what she'd anticipated after the start to her day, but perhaps the universe was throwing her a bone — and it was one she was happy to accept.

Her bruised knees and grazed ego were forgotten as she took in the place that could soon be her home: so far, the viewing was living up to its promise. Polished parquet floors the colour of autumnal conkers; a cream kitchen that looked almost brand-new; and breakfast bar stools that gleamed despite the lack of sunshine.

She'd only been in the door five minutes, but she could already sense her spirit rolling around on the wooden floor, claiming the space as her own. She wanted to move in on the spot, but she knew there might be some other things to consider first.

She walked over to the floor-to-ceiling glass wall that opened out onto the balcony overlooking the river, raindrops sliding down its surfaces. She took a deep breath in: the smell of coffee was alluring, and she was grateful for the cup she was holding in her hands. It had steadied her shredded nerves, helping her focus on what was important today: this flat.

Jenny had been very clear there were many interested parties, telling her if she wanted to move on this apartment, she'd better do it quickly. This one was pulling on her heartstrings, even though some of her exes would probably say she didn't have a heart, let alone any strings. But Tanya knew better.

"So, what do you think?" Jenny was sauntering across the room, her heels clicking on the parquet floor. If Tanya bought this flat, she'd be telling Jenny to take those off straight away. "Done to a high spec, isn't it?"

Tanya nodded. "It's incredible — more than I was expecting." She put her hand to her heart. "It's made me a bit emotional. It's even better than it looks online."

Jenny was nodding, a satisfied grin on her face. "Told you. You've got all that money burning a hole in your pocket, this could be the one to relieve you of it." She paused, coming to a standstill beside Tanya. "But remember, I've got three other couples viewing it later. So if you want to move, do it sooner rather than later. And you're in a better position than most."

Tanya sucked on her bottom lip. "I know." She strolled forward to just before the balcony doors, smiling as the river breeze tickled her face. Yeah, she could see herself sitting out here of a weekend, drinking her coffee, reading her tablet, watching the world go by. Well, the birds at least, seeing as she was on the 30th floor. Or maybe she could do some naked sunbathing — it wasn't like she was overlooked. This almost-penthouse apartment could be just what she'd been waiting for.

"Can you see yourself here?" Jenny asked, her painted lips inches from Tanya's as she turned to face her. Not for the first time, Tanya wondered if Jenny was on her team.

Tanya nodded, running a hand through her shoulder-length hair. She could totally see herself there: it was her time to step into the spotlight, in a whole new area with a block of people to get to know. Including the woman from the lift earlier, although she might have some reputation restoration to do with her. Tanya wanted to know more about her, though: she'd piqued her interest, as well as being gracious after Tanya had been anything but.

"I can, actually," Tanya replied. But could she afford the mortgage? Did she have a big enough deposit to put down? She did the figures in her head one more time, but with her gran's help, she had the collateral. "I think this one, finally, could be it."

She turned to face Jenny, scanning the lounge with its built-in shelving lining the walls, great for all her framed photos and treasured ornaments. First to go on the shelving would be the photo of her and her gran in happier, healthier times, before her gran got sick. But her gran wasn't dead yet, and she had to concentrate on that.

And what had she told her the other day? "Spend my money, make me proud."

And Tanya was going to follow her advice. She walked through to the master bedroom again, with its muted cream walls, its boutique en-suite, its effortless style. This was exactly what she'd been after: her search was over. She turned on her heel and walked back into the lounge, where Jenny was waiting.

"I'd like to make an offer. Ten grand under the asking price, so long as he agrees to leave all the white goods and that dining table. Can you do the necessary?"

Tanya's heart was pounding, but her words were coming out just fine: loud, strong, in control, like she knew exactly what she was doing. And she was pretty sure she almost did. Tanya was buying her own piece of London real estate, in the process spending the most money she'd done in her entire life, on a purchase that she'd seen for precisely six minutes.

She spent longer pondering a £60 pair of jeans.

Did this feel right? Would it go through? Would she get into a bidding war and be gazumped at the last minute? She'd never know until she tried. After all, like her gran always said, you've got to be in it to win it.

Seeing pound signs light up in her commission, Jenny grinned anew. "I certainly can," she said, grabbing her phone from the kitchen counter and pressing one of the buttons before holding it to her ear. She nudged Tanya with her elbow while she waited for it to connect.

"I'm so excited you've finally found your flat!" she said. "I've got a good feeling about this: it's got your name written all over it."

Chapter Five

"And what time do you call this?" Rachel asked, walking into the living room just as Sophie added milk to her cup of tea. Rachel was dressed in blue-and-white striped pyjamas, her dark hair sticking up at the back, showing she'd just got up. But even with that, she was still amazingly fresh-faced: it ran in her family, as she'd told Sophie numerous times. Rachel came from an Irish background, so her dark hair was set against milky-white skin. She also had the straightest teeth in the history of the universe.

"I'd call it Cup of Tea O'Clock?" Sophie said. "Want one?"

Rachel nodded, sitting down on the sofa with a groan. "Of course," she replied.

Like most modern London flats, their kitchen sat in one corner of their living room. They had no dining table, but Rachel had a free-standing butcher's block, which served simultaneously as a wine rack and an island. The lack of a table had also allowed room for Rachel's massive and soothing mustard sofa, where Sophie had conked out on numerous occasions — and it was what Rachel was sinking into now.

"It's also way past your curfew," Rachel said, but Sophie could hear the smile in her tone.

"I have a curfew?"

Rachel nodded. "Since you can't be trusted to do the right thing. Because getting in at this time means only one thing."

"That I got up really early and went for a jog along the river?" Sophie placed Rachel's tea on the coffee table and sat down next to her.

Rachel smirked. "In the same clothes you were wearing last night?"

"I changed already — I've had a really productive morning."

Rachel rolled her eyes. "I don't know when you became such a floozy."

"Am I not floozy material?" Sophie asked, her face the picture of innocence.

"You are now, sitting here all chipper after a night of sex," she said. "But you're not when you're moaning that Helen isn't giving you what you want, that she isn't treating you more like a girlfriend," Rachel replied. "I've got nothing against casual sex — chance would be a fine thing — but it's not casual for you, and I worry about your fragile heart."

Sophie smiled at her, rubbing her arm. Rachel always had her back, she knew that. "I know you're right, it's just that I like her," Sophie said. "And she's lovely in many ways."

"Apart from not wanting to have a relationship with you?"

Sophie stuck her tongue out at her best friend in response.

Rachel laughed. "Very mature," she said. "But seriously: picture your ideal romance and I bet it doesn't look like what you've got now. That's what you should be aiming for — it's what I do with my affirmations every day." Rachel paused. "I will find that special woman, I am worthy of love."

Sophie smiled: Rachel was all about bettering yourself and self-help. "Yes, but you're into all that hippy shit. I'm not."

"And who's happier?"

"I'm happy with Helen," Sophie said, retreating into a ball on the sofa.

Rachel snorted as she sipped her tea. "Sure you are." She nudged Sophie with her elbow. "What would your perfect romance look like?"

Sophie frowned as she tried to conjure up her ideal relationship, but nothing came. She let her mind wander over her teenage years, her ill-fated outings with boyfriends, her gradual realisation she was more into girls. And then, just as she'd joined the dots, her homelife had been turned upside down and her romantic dreams had stalled. She'd been chasing love ever since, but it had proved elusive.

"I haven't really given it much thought, but I suppose what everyone wants — someone who's there for me, someone to love. Good hair, not an idiot, and hot, obviously."

"Obviously," Rachel replied. "But you should know what you want — then you'll recognise it when it arrives."

Sophie let Rachel's words roll around the room. "You know, you make a surprising amount of sense at times," she said eventually.

"High praise from the romance dodger," Rachel replied.

Sophie folded her arms across her chest. "But who's to say me and Helen aren't destined to be together? You never know what's around the corner — and she does have good hair."

"Do you really think that?"

"That she's got good hair?"

Rachel gave her a look.

Sophie smiled, before shaking her head. "Not really."

"Good, because you can do so much better than Helen," Rachel replied. "She treats you like dirt and you let her. And I know that deep down you want a girlfriend: a proper, honest-to-goodness woman who might let you stay in her apartment later than 10am." Rachel paused. "When you do meet someone who's a game-changer, you're going to fall so hard, you'll spin."

"Sounds painful," Sophie said, flexing her shoulder, still feeling the impact of the mysterious lift woman in her bones and in her blood. Her swirling green eyes, her penetrating stare that had reached in and grabbed Sophie's attention. Did *she* kick women out at ungodly hours?

Rachel nudged Sophie with her elbow. "It's going to be magnificent, I have a feeling. When you do eventually fall in love for the very first time, it's going to be mega. There will be love songs written about it. Sonnets. Poems. Flash mobs. The works."

Sophie laughed. "I love your faith in romance, you know that? You always believe in happy endings."

"That's because happy endings never go out of fashion."

Sophie gave a deep sigh before the next words came out of her mouth — and as soon as she said them, she knew they were the absolute truth. "Helen isn't my happy ending, is she?" She took off her glasses and rubbed her face with both palms, before peeking through her fingers at Rachel. "I've got to end it, haven't I?" Her voice was hardly audible.

She couldn't see Rachel clearly, but she could see she was nodding. "You do. For your sanity, and for your health. And because the sooner you do, the sooner you can open yourself up to the possibility of a real-life relationship. You know, with responsibilities, love and commitment involved."

Sophie shuddered: while it was what she wanted, it also scared the living daylights out of her. "Why would you say those words?"

"Because they can be great," Rachel replied, rolling her eyes. "And because, when you get deeper into a relationship, the sex can be mind-blowing."

"Now you've got my attention," Sophie told her, sitting up with a smile. Rachel's words were getting through to her this morning.

"Talking of difficult women," Sophie added, dropping her hands and put her glasses back on.

"Were we?"

"We are now," Sophie said. "We might be having a new lesbian moving into floor 30 — she's quite hot but she's got the social skills of a gnat. She just barrelled into a woman in the station, and then nearly crushed me in the lift — and I had to draw the apology out of her. Manners are not high up on her list of daily objectives, and you know my pet peeve with manners and Londoners."

"Because Helen's got loads of manners," Rachel replied, almost choking on the words.

"Helen's not that bad," Sophie said, knowing it was a lie even before it left her lips.

Helen was a lazy, dirty scoundrel.

A sexy, lazy, dirty scoundrel.

Rachel didn't even respond, she just spluttered, but luckily her mouth was tea-free.

"Okay, okay, maybe she's a little bad. But this woman — she was willing to trample over anyone in her way to get to where she was going. So we have a charmer moving into the building, FYI."

Sophie paused, remembering the woman pressed against her, almost the whole length of their bodies touching. Her hand on Sophie's breast, then on her elbow, grazing Sophie's hip as she stood and regained her balance. And most of all, her heated stare, her intriguing smile. Despite everything that was coming out of her mouth, Sophie already knew she wouldn't say no to being trapped in that lift with her again.

"I repeat, sounds like just your type," Rachel said. "Your choice in women has always been terrible — that's something you need to work on." Rachel paused, glancing at her friend. "But at least you meet women, whereas with my unsocial chef hours, I never meet anyone. I'm destined to end up alone, surrounded by cats." Rachel gave her a perfect pout, followed by a deep sigh.

Sophie smiled at her, rubbing her arm. "What happened to your affirmations: 'I am the greatest lover ever, I will find a drop-dead gorgeous woman any minute now'?"

Rachel gave a gentle laugh. "They're not bad, maybe I should change to those."

"You'll be fine — your ideal woman is just around the corner. And you're a chef, which means you have a secret weapon. Who doesn't like a woman who can cook? Once they taste the food at your place, you'll be fighting them off," Sophie replied, squeezing her friend's leg. "Anyway, I've got to go and have a shower, and then I'm going to bed. I didn't get much sleep last night, if you know what I mean."

Rachel screwed up her face like she'd just eaten something particularly distasteful. "Spare me the gory details," she replied. And then she reached over and sniffed Sophie. "And correct me if I'm wrong, but I can smell cigarettes on you. I thought you agreed you'd try to give up?"

Sophie sank back into the sofa. "I did agree, and the key word in that sentence is try. I was absolutely trying to give up, but you can't expect me not to have a smoke when (a) my lover chucks me out at stupid o'clock, and (b) I nearly get killed by a crazy woman on the way home. Everyone has their limits."

"Did anyone ever tell you you're a drama queen?"

Sophie grinned at her. "Never," she replied.

Chapter Six

Tanya was standing with her hands in her pockets, staring out of her office window after a morning of back-to-back meetings. She jiggled her back one way, then the other, as she did whenever she'd been sitting for too long, and today certainly qualified.

Buttery sunshine was sliding down the windows of her statuesque office block in Canary Wharf, where she worked as a member of the legal team of LogicOne Bank. Tanya was situated 22 floors up with views over the Thames and the O2, along with the bonus of spectacularly framed summer sunsets and winter downpours. She never got bored looking out of her office window.

Tanya had been working there for a little over six months, and she was just about settling into her new role in Mergers & Acquisitions, which was a cosmic shift from her former life as a barrister.

She'd been nervous about making the switch from court room to corporate office, but it'd turned out to be the best move. Being a barrister had lost its shine; she'd started resenting her clients and their pull on her time.

She'd trained for the bar because the tradition appealed, and she wanted to prove she could do it: that a working class girl could make it in a man's world. And she had. She'd worn the robes and eaten formal dinners in great banqueting halls — she'd done her time.

However, the day-to-day reality of the job had proved humdrum, and after a while, Tanya had begun to wonder if this was what she wanted to do with the rest of her life: the ultimate answer had been no. The reality of being a barrister had proved far removed from her movie-inspired ideal. The job had sucked the thrill from her life, chewed up her evenings and weekends and left her depleted, with grey bags around her eyes, the light behind them dimmed.

In this new job, the lights were beginning to be turned back on and her weekends were her own, which still left her slightly giddy. She'd even found time to join a gym and actually go — wonder of wonders.

This morning had been particularly fruitful for the company merger she was working on, including a productive breakfast meeting with her boss, before chairing meetings with both the seller's legal and compliance teams — and everything appeared to be progressing as scheduled. Her boss had been chuffed with the progress, which meant Tanya was, too.

Her phone ringing interrupted her thoughts and she grabbed it from her desk. She checked the number that flashed up on the caller ID screen and smiled as she spoke into the receiver.

"To what do I owe this honour?"

Tanya's best friend Alice chuckled down the line at her greeting. "Aren't you meant to answer the phone with something like, 'Tanya Grant, high-powered exec, fighting world superpowers daily, how can I help?' That's what they do in the Hollywood movies, at least."

Tanya grinned. "Last time I checked, I wasn't engaged in mortal combat with many world superpowers. Excel spreadsheets and paper cuts, maybe, but not many superpowers."

"Hey, if you can master Excel, I'm sure you can conquer world superpowers. Or at least make them pivot and get all confused."

Tanya and Alice had been friends since university, with Alice being Tanya's regular sounding board on matters of life and the heart. They didn't see each other as regularly as Tanya would like, what with her work schedule and Alice's recent acquisition of a boyfriend named Jake. She gushed about him on every phone call they had, and Tanya could tell she was smitten. She envied Alice that — she'd met someone who she loved and trusted completely, which is what Tanya was after. Although perhaps she should learn to love and trust herself first.

Alice worked as the head of art and design for the local college, a job she loved and hated all at the same time. Her love for it was simple: she believed in the power of art, and she adored working with students and unlocking their potential — her eyes lit up whenever she spoke about it, which had often made Tanya envious. However, her hate was simple, too: the endless admin and the ongoing struggle with budget cuts that always seemed to hit the arts hardest.

Tanya sympathised, even though she and Alice sat at opposite ends of the spectrum when it came to politics and careers. However, their friendship had remained strong despite their differences, because when it came down to it, they were still the same two girls who liked to meet, drink beer and gossip.

"Anyway," Alice continued. "This is a social call. I'm currently out shopping, just a stone's throw from your building and wondered if you were free for lunch? I've already bought two pairs of trousers, one skirt and a shirt that's slightly too small for me but was in the sale, so it's still a bargain. I need someone to come and stop me buying anything else while I'm in this drugged-up shopping spree state." She paused. "Are you that woman?"

Tanya checked her watch. "I can meet you in half an hour? Give me some time to reply to a couple of emails first?"

"Meet me at Carluccio's at 12.45pm and don't be late."

"12.45, I'll be there. Try not to buy anything else in the half an hour till then."

"I can't make any promises," Alice replied, before hanging up.

Tanya replaced her phone on its base and pulled down the cuffs of her baby blue shirt. Lunch with Alice was just what the doctor ordered — they hadn't caught up in person in ages, not since she'd started seeing her personal trainer, Jake, five months ago.

Tanya woke up her screen and started replying to her lengthy list of emails.

Chapter Seven

"Hello, gorgeous." Alice got up from her chair and gave Tanya a hug. When she let her go, she held her at arm's length. "You know, this new job really suits you. You look at least 20 per cent more attractive to me today. And I'm pretty firmly in the straight camp, as we know."

When Alice let her go, Tanya pulled out a chair and sat down, folding up her sunglasses and placing them on the table. "What do you mean, 'pretty firmly in the straight camp'? Are you having an early midlife crisis I need to know about?"

Alice peeked out from behind her large menu. "You know what I mean," she replied. "Anyway, I was reading about being pansexual and thought maybe I might try that."

Tanya smirked at her friend. "Do you even know what it means?"

"Something to do with Peter Pan?"

Tanya let out a peel of laughter. She loved Alice for many reasons, but a key one was her unique view on the world. She was a voracious reader and super smart, but she preferred to underplay what she knew with humour.

So Tanya was sure she knew full well what being pansexual actually entailed, but she was going for the Peter Pan angle for now.

"Was it the green tights and jaunty hat that were the main appeal?"

Alice gave her a grin. "That and the never having to grow up bit — green tights and not being an adult, what's not to like?" She paused. "Have you eaten here before?"

"Hasn't everyone eaten at a Carluccio's?"

"Bit fancier than Pizza Express."

"It might look it, but it all tastes the same: Italian and tomato-ey."

"Perfect," Alice said. "I'll have the lasagne. I need to fill up with an afternoon of shopping ahead."

Tanya clicked her fingers together. "Of course, it's the Easter holidays, isn't it? I thought you might be playing hooky."

Alice smiled across the table. "I don't play hooky — I'm a teacher, remember?"

"Does that discount you?"

"Absolutely — I'm the epitome of a moral, upstanding and responsible person."

"Right," Tanya replied, chewing on a slice of focaccia the waitress had just delivered.

They ordered their food and drinks from the short-haired woman who Tanya got definite vibes from, before settling down to more chat.

"You could definitely have her, if you're thinking of

experimenting." Tanya inclined her head towards the retreating waitress.

"What?" Alice said.

"The waitress — there were clear signs going on then. She wanted you." Tanya raised an eyebrow at her friend.

It wasn't the first time this had happened, and Tanya knew it wouldn't be the last. Tanya, after all, was the one who wore heels, skirts and longish hair; while Alice was rocking short hair, distressed jeans and a chequered shirt, topped off with a pair of DMs. As Tanya had told Alice many times, lesbian style and artistic style had a lot of crossover. Alice matched the dyke template perfectly — apart from the sleeping with women bit.

Alice twisted in her seat to check out their waitress, but she turned back and shook her head. "Not my type," she told Tanya. "Her arse was far too small — I'd get a complex. Which is why I much prefer dating men: bigger and hairier arses, no competition."

Tanya crinkled her nose. "And that's exactly why I date women." She took a sip of her fizzy water.

"So anyway," Alice said, clapping her hands together. "Tell me about this flat. I want to hear everything about it: how it felt, what it looked like, who would play it in a movie."

Tanya cocked her head. "It's a flat, not a person."

"Flats have personalities, believe me. And they can be haunted, too. In fact, it'd be quite cool if it was haunted, wouldn't it?"

Tanya shook her head. "For you maybe, but not for me — I'd have to live there."

"Ghosts are just dead people, they're nothing to be scared of."

"Are you feeling okay today?"

"So anyway, the flat."

Tanya cast her mind back, remembering her Saturday morning in all its glory: the highs of seeing the flat, the lows of ending up on her arse. And then an image of Lift Woman popped into her head, all tussled hair and vexed, those piercing blue eyes glaring at her. Tanya would be happy for her to glare at her all day long — she was a sucker for a woman in an army jacket. However, she would rather Lift Woman wasn't quite so mad at her in the first place.

"It's perfect — it's got the open-plan living I wanted, two bedrooms, balcony, river views. And it's high up, so I'm not overlooked."

"How high?"

"30th floor."

"You better hope the lift never breaks down and you have to carry your shopping up all those stairs."

"I will start praying today."

"So you're thinking you're going to put in an offer?"

"I already did. The estate agent thinks it's a done deal, but I'm still waiting to hear for sure — the owner's on some exotic holiday where there's no reception."

Alice's eyes widened to the size of moons, her mouth also dropping open in cartoon fashion.

"What?" Tanya asked.

"And you've only just told me this now!?"

"I've been processing," Tanya replied, grinning as her friend got up and gave her a hug, which she accepted readily.

"But this is big news! You've been looking for a flat ever since you split from Meg, and that's nearly two years ago. And now you look at one, casually put in an offer and don't tell me?"

When she put it like that. "Sorry." Tanya said, looking Alice in the eye. "Hey, Alice — I put in an offer on a flat!"

Alice raised an eyebrow. "You're not an easy woman to love. God help the next one who tries," she said as she sat down again. "You've got to open up to people and share, let people in. It's been a nightmare pinning you down for a weekend, and don't tell me your social calendar is full up, because I don't believe it." Alice gave her a look to back up her statement.

"I've been flat-hunting, that takes time." Tanya paused. "But that hunt is now over. Now I've just got to work on getting to know my new area and my new neighbours. Which might be easier with some than others."

Tanya sucked on the inside of her cheek, thinking about Lift Woman again. When she'd relaxed, Lift Woman had taken on a whole new persona, one Tanya wanted to get to know better. There was something about her that had made Tanya sit up and take notice — and right now, it was making her heart beat that little bit faster, warming her very insides.

"Meaning?" Alice asked.

"Meaning I might have been a bit rude to one of them already, a woman about our age who tried to help me when I tripped coming out of the tube." Tanya held up a hand. "And before you have a go at me, I know I was in the wrong and I will make amends when I move in. Let's just say when it came to her, I was tripping up with my mouth as well as my feet."

"You fell over? Were you hurt?"

"My pride was."

"And she offered to help?" Alice raised an eyebrow at Tanya.

"She did."

"And let me guess, you turned her down."

Tanya looked away before replying. "I might have given her the wrong impression. And I did try to change it, but my mouth refused to comply with my brain."

"How many times have we gone through the fact that asking for help and accepting it doesn't make you weak? Not asking for help and doing it all yourself is the stupid option. She was being nice and you were being an idiot."

"I know," Tanya said: she'd heard this particular tune from Alice and other friends a few times before.

"You say this every time — loosen up a little, Grant."

"You sound like my gran."

"Your gran is a wise woman," Alice replied. "How's she doing, by the way?"

Tanya shook her head. "No change, still the same."

She felt her mood start to slide, but shook herself, dragging her mind back to Lift Woman.

"Anyway, then I clattered into her in the lift, too. Can you believe she lives in the same block? So I might have to start again when it comes to me and her, make a better first impression the third time around."

"How, exactly, do you manage to clatter into someone in a lift?" Alice asked, cocking her head.

Tanya blushed despite herself. "I was late for the viewing, so I was running and didn't judge the distance very well." She looked down, before looking back up at Alice. "I kinda landed on top of her, crushing her against the wall. I was mortified."

Alice began to laugh gently, her body shaking as she did. "This gets better. So let me get this straight: some woman tries to help you, you rebuff her, then you crush her in a lift." She paused, still laughing. "And did your hands land anywhere they shouldn't have?"

Tanya's cheeks flooded again. "I was just trying to save myself," she said, not looking at Alice. "Her tits might have got in the way."

Alice let out a bark of laughter at that, wiping some tears from her eyes. "Her tits got in the way?" she said, her voice now at a high pitch of amusement. "That, my friend, is the lamest excuse for feeling someone up I've ever heard."

Their food arrived, which cut the conversation for a few seconds. She thanked the waitress as she deposited

Tanya's salad and Alice's lasagne on the wooden table, but then Tanya dived straight back in to close down the subject.

"I was *not* feeling her up," Tanya replied, rolling her eyes. Although they had felt firm under her touch, and she had let her mind wander to what they might *actually* look like. "I was just…" she said, remembering the woman's smile, her strong aura. What was it about her? Tanya wasn't sure, but now wasn't the time to analyse. "Look, never mind. Let's eat our food and talk about something else. Like the fact that when I move in, you can come over and see me on the weekend — I'm going to be at your disposal all the time."

Alice nodded through a mouthful of lasagne, clearly happy to let the subject lie for now. "Good to hear it," she said when she'd finished chewing.

"I was even thinking of asking Alan if Gran would be up to a visit — it'd be nice for her to see the flat her money contributed to." Her gran had given her £100,000 towards the flat, telling her she'd rather she took the money now in case her mum tried any tricks when she was gone. Alan was her gran's best friend and also her parents' neighbour.

"She's too ill, surely?"

"Maybe, but no harm in asking." Tanya pushed her salad around the plate as she thought about her gran. Her health was touch and go these days, and Tanya really should get up to see her again soon because of that.

However, going home meant being in proximity of her mother, and that fact still gave her the creeps.

"I'm going to take her a bottle of wine when I move in, to say hi. Does that meet with your approval?" Tanya added, zig-zagging on the conversation.

"Your gran?" Alice asked.

Tanya shook her head. "No, my new neighbour."

"Oh, we're back to her," Alice replied, fork in the air. "Well, it's a good start," she said. "And tell me — is this woman cute?"

Her image flashed into Tanya's mind again, along with the moment Tanya's body had pressed up against hers and they'd shared a moment, a connection. Or had that just been Tanya's imagination?

"She's okay," Tanya said, underplaying it like a boss. "She had a nice jacket on."

Alice gave her a knowing smile. "She's okay *and* she had a nice jacket? That's code for 'Hell yes, she was cute and stylish!' in your world. So take her a nice bottle of wine, not just what's on offer in the Co-Op. Goddit?"

Chapter Eight

It was 8pm and the bar was packed solid with thirsty drinkers, the air thick with Friday night exuberance. Sophie scanned the waiting punters as she gave the previous customer her change, receiving no thanks in return. At one end, a suave woman in a stylishly cut black suit was waving a £50 note in Sophie's direction. In front of her, two guys were arguing about how many shots they needed and what variety. Behind her, Helen swept past Sophie, stopping briefly to whisper in her ear.

"Are you coming back to mine tonight?" Helen's breath was hot on Sophie's lobe.

Despite herself, Sophie felt it all the way down to her toes. "If you play your cards right," she replied.

Damn — there went all her good intentions. But seemingly, where Helen was concerned, Sophie was an easy touch.

"I'll look forward to it."

Before Sophie could reply, Helen was off down the bar, ignoring other customers' pleading eyes and making a beeline for the good-looking suit with the £50 note. Typical Helen.

"You serving?" asked one of the men in front of her who'd been discussing the shots. His eyes were bloodshot and he was already squinting.

"Sure am," Sophie replied. "What can I get you?"

* * *

Getting customers into the bar was never an effort — it was getting them to leave when the bar shut at midnight that was the problem. However, their security duo were doing a professional job tonight, gently encouraging people to drink what was left in their glasses, or offering them a plastic cup to takeaway. It was another 15 minutes before the final customer tottered out clutching a half pint of white wine; another half an hour till the chairs were stacked, the pipes covered and the surfaces wiped.

Helen was leaning on the bar filling in her shift sheets when Sophie sat down on a barstool opposite.

Helen gave her a smile. "Fancy a drink?"

Sophie nodded. "A beer would be good."

"Coming up." Helen signed the bottom of her shift sheet, then went to the fridge and pulled out two bottles of beer from a local brewery. On opening, they offered a satisfying hiss and she clinked Sophie's bottle before they both drank.

"Crazy night tonight."

"Always is on a Friday," Sophie replied, picking at the label on her bottle.

"And did you see that woman flashing the cash at the

end of the bar?" Helen paused, fishing in her pocket. "She gave me a £20 tip. £20!" Helen waved the note in front of Sophie's face. "I love Americans. We should encourage them to drink in here more often. Do a US promotion or something." She paused. "I'm buying us a fancy bottle of wine on the way home with this." Helen pocketed the note and took a slug of her beer.

"Planning on getting me drunk and seducing me?" A smile played on Sophie's lips as she said it.

"Damn, you've seen through my dastardly plan." Helen flashed Sophie her sexy smile and Sophie's heart stuttered. Damn, she wished she wasn't such a pushover when it came to her boss.

"And have you worked out about Wednesday yet?"

Helen smiled with her mouth, but the rest of her face didn't follow suit. "Wednesday?" Her tone was questioning.

Sophie sighed. "Yes, Wednesday — you know, Rachel's restaurant?" Rachel was having a tasting evening at her restaurant, and Sophie had invited Helen weeks ago.

It wasn't that she wanted a girlfriend to go with, it's just that she thought it might be fun for them to go, to do something other than work with each other and have sex. Something that involved being outside together, chatting like normal people.

"Right, that." Helen took a swig of her beer and looked away, before shaking her head slowly. "I don't think I'm going to be able to make it, can't make the shifts work."

Every muscle in Sophie's body stiffened. "You've known

about this for over a month and you're the manager of the bar. I think if you want to take a night off, it's pretty easy to do."

Helen shrugged, her cropped black hair not moving as she did so. "This week isn't great, especially with the good weather forecast. You know that. People drink more in the sunshine, so we need more hands on deck." Helen looked away. "It's just how it is."

Sophie's spirit sagged, her heart slowing down just that little bit more every time Helen disappointed her. It was getting more and more often of late, because they no longer wanted the same things.

Sophie wanted a relationship.

Helen didn't.

"It sounds to me more like you don't want to take the time off," Sophie said, fed up of the lame excuses.

"Sophie," Helen said, her tone a warning. "You know the deal, I've never been any less than honest with you. I don't do relationships. I like to keep my freedom." Helen paused, stroking the side of her angular face nervously. "But let's not ruin tonight by talking about it. Me and you, we've got something good going here — I thought we both agreed? No need to spoil it, is there?" Helen reached over and laid her hand on top of Sophie's.

A banging on the door interrupted the moment.

Helen looked up and swiftly let go of Sophie, her face falling fast.

Sophie turned her head to see a woman at the door,

around their age with long blonde hair, smiling and waving. Sophie had no idea who she was: possibly a drunk? They got a lot of them at this time of night.

But Helen was on the move, rushing to the end of the bar, her jaw clenched, not looking back.

And when the door opened, Sophie's already flagging emotions sank without trace as the woman stepped inside, wrapping her arms around Helen's neck, giving her a long, lingering kiss on the lips.

"Hey you!" she said, pulling back, a smile painted on her face. "I was just on my way home and thought I'd get off the tube early and surprise my girlfriend."

Girlfriend? Had Sophie just heard right? Helen, the no-strings-attached woman, had a girlfriend? What the actual fuck?

This explained so much. Yes, Sophie had accepted that Helen saw other women, but she'd also thought that perhaps she was special, that she was the one who had the potential to pick the lock of Helen's heart. How very wrong she'd been.

A ball of nausea worked its way up Sophie's windpipe, quickly followed by anger as she sat, jaw slackened, taking in the floorshow in front of her.

"You certainly did that," Helen replied, unhooking her girlfriend's arms from her. "I thought you were staying at Nessa's tonight?" Her voice was calm, believable.

Which was kinda unbelievable to Sophie. She hadn't realised what a good liar Helen was until that moment, but now she saw she was a master of deception. She'd deceived Sophie; she'd deceived her girlfriend; and who knew just who else?

"Change of plan — Nessa had a fight with her boyfriend. She thinks he's cheating. I mean, he says he isn't, but she doesn't believe him. Anyway, she thinks he's with her tonight, so she's gone to confront them."

Helen's girlfriend began to walk towards the bar, noticing Sophie as she sat on a stool. "Oh, hello! Sorry, I didn't see you there." She gave her a happy smile as Sophie walked past her and round the bar to grab her coat and bag.

Sophie didn't want to stay in this bar for any longer than she had to. If her skin hadn't been attached to her, it might have crawled off her body in shame.

"No problem," Sophie said. "I was just leaving." She glanced over at Helen, who was watching the whole interchange with a glazed expression on her face. What was she thinking?

Her girlfriend, oblivious, stuck out her hand. "I'm Polly, by the way, Helen's girlfriend."

Sophie smiled, nodding her head as if on auto-pilot. And then her politeness forced her to shake Polly's hand.

She hated her manners sometimes.

"Sophie," she said. "Anyway, I really do have to go."

"The famous Sophie!" Polly said, grinning. "If there's one person Helen talks about more than anyone else at work, it's you."

What could Sophie say to that?

The silence from Helen was deafening.

Once outside, Sophie broke into a little jog: anything to get her body moving, to do something to take her mind off what had just happened. Sophie had always abhorred affairs, but unwittingly, she'd fallen into the trap of being the other woman. She couldn't believe she'd been so stupid.

Maybe there was something in those affirmations that Rachel spoke about. Maybe she should start doing them tomorrow morning. From now on, Sophie was going to put herself first and go after a real relationship, not a part-time one.

She reached into her bag and got out her packet of cigarettes, but when she opened it, it was empty.

Damn it.

She threw the packet into a nearby bin and raced up the stairs to the train platform at Canary Wharf, replaying Polly's trusting smile over and over again in her mind. It wasn't Sophie's fault, but somehow she felt responsible.

As the DLR train pulled up, Sophie had much to ponder. In one short night, she'd lost her job and her lover.

Chapter Nine

The flat was hers: she'd just heard back from Jenny. When Tanya had got the call, her skin had broken out in goosebumps all over.

Maybe, just maybe, after a rough two years, things were starting to fall into place. She allowed herself to feel hopeful for the first time in a long time, tapping her desk, leaning back in her black leather office chair, looking out over Canary Wharf.

The office blocks dazzled in their metallic splendour, the windows darkened, keeping the mystery inside to the casual observer. When Tanya had first begun working here a few months back, she'd been impressed by the towering structures all around her every day, overwhelmed by their presence. She just took them for granted these days, along with the thousands of others who worked here daily.

And now she had a flat beside the Thames, too, just a 20-minute train ride from where she was sitting this morning. Her stomach knotted as she thought about it, and she wondered again if she'd done the right thing. Was buying a flat in today's climate the right thing? She had no idea.

But she needed somewhere to live, and the world kept on turning, despite the economy being on a knife-edge. She was 80 per cent sure, and that would have to be enough today.

Her phone pinged and she looked down at the screen: she had a meeting in 15 minutes and this was her reminder. She opened the files for the project on her laptop and began reviewing them. However, she was only halfway into the second paragraph when her phone began to ring, with a number she didn't recognise. She stared at it, then pressed the green call button.

"Hello?"

"Tanya?"

She might not have recognised the number, but she'd recognise that voice anywhere. It'd been a few years since she'd heard it, but it was filled with the same hesitancy as always, its edges softened with love.

Just hearing his voice made her recall the times it had cushioned her when she needed it.

And also, the times when it hadn't.

"Hi, Dad."

"Hello, love." He paused. "I have some bad news." His voice went down at the end, as if he was reading a football result and the team had lost.

All the good vibes that had been circulating her body fell over, tumbling to the floor like dominoes.

She knew what the news was, of course she did.

Yet she didn't want her dad to say it, because that would make it true.

Tanya gripped her desk and prepared for the words. "Is she okay?" she asked.

Her dad cleared his throat before replying. "She's not. She passed away in the night. She didn't suffer, she went peacefully. I thought you should know."

Tanya held her breath, and then completely forgot how to breathe. How could she do anything when her gran had just died? The wonderful, caring woman who had always loved her, no matter what. The woman who'd told her she could be anything she wanted to be, wherever she wanted to do it. The woman who'd made her laugh more than any other, who'd taught her how to bake a sponge cake, who'd held her when she cried. How was Tanya meant to go on when this whirlwind of positivity had suddenly been sucked from her life? Was she just meant to talk on the phone, like everything was normal?

Apparently, the answer was yes.

Keep calm and carry on.

Tanya wasn't sure she was capable.

"But I spoke to Alan on Monday and he said she was rallying. I was coming to see her this weekend." Her mind was whirring with the news, like a child's spinning top. Round and round it went, never stopping for anyone. "Are they sure? Absolutely positive?"

"They're sure. She's gone, I'm afraid. And the funeral won't be for a while because they've got a backlog. They're saying a month till they have space — I'll send you an email to let you know the details when we get them."

"A month?" Did bodies survive that long?

"Apparently." Her dad paused. "Your mum's beside herself, of course."

Tanya stiffened at the mention of her mother. She supposed her mum might be upset that her mother had died, but then again, she didn't show much care for gran when she was living. But grieving for the dead was expected, and her mum was a stickler for convention and tradition: it's the code she lived her life by.

"And how are you?" Tanya asked.

"Coping, you know. It's hard, but it's probably for the best. Your gran's quality of life wasn't really there anymore."

He cleared his throat again. The conversation between father and daughter should have been smoother, but Tanya wasn't surprised. Theirs was not a relationship that anyone was going to write a sitcom about.

"I guess not," Tanya replied. She knew her dad was telling the truth, but she'd never be ready to let go of her beloved gran. Not today, not tomorrow, not any day. And she was almost offended her mum was grieving for her. As her gran's only child, she was considered the chief mourner, but she didn't deserve that title.

Her mum didn't deserve much of anything.

"Will you be coming for the funeral?" her dad asked, after staying silent for a good few seconds.

Tanya sighed and stared at the sunshine out her window. Just a few minutes ago, she'd been admiring its silky rays. Now, there was a jagged edge to its light: the rays didn't slide down the buildings, they sliced them in two.

"Of course I'll be coming," she replied, unable to keep the peeve out of her voice. Her dad knew what her gran had meant to her, did he think she was a monster?

"Good," he said, quickly. "Only I wasn't sure, because… well, you know."

"Because I haven't been home since mum told me I wasn't welcome? That doesn't mean I've stopped coming to see gran. I've been up regularly to see her in the past few years. Life doesn't stop just because Ann decides she no longer has a daughter."

Silence.

Tanya chewed her bottom lip, wincing as she heard her words echoing down the line. They'd come out harder than she'd wanted. This wasn't the time to lay into her mum, she knew that.

Today wasn't about her mum.

Today was about her beloved gran, and how cancer had stolen her life sooner than anyone wanted. Way sooner.

Eventually, her dad spoke. "I would have liked to have seen you, I told you that."

Tanya sighed. "You did, Dad. But you never came to see me, so what am I meant to think?" She felt sorry for him even though she was angry at him.

Yes, it was her mum who made the rules, but it was

her dad who abided by them. Tanya had always hoped he'd try to stick up for his only daughter, but it had never happened.

"If you're coming home, will you stay with us?" he asked.

A chill ran through her, causing every hair on her body to stand up straight.

Every fibre of her being screamed "No!" at the top of its voice.

"I don't think that's a good idea, do you?"

He was silent again for a few more seconds. "I do, actually. I'll talk to your mother, but it'd be nice to have you home." He paused. "I'd like to have you home."

"Is Jonathan coming?"

"He says he can't get the time off work."

The coward. Maybe she'd email her brother and ask him to come for some moral support. After all, Jonathan was the only one who fully understood.

"I'll speak to him. But it might be better if I got a hotel. You can speak to Mum till you're blue in the face, but can you truly tell me she'll be happy to have me home?"

He cleared his throat again, a stalling tactic she was well used to. "She will be. She misses you, she just finds it hard to express her feelings."

Tanya sighed. "Let me know the moment you find out any details for the funeral, okay?"

"I will."

"And do me a favour?"

"Anything," he replied.

"Don't let Mum throw out all of Gran's stuff before I get there. You know what she's like, getting rid of things, putting things out of sight. I want a couple of keepsakes, so promise me that?"

Another clearing of his throat. "I'll do my best," he replied, and then she heard him speaking to someone else: her mother. "Nobody, just a sales call, be there in a minute," he said, covering the receiver to spare Tanya.

But Tanya heard what he'd said, and her heart drooped. Whatever her dad claimed, nothing had changed. Her mum still ruled the roost and he still toed the line, just like always.

"I've got to go," he said, his voice now spiked with tension. How he lived like that, she'd never understand.

"Bye, Dad," she said, and hung up.

In all the emotional commotion that call had entailed, she'd almost forgotten the reason for it.

Her gran was dead. Her beautiful, funny, warm gran.

Tanya waited for the emotions to spill down her like raindrops, but nothing came. She just felt numbness, from the top of her head to the tips of toes. Gran was gone for good. No more smiles, no more laughs, just the dull ache of a life well lived.

Her phone beeped: she was due at her meeting.

She took a deep breath, gathered her thoughts and stood up.

The show must go on.

Chapter Ten

"Hi Alan — it's me," Tanya said, relief flooding through her. Alan was her gran's best friend and also her parent's next door neighbour. But more than that, he was another place Tanya called home.

"I've been expecting your call," he said, his voice soft and familiar. "I'm so sorry, pet. How you holding up?"

Her dad had never asked that once in their chat earlier.

"I'm... I don't know. Better for hearing your voice. I just spoke to dad and he was as useless as ever." She'd made it through her meeting in a daze, and now she was just glad to hear a friendly voice.

There was a pause on the line. "He does his best," Alan said eventually.

But her chat with her dad was still fresh in Tanya's mind, as was the way he'd pretended she was a sales call. "I don't want to talk about him. It's all been said before."

"I know," Alan replied, because he did.

He'd been there after the fallout ten years earlier, and he'd been there ever since. She could imagine him sitting in his lounge, his beloved pooches at his feet, a tot of brandy at his side. The familiarity warmed her: when Alan died and her final loving connection to her childhood disappeared, she might just fall to pieces.

But Tanya put that thought to the back of her mind: she couldn't deal with that today.

Now, she had to focus on her gran.

"I'm at a loss, really," she replied. "I mean, she was my one and only, the one I truly loved my whole life." She paused. "Along with you, of course."

He laughed at that. "I don't think I can hold a candle to your gran."

"You gave her a run for her money," Tanya told him. And he had. However, it was her gran that she judged all other women by, her gran who'd shown her that love could be pure, never expecting anything in return. Her gran who'd taught her what love should feel like.

"When are you coming back?" Alan asked, interrupting her thoughts.

"Whenever the funeral is — Dad said he'd let me know."

"Are you staying there?"

"He wants me to, but it doesn't feel right." That was the understatement of the year. "We left it up in the air, but you know how things are."

"He does want you to, he's told me."

Tanya sighed. "It's not as easy as that though, is it?"

They both knew the answer.

"If it makes it easier, I've got a room you're welcome

to," Alan said. "You'd be close by and we'd all welcome you with open arms: me, Bouncer and Margo."

Tanya smiled at the mention of Bouncer and Margo, Alan's two dogs. Bouncer was an arthritic golden labrador, while Margo was a poodle-terrier mix and always up to mischief.

"I might take you up on that."

"I'll make the bed up just in case," he replied.

"How are you doing with it all?" Tanya asked.

Alan paused, and Tanya pictured his sad smile sitting underneath his thick shock of grey hair. He might be 70, but he'd always been a snappy dresser, and his hair was always just-so.

"I'm fine," he replied. "Trooping on, you know. I'm the wrong side of 65, so I'm a little more used to people disappearing. It doesn't make Celia's loss any less acute, but she was ready to go. Honestly, I've been to more funerals than anything over the past year. It can make a man paranoid."

"You're not allowed to die, Alan, okay? You're bullet-proof. You and gran were my safety net. And now she's gone, there's only you."

His gentle laugh soothed her down the phone. "I'll do my best — but you never needed a safety net. You were always far braver and wiser than I've ever been. You lived your life out and proud, and never took any bullshit. Celia was proud of you and I am, too."

Hearing him swear made Tanya sit up: Alan wasn't

normally one to have a potty mouth. "Are you trying to make me cry?"

"Just telling the truth," he said. "And I know it's going to be a sad occasion, but I can't wait to see you. And try not to be too sad, your gran wouldn't have wanted it. We'll make it a celebration of her life, okay?"

Tanya nodded, her eyes brimming with tears. "Okay," she agreed.

But even as she clicked off the phone call, Tanya swore she felt her heart break just a tiny bit, a hairline fracture that started in the centre and then simply carried on, with no end in sight.

Chapter Eleven

Sophie was taking a drag of her second cigarette of the day, the sole of her right trainer flat against the station wall when she saw her dad's white van trundling up the street. The van could do with a wash, but then, it always could.

Her dad was a builder and carpenter, and Sophie knew the back of the van would be a mess of tools, wood and dirty boots, all covered in a fine layer of dust. She ground out the stub of her cigarette under her foot as he pulled up, blowing the smoke out of her mouth and replacing it with a grin.

Sophie opened the passenger door and it creaked, as it always did.

"You should get some WD40 on that, you know."

She'd been saying that for the past two years. She smiled across at her dad, his bald head the colour of the wooden coffee table they'd had growing up, a hazard of working outdoors.

Nick London was a six-foot bruiser of a man which had always come in handy if anybody had tried to pick on Sophie at school — once they saw her dad, they soon shut up. He was also the archetypal softie: tough on the outside, a marshmallow underneath.

"You should stop smoking; it's a disgusting habit." Her dad threw her a grin as he replied, playing his traditional role in their standard conversation.

But Sophie wasn't listening — she already had her arms around the family border collie, Doris, ruffling her thick black-and-white fur, and Doris in turn was licking her face with wriggly enthusiasm.

"How's my gorgeous girl? How's my favourite girl in the world? You're such a good dog!" Sophie placed a kiss on Doris's face, and she barked in return. She'd been their family dog for the past nine years, and when Sophie had moved out, leaving Doris had been almost as hard as leaving her dad. Sophie still worried about them both.

"How come I never get that greeting?" her dad asked.

"Because you're never *quite* as happy to see me as Doris. If you panted in my face, I'd pat your head, too."

In response, her dad gave her a broad smile, before sticking out his tongue and panting at her.

Sophie rolled her eyes, before ruffling Doris's fur, letting her spread out on her lap. She put an arm around the dog to hold her in place, and they pulled away, their destination unspoken, but known: Epping Forest, her dad's favourite place to walk Doris. He lived nearby, north London being his manor.

Fifteen minutes later, they parked up. Sophie snapped

a lead on Doris, who gave her a look as if to say 'how dare you!'. But once they were out of the car park and into the forest, she set her free and Doris galloped off, as if she'd been locked up for days. Her boundless energy had dwindled over the years, but even now at nine years old, she still ran rings around the humans in her life.

"So how's tricks? You're looking thin — is that the fashion these days?" Her dad's grip tightened around her shoulder as they walked, and Sophie leaned into his embrace.

"That's what Mum said when I spoke to her on Skype the other day."

Her dad stiffened at the mention of his ex-wife. "Did she?"

Sophie's parents had split up eight years ago when her mum walked out one day and never came back. She left her dad, Sophie and her brother Luke without so much as a note, taking a shiny blade to their perfectly embroidered lives and slicing it in two.

Her mum had since emigrated to Portugal where she was now living with a man named Rui, leaving the others to pick up the shreds of their family life and restitch it in a whole new way. It was only in the last couple of years that her dad was starting to get back to his old self, going golfing again and meeting up with friends. He'd worn the embarrassment of being abandoned like a dark cloak for years, but gradually, he was coming back to life.

"And how is she?" her dad asked, his face pinched.

"She's fine, you know Mum. She's got sunshine and wine all year round, so she's happy."

Her dad nodded knowingly. "She always did enjoy the sun." Looking at his face, Sophie was certain he was thinking about all the family holidays they'd taken to Spain and Portugal, the photos showing a happy family with two chirpy kids. But nothing was quite that simple.

"No plans to run off to Portugal with your latest squeeze, I take it?"

Sophie smiled. "None whatsoever," she replied, her stomach flipping when she thought about the other night in the bar. She still hadn't told anyone about it, not even Rachel. She was still coming to terms with being played so blatantly. "In fact, there is no current squeeze — I'm like you, footloose and fancy-free."

Her dad laughed as he leaned down and picked up a stick, before throwing it for Doris. The Collie chased it with gusto and not for the first time, Sophie wished life could be as simple and as satisfying as it was for a dog.

"Footloose and fancy-free: is that what I am?"

"As well as being an eligible bachelor," Sophie replied, giving him a grin.

"You're a kind daughter, you know that?" Her dad kissed the top of her head and they walked on, the only sound around them in the forest being the birds tweeting and the snap of twigs under Doris's clumsy paws. It was a beautiful early spring day, the weather on the turn from crisp to hazy, the smell of the soil and surrounding greenery seeping into their airwaves.

Her dad grabbed the stick from Doris's mouth and threw it again, Doris gamely giving chase. "And how come you're single again? I thought you had high hopes for this one?"

Sophie sighed. "I did, but I think my hopes might have been misplaced. Turns out the reason she didn't want to commit was because she had a girlfriend."

"A girlfriend?" her dad replied, his tone telling her he couldn't believe it.

Sophie gave him a wry smile. "I know — you're the first person I've told." She blew out a long breath and prepared to be overwhelmed with embarrassment. However, instead she just felt lighter after revealing it, which in turn made her next step lighter, more relaxed. Deep down, she knew it wasn't her fault, even though that's how she'd taken it over the first few days.

"Well, I'm honoured," her dad said. "How did you find out?"

Sophie risked a glance his way, but all she saw were his hazel eyes sparkling with concern. She should have known he wouldn't stand in judgement — after all, her judgement was always going to be the harshest around.

"Her girlfriend paid her a surprise visit in the bar, and I was still there — and the less said about that awkward encounter, the better. So now I'm single again and jobless." That night, she'd crawled into bed, too numb to even cry. The tears had come the next morning, but later she'd realised they hadn't been for Helen. Rather, they were for the loss of yet another relationship, even if it had been completely the wrong one.

Sophie dug her hands deep into her pockets and hunched her shoulders. She was glad to be rid of Helen and her dead-end job — but the loss of both at the same time had left two gaping holes in her life. A shard of sunlight broke through the trees, making her hold up her hand to shield her eyes.

Her dad winced, putting an arm around her as they continued up the forest path. "Sorry to hear that, but it's probably for the best. Better to find out she's a cheat now than months down the line."

Sophie buried her hands deeper and nodded. "I know you're right, I just feel a bit stupid for being so gullible. I'm a grown woman after all, I shouldn't be able to be duped so easily."

Her dad gave a short, sharp laugh. "Don't be so hard on yourself. When it comes to love and relationships, normal rules fly out the window." He put a finger to his chest. "Look at me — I've got a successful business and two great kids, but my wife still walked out on me for no apparent reason and I never saw it coming." He paused, and Sophie knew he was thinking about her mum and their life together, which she'd so casually and thoughtlessly rejected.

"And I'm not saying it runs in the family, far from it. When the right woman comes along, you'll know, that's all." He squeezed her shoulder hard. "And I never thought this one sounded right, anyway. It wasn't even that she was your boss — you just never had any excitement in your voice when you spoke about her, and that's important."

Sophie looked up at her dad's stubbled face and gave him a slow smile. "That's true — I wanted to be excited, but I wasn't." She took a deep breath before continuing. "So what happened was probably what I needed: it's forced me into a fresh start, a new challenge. So I'm looking for a new job at the moment."

Doris interrupted their conversation, circling them while she barked, the sound echoing around the forest.

She was stickless.

Sophie bent down and picked up the nearest replacement, wiping the dirt away as she did. She threw it and Doris chased obediently, then ran back towards them with the stick protruding from both sides of her mouth.

"Is she grinning? I swear she's grinning," Sophie asked, grinning herself.

"She's always grinning — what's she got to frown about?"

Her dad grabbed the stick from Doris's mouth and threw it, smiling as she scarpered after it. "So what's next for you jobwise? Are you going to stick with the same kind of work or do something different?"

Sophie rolled her shoulders before replying. "I'm not sure, but I feel like I need to shake up my life — start focusing on me again. I need to stop smoking and get healthy, then get a new career. The problem is I dropped out of uni and my skills are admin, bar work and catering. And I've done that for the past ten years." She took off her glasses and wiped her eyes. "I feel like I need a change."

"Now's the time to do it — you're young, you've got your whole life ahead of you."

They both fell silent for a moment, monitoring Doris who was saying hi to another dog on the path ahead of them. There had been a spate of dog attacks in the area recently, but Doris's new friend seemed harmless enough. When the dog left Doris alone and she wandered back to them, they resumed their conversation.

"Why don't you take the time to think about what you'd like to do? I can give you some money to tide you over for a few months, you know that." He stopped walking and turned to face her. "And I've told you enough times you can come and work for me — Luke was never interested, but you could join the family firm." He swept his hand across the air above him as he spoke. "London & Daughter: got a nice ring to it, don't you think?"

Sophie couldn't help but laugh. "Until you remember I'm terrible at DIY, so not a great choice to be a builder or a carpenter."

"I could teach you," he replied. "And you've got more aptitude for it than Luke, that's for sure. You're a doer, and you know what he's like — he's a thinker, doesn't like to get his hands dirty. Whereas you — I've always thought you'd make a great worker."

Sophie hugged him and felt his strong, protective arms around him. "Thanks, Dad."

"What for?" he asked, pulling away.

"For believing in me. Sometimes, it's nice to hear even when I know you're humouring me."

Her dad laughed, the vibrations rattling through both their bodies. "I'm only half-joking," he replied, letting her go. When she stepped back, Doris was yapping at their feet, feeling left out of the love.

Sophie got down on her haunches to pet her, which Doris was thrilled about. "You know," she began, letting Doris smother her in kisses. "The only thing I really would love to do is work with animals. I love Doris, and I loved Sparky when he was around, too." Sparky had been their dog when Sophie was a child, a feisty Jack Russell who thought he was ten times bigger than he actually was.

"So why don't you retrain to be a vet?" Her dad leaned over and petted Doris as Sophie got back to her feet.

"Too time-consuming — doesn't it take like, eight years?"

"It does," her dad said. "But we paid for Luke to go to university, and I can pay for you, too. Or I could give you money to start a business, I've told you before." They continued to walk. "What about working in an animal centre? Or you could become a vet's assistant."

Sophie nodded. "Maybe," she replied. She'd been over this, but at 30, she didn't want to be at university for the next few years. She had itchy feet for life, and she wanted to be out there, living it. A vet's assistant might be the way forward, or perhaps some other kind of job working with animals? She'd been searching the internet for inspiration since her job had come to such an abrupt end, but she hadn't arrived at any decision as yet.

Just then, a woman came into view with three dogs on leashes. They watched her walk past them and both stared at each other at the same time.

"Or you could become a dog walker?" her dad said. "Big business in London: people want dogs, but they don't have time to walk them. Ridiculous if you ask me, that's the whole point of having a dog, but it's modern life."

Sophie slowed to a halt. A dog walker. Why hadn't she thought of that? She loved dogs, she loved being outdoors, and she could be her own boss. But was it that simple? Could you just start walking dogs? Set up a business just like that and boom, money started to roll in?

"And if you became a dog walker, I could be your first client — well, Doris could," her dad continued.

"I thought you said dog walkers were stupid," she said, grinning at him.

"They are — unless they're my daughter."

Sophie nodded her head, turning the idea over in her mind. Every other business idea she'd dreamed up had always had something standing in the way — but with this one, she couldn't see a downside. Her dad might just have stumbled upon her ideal job.

"You know, you might be onto something," Sophie

said. "Low start-up costs, I could start immediately and the only thing I need is to build a website."

Her dad nodded. "Exactly — and you did that for me, so that's a piece of cake." He paused. "I really think you should do this — get out of hospitality and try something different. You love dogs!"

Sophie grinned. "I really do." She hugged herself thinking about the possibility. "You know what — I think I might do this. So long as that loan's still on offer while I get on my feet."

"It's not a loan, it's a business investment," her dad replied. "And it's there whenever you want it."

Chapter Twelve

Today wasn't the day Tanya needed to have period pains from hell, but that's what she had. Still, she was trying to put on her happy public face for Alice and her boyfriend Jake, who were helping her move house, even though it currently felt like there was a shooting match going on in her stomach. She gripped the warm, plastic seat of their hire van as nausea rolled through her for the umpteenth time that day.

Dammit, some days she really wished she'd been born a man. Especially on a day like today, when she should have been focusing on her new start. But all she was actually thinking about was how she wanted to vomit.

"Is that it?" Jake asked, peering into the sunlight, looking directly at a block that rose many stories into the sky, glinting in the Saturday morning sunlight with its sleek steel and glass exterior.

"Yep, home sweet home," Tanya replied. And then, despite her nausea, a tingle of excitement rushed through her, starting in her stomach and reaching her earlobes. This was it, the start of her new adventure.

"Looks smart," Jake said, his curls bobbing around his ears as he smiled at Tanya. "Can't wait to see it!"

Tanya smiled over at Alice, who was nodding at her: she could see the appeal of Jake, his excitement was infectious. Tanya was grateful for his pep this morning, along with his offer to drive the van when she thought she might throw up on the steering wheel.

Minutes later Jake pulled on the handbrake and the van came to a halt in front of her new building. With a sudden burst of energy, Tanya jumped out and consulted with the concierge, who gave her the go-ahead to park there while she unloaded. She could have kissed him.

And she also could have kissed the weather gods, who'd selected the dry, sunshiney button for London today, meaning her move was going to be plain-sailing and not drowned as it had been when she and Meg split up. This move was getting the thumbs-up from on high. She was sure that had something to do with her gran.

"Shall we go up, first?" Alice said, her face illuminated by the sun.

Jake was already unloading, but he nodded. "You do that, I'll start getting stuff down and ready to go."

Tanya gave him a grin. "I like your thinking," she said, as Alice weaved an arm through hers and they advanced to the lift. A flashback of a few weeks earlier sprang to mind and Tanya felt her cheeks redden at the thought. She'd been thinking about Lift Woman last night when she was doing her final bits of packing, wondering if they might meet up again soon — she owed her a bottle of wine, after all. What was Lift Woman doing this morning?

As if reading her mind, Alice turned to her with a grin on her face. "So, you want to re-enact the lift scene for me? I'm that woman and you're just about to land on me?" she said, pressing the button and the lift door opening. "It'll be like a scene from a gorgeous love story. Ready?" Alice flattened herself against the lift wall as the doors closed.

Tanya simply rolled her eyes. "Get this out of your system now, please — at least that way you won't be doing it whenever you eventually meet her."

"I'm dying to meet her. You think she might be lured out here by the scent of you moving in?"

"The scent of me moving in?" Tanya repeated. "What on earth does that mean?"

Alice gave her a slow smile. "You know, lesbian speak. When one moves into the building, the others get a tingle in their spider senses and flock to help. Or offer herbal teas, that sort of thing."

"I don't drink herbal tea."

"That's because you're a very bad lesbian, we've already established that. Meat-eater, no pets, capitalist, severe lack of chequered shirts."

"When you're done with my character assassination, let me know," Tanya replied, as the lift stopped at floor 30. It'd always been the same with them, as was their running joke — Alice was more the lesbian in looks and politics, yet Tanya was the full-on ladykiller. Well, she had been at least, some years ago. "And anyway, I never once said I thought this girl was a lesbian."

But even as the words tumbled from Tanya's mouth, she knew she'd *hoped* she was, because otherwise, all of her recent thoughts about her would be for nothing. She certainly didn't fancy seeing her stepping out of the flat hand in hand with her boyfriend — there was nothing quite as crushing to any lesbian's soul than that particular scenario.

Alice raised an eyebrow as she followed her out of the lift. "You didn't need to — I could tell by your tone you thought she might be. You're always instantly dismissive of women you think are straight, whereas this one... you said nothing. You almost seemed hopeful."

"Hopeful I could knock her over again and make more of a fool out of myself?" Tanya replied, grabbing her new keys from their envelope. Alice was right: she was hopeful, but she wasn't going to tell her that. Instead, she held up her keys and gave them a shake. "Ready for the big unveiling?"

Alice clapped her hands as Tanya came to a halt outside flat 116. "I can't wait — I'm so excited!"

Tanya grinned as she put the keys in the door, Alice's excitement rubbing off on her, too.

When they walked in, Alice clapped a little harder. "Nice plush carpet in the hallway," she said, bouncing on the balls of her feet. "I like that a lot, it says opulence."

But Tanya wasn't listening. Instead, she was off down the hallway, past the bedrooms, the bathroom and the airing cupboard, and into the main room that had sold it: kitchen in one corner and huge living space with balcony overlooking the river.

Alice barged her shoulder as she walked past, but then she stopped, her mouth open. "Wow," she said. "Now this is a view that says you've made it." She twisted to look at Tanya. "You've made it, my friend. I'm so happy for you!"

Alice gave Tanya a hug, and she smiled as she was engulfed.

Yep, she'd made it.

However, the one person she'd have loved to see this view the most wasn't around anymore to do so.

* * *

Sophie was sitting in the lounge on her laptop when Rachel wandered through in her dressing gown.

"Morning!" she said, a chirp in her voice as had been the case since she'd decided on her future. "There's fresh coffee in the pot and guess what?"

"What?" Rachel asked, her voice studded with sleep.

"I have my first client for dog walking! Can you believe it — I only put a few flyers up around here this week, and I've already had three enquiries. Imagine what will happen when I put the website up." She paused. "And this one is from a lesbian, too."

Rachel turned as she picked up the coffee pot. "How do you know it's from a lesbian? Did she say that in her email?"

Sophie shook her head. "No, I cyberstalked her and her Facebook page is public." She paused. "The fact she's engaged to a woman was a bit of a giveaway."

"No flies on you," Rachel said, sitting down on the sofa next to her. "But well done — first client! When are you meeting her?"

"She asked if I could do today."

"Today?"

"I know, super-keen." Sophie shrugged. "But I can, and it means I'm making money and getting some exercise. It's a win-win."

Rachel yawned. "If you say so."

"Late night last night?" Sophie asked.

Rachel nodded. "The restaurant was crazy busy, and then we went for a drink afterwards at The Stage. Didn't get in till 2.30 this morning, and I'm back on in four hours. Somebody shoot me."

"Seems a bit extreme," Sophie replied. "Anyway, I'm going to give this woman a call and arrange to go round to meet them and their dog." She jumped up from the sofa, depositing her laptop on the coffee table.

"Them?"

"She's called Jess, her fiancée's called Lucy."

"You should ask if they have any single friends."

"I'm not in the market — not after Helen. I'm focusing

on me, remember? I'm on a romance sabbatical," Sophie replied.

"A romance sabbatical? When did you come up with that?"

Sophie puffed out her chest. "Just now. You like it?"

"It sounds very mature and like you know what you want in life," she replied. "Which is why I was sceptical when it came out of your mouth."

Sophie shook her head, drawing in a long breath. "Mock all you want my friend, but this woman is on the up," she said, pointing to her chest. "New life, now outlook, new me."

"And the new you doesn't want to get laid anymore?" Rachel asked, crinkling her forehead.

The rude woman from the other week flashed into Sophie's mind, her body flush against hers in the lift, which still caused her blood to fizz when she thought about it. Damn her for being such an idiot; it had ruined many sexy daydreams Sophie's mind had started.

"The new me is way above that," Sophie replied, almost believing it herself.

* * *

"I just love this kitchen — you've got an island. I can just imagine chopping and cooking, looking out at that view." Jake was still a ball of energy, despite the fact they'd been lugging Tanya's stuff up in the lift for the past hour.

They'd just finished their coffee, Tanya giving up on finding her kettle and instead running down to the local café to buy them. Now, they were leaning on her new island, the balcony doors thrown wide open, with sunshine licking the windows. And this despite the fact it wasn't quite al fresco weather just yet, the calendar year having just flicked into April.

"She's living the dream!" Alice said.

"I will be, just as soon as I can find my damn chopping boards and knives," Tanya said, laughing. "But seriously, thanks for helping today — you've both been lifesavers. And to thank you, my first meal here will be with you two — name the date and I'll consult my Nigella Lawson cookbook, okay?"

"You're on," Jake grinned. "Shall we go and get the last few boxes and bring the sofa up?"

Tanya nodded. "Absolutely."

They got the lift down, Jake checking out his curls in the mirror, Alice playing with a spot she'd been moaning about all morning, and Tanya frowning at her pale skin. Periods always took it out of her, plus she hadn't put any make-up on this morning, figuring she was going to get grimy anyway. She just hoped she didn't run into anyone she knew, or anyone she'd like to get to know.

That thought was stuck in her head as the lift stopped at floor 20 and Lift Woman got in, looking down at her phone. She was dressed casually again in jeans, green-and-yellow trainers, and she was wearing the same green army jacket as she had the other day. However, she seemed calmer, more relaxed than when they'd first met. But Tanya guessed that was because she hadn't just landed on top of her.

Great. Now she was meeting Lift Woman on a bad period day, sans make-up. Thanks, universe.

When the woman eventually looked up, she did a double-take, as if she wasn't expecting three other people, never mind one of them being Tanya.

When she saw Tanya, her face froze. "It's you," Lift Woman said, her tone not filled with quite as much happiness as Tanya might have hoped.

She'd been anticipating their first meeting to be one where Tanya would make light of what had happened before, she'd apologise and then they'd go for coffee, where they'd be laughing together within minutes. She hadn't anticipated it being in a lift with her best friend and her boyfriend, and with world war three going on in her stomach.

"We must stop meeting like this," Tanya said, and then immediately regretted it.

Why had she said that?

Tanya could feel Alice's eyes getting wider by the second as her gaze ping-ponged between the two of them.

"Going down!" the lift announced, the doors sliding shut. Going down? An image flicked into Tanya's mind and she quickly banished it, feeling her cheeks darken, not daring to look at Lift Woman now.

"You two know each other?" Alice asked, not waiting for a response. "Hi, I'm Alice." She held out her hand and Lift Woman shook it.

"Sophie," Lift Woman said. "Nice to meet you."

"Lovely to meet you, Sophie," Alice replied, looking from Sophie to Tanya.

But Tanya was struggling with words, not quite sure what to say in case she buggered it up again. And she really, desperately didn't want to bugger it up again.

"And this is my boyfriend Jake," Alice added, filling the blank air with her words.

Jake shook Sophie's hand, but all the while she was glancing at Tanya.

Tanya couldn't read her expression. She hoped it was more along the lines of curiosity rather than annoyance. Eventually, she held out her hand. "Good to see you again, I'm Tanya," she said.

Sophie pressed her hand into hers, and a warm rush shot up Tanya's arm, through to her core. She shifted her gaze to Sophie's face, to those scorching blue eyes she recalled so well. Tanya swallowed down hard. Then she glanced down at their hands, still joined, feeling her pulse accelerate.

When Tanya looked up, Sophie's gorgeous gaze was on her, assessing her as if for the first time. "Nice to put a name to the face," Sophie said, before dropping Tanya's hand. "So you took the flat?" she added, her lips a portrait in cerise.

It was entrancing, but Tanya tried not to stare, instead concentrating on her words coming out in a straight line. "Moving in today, with a little help from my friends," Tanya replied, indicating Alice and then Jake, who gave Sophie a little wave.

Sophie smiled at that, but her gaze was rarely off Tanya, something Tanya was acutely aware of. Her skin prickled and she cleared her throat for want of something to do. She had to get out of this lift as soon as possible — with four people, it was far too crowded. Tanya's optimal number was two, and if she had to choose with who, she knew she'd choose Sophie.

The lift made it to the ground floor and the doors slid open. Tanya walked forward first, at the same time as Sophie, and their bodies pressed together again, more familiar this time. Was it just Tanya's imagination or did Sophie lean in slightly?

She knew she had.

When Tanya glanced up at Sophie, their eyes met once more and for a split second, the world wobbled, just as it had before a few weeks back. Did Sophie feel it, too? Or did she still think Tanya was the world's biggest idiot? Tanya would love to know, but now wasn't the time to ask. Not with a house move to do, and Alice and Jake behind them.

"Sorry," Sophie said, her gaze sliding down Tanya's face as she bit her lip.

All of which made Tanya wobble that bit more internally, but from the outside she hoped she looked cool, calm and collected — it was, after all, Tanya's signature brand.

"My fault," Tanya said as she waved her arm, waiting for Sophie to walk ahead.

This morning, Sophie looked very different to how she had when Tanya had first run into her, and it wasn't simply that her hair was styled just-so and she looked shower-fresh. She was also exuding an air of confidence that hadn't been there before, one Tanya was instantly drawn to.

"So I'll see you around, now we're neighbours," Tanya said, controlling her breathing and hoping her cheeks weren't actually alight as she imagined they were.

"I'll probably see you in the lift," Sophie said with a tiny smile, glancing at Tanya. Then, just as quickly, she checked her watch and turned on her heel. "I've gotta run — but if you need anything, Rachel and I live in flat 20, so just knock." She turned to Alice and Jake. "Nice to meet you both, good luck with the move!"

With that, Sophie gave Tanya a wave, before hesitating, shaking her head and walking off.

"So I take it that was the woman you nearly knocked out when you were checking out the flat," Alice said, watching her go.

"The very same," Tanya replied, her heartbeat pounding in her ears.

"What you failed to mention in your original report was that she was stunning. I mean, did you see the eyes on her? And her perfect figure? Honey, I'd turn for her."

Tanya rolled her eyes. "You're straight, remember?" She paused. "But anyway, she just told us she lives with Rachel, so she's not available." Tanya didn't want to discuss this any further with Alice this morning: she was only just digesting the new and improved Lift Woman, whose name she now knew was Sophie. She'd never met a Sophie before.

Sophie sounded exotic, a little French, like a movie star from the golden era.

Sophie. Tanya liked the way the name rolled around on her tongue. She liked the way it tasted.

She shook her head to clear her thoughts. She had a sofa to move, no time to ponder a new woman on the horizon. Today was all about settling in and getting her bearings. And first of all, moving the damn sofa.

She flicked her head towards the van, where Jake was already up and shifting the sofa to the edge of the van's floor. Tanya and Alice ran to the back of the van to help him.

"If I shove this over the edge, are you two ready to catch it?" he said.

Alice gave him a look. "Ha ha, very funny."

"It's not that far off the truth — I'll hold it, but you're going to have to take its weight. Ready?"

Tanya nodded up to Jake, holding out her arms. "I'll get this end, you get the other, Alice, okay?"

"On it," Alice said, holding out her arms, too, as Jake shifted the sofa over the van's edge.

"Okay?" he asked as the sofa slid forwards and then

pitched down sharply, quicker than Tanya had imagined. Tanya let out an 'ooomph!' as the sofa landed heavily in her midriff, but she caught it. However, the force of it meant she staggered backwards a little, but she took a moment and managed to hold it.

"You okay?" Jake asked, concern on his face as Tanya looked up.

"I think so," Tanya said, trying to balance the sofa's weight. "Yeah, I think I'm okay." But then she glanced left, where Alice's features were creased with concern. She was struggling to hold the sofa.

"You got it, Alice?" Jake asked.

"I have, but the leg is stuck in my ribs. It really hurts!" Alice replied.

Tanya could see the sofa was lurching left where Alice didn't have it balanced. She thought hard for a solution, but she couldn't see an obvious one.

"I can't move or I'll drop it, and then you'll have more weight," Tanya said, her voice rising. She didn't want anyone injured and she didn't want a buggered sofa. They were in a pickle and she leaned backwards, trying to get the attention of Roger the concierge, but he was on the phone.

"And if I let go you're both buggered," Jake said from above them, where he was still holding onto the other end of the sofa.

"Should we try to push it back up and try a different angle?" Tanya asked.

"Maybe," Jake replied.

"Can I help?" said a voice from behind.

When Tanya turned her head, that voice belonged to Sophie. "I forgot my headphones, just came back for them." She immediately sprang to the middle of the sofa and took the weight, which freed the leg from Alice's ribs.

"Oh, thank god. I thought I was going to puncture a lung," Alice said, breathing out.

"No problem," Sophie replied, smiling at Tanya.

"Alice — if you let Sophie take your end, you can you take one side of my end, then hopefully we can get it down?" Jake said, pointing.

Alice made sure Sophie was okay, then she ran around and did as Jake instructed. Together, with lots of shouting and coaxing, they managed to get the sofa to the ground unscathed. When its legs touched the floor, Tanya let out a sigh. "Thanks so much, we nearly had casualties then," she said, smiling at Sophie.

"You need a hand getting it up the stairs, too?" Sophie asked.

"We might," Tanya said. "Do you have time?"

Sophie nodded. "Sure."

Tanya tried not to focus on Sophie's strong build as they lifted the sofa on the count of three, getting it through the front door with the help of Roger the concierge holding the lift door. Then they all wedged themselves and the sofa inside — it was a tight squeeze. It was only when the doors shut Tanya realised Sophie was stuck on the back wall again, this time pinned by her sofa.

"I seem to do this to you a lot, don't I?" Tanya said, grinning.

"I guess I'm coming to floor 30 with you," Sophie replied.

Chapter Thirteen

Sophie followed Tanya out onto the balcony, accepting the offer of a river view. Alice and Jake had disappeared downstairs to get the last few boxes, which left just the two of them. However, it didn't feel as awkward as their first exchanges — perhaps Sophie had been a little hasty in judging her new neighbour.

"Like I said, if you need anything, let us know. Not just a cup of sugar or a stick of butter, but good pubs to go to, restaurants, shops. We've lived here for a year, so we're locals now."

"I'll do that, thanks," Tanya said.

"This really is a lovely flat — two bedrooms as well. Are your friends moving in, too?" Sophie's gaze was raking the view, revelling in the lunchtime sunshine. She checked her watch: she needed to get a move on if she was going to make her appointment, but she didn't want to move from this particular spot. Outside space was at a premium in London, and it was what she missed the most living in her flat.

Tanya shook her head. "On my own — Alice and Jake are just helping me today."

Sophie tried to keep a hold on her facial muscles, but she knew they'd gone into surprise mode. "Wow," she said. "Are you a not-so-secret millionaire?" Sophie knew what these flats went for, and it wasn't anything near what she could afford. Then again, that would be something no bigger than a shoe box, so it wasn't an ultra-reliable barometer.

Tanya laughed, and her face lit up when she did. She was so different from that first morning they'd met: friendly, helpful, grateful for Sophie's help. Sophie much preferred this version than what she'd got on day one.

"Not a millionaire, no. But my ex and I sold a house when we split up two years ago, so I had money from that." Tanya's face clouded over then. "Plus, my gran gave me some cash, so there was that, too."

Sophie's stomach dropped: she shouldn't have pried, Tanya's whole persona had changed in an instant. She'd gone from sunshine to stormy in the blink of an eye. "I'm sorry," she said. "I shouldn't have asked."

Tanya shook her head, painting a water-coloured smile on her face. "It's fine — I've just been lucky in some ways, buying and selling at the right time. My ex is still sitting on her pile of cash, so she's lucky, too. And now, here I am." Tanya splayed her hands wide. "On the waterfront in Woolwich. A far cry from where I was living in Finchley, but I think it was the right move. At least, I hope it will be."

Sophie smiled at her new neighbour: so Tanya's ex was a woman *and* she had a balcony to die for. She chewed over those bits of information before replying. Tanya was a lesbian, which she'd thought she might be. However, now it was confirmed, Sophie was inordinately pleased, a happy grin tugging at the corners of her mouth.

"I'm sure you'll be happy in this flat, how could you not be?" she said. "And if it helps, Rachel and I — my flatmate by the way — we did the same. We moved from north London to south, and contrary to popular belief, the world did not end."

Sophie still recalled her dad's horror when she'd told him. "My dad thought I was selling my soul to the devil, but even he can see the benefits of living here. We just rent, but one day, I'd love to buy a flat as nice as this one." Sophie gave Tanya a smile and wandered back into the living room. "You've done really well."

"Thanks," Tanya said. "And thanks again for your help, too."

Sophie checked her watch again. "No worries," she said. "But I have to dash, I've got a client I have to meet. My first one."

"Client? What do you do?"

"I've just started a dog-walking business. New venture, new horizons."

Tanya gave an impressed nod. "For you and me both," she said, sweeping her hand around the flat. "Good luck with your new client. And I hope to see you around."

Sophie gave her a full-beam smile.

Much to her surprise, she hoped so, too.

Chapter Fourteen

"I can't believe it — you're finally a home owner!" Meg hugged Tanya as she sat down opposite her in a café called Porter's. Seemingly custom-made to make you feel good about yourself, it was a mass of huge windows that bathed you in natural light, coupled with righteous coffee and incredible-looking food.

Meg was Tanya's ex-girlfriend, and after some time navigating their post-relationship status, they were now back to being friends. Tanya was thrilled it had finally happened — she never wanted to be without Meg in her life. Porter's was just around the corner from the flat Meg shared with her wife Kate, and Meg was clearly a regular, greeting all the staff like they were long lost friends.

"I am indeed," Tanya replied, leaning back in her wooden chair. Her new place was all hers, the first time she'd owned something on her own and that was an amazing feeling. To be able to sit here with Meg and say that showed just how far they'd come in the two years since they split up. It seemed like a lifetime ago.

"The pictures you sent me looked fantastic. And that

river view! I can't wait to come over and see it." She paused. "And did I spot an island?"

Tanya nodded, a wide grin on her face. "And a wine cooler. Did I mention I own a wine cooler?"

Meg shook her head. "You did not. I'm so jealous now." She paused. "Did you buy some wine to put in it?"

"First thing I did," Tanya replied. "And I'd like to tell you that's not true, but I'd be lying." She paused as their coffees arrived, brought by a smiling woman with awesome hair, shaved up one side. Tanya had always wanted to do that, but she'd never had the guts. Plus, she worked in finance, where it wasn't really the done thing.

"Thanks, Jess," Meg said, a smile on her face. "Jess, this is my friend Tanya and she's just moved to Woolwich — so you're going to be neighbours!"

Jess put out a hand and Tanya shook it. "You live in Woolwich?"

Jess nodded. "Yep — we moved down there six months ago, one of the new builds on the river. My girlfriend opened a new optician's nearby, and I'm opening a café there, so it was a no-brainer." She paused, putting one hand in the back pocket of her jeans.

"She's your fiancée, not your girlfriend," Meg corrected.

Jess gave her a smile. "I keep forgetting — it's still new." She turned her gaze back to Tanya. "Whereabouts are you?"

"On the river, too — just moved in this week."

"In that case, we should have a drink in the pub —

and then you must come into the café when it opens for coffee and cake."

"Definitely get the cake," Meg agreed, laying her hand on Tanya's arm. "Jess makes the best cakes, as does Mark, her business partner. In fact, I will demonstrate — can we get some now?"

Jess nodded. "Salted caramel?"

"God, yes," Meg replied, as if Jess had just offered her a massage with a long-lasting, happy finish.

"After a reaction like that, this cake has a lot to live up to," Tanya said, laughing.

"It's never let anybody down yet," Jess replied. "Be right back."

Tanya watched her leave, her mouth watering at the sound of this apparently legendary cake. But then she thought of her gran baking in her bright yellow kitchen, the smell of chocolate and vanilla wafting around her house just like always. A wave of emotion welled inside her, but she pushed it down and turned her mind back to today, away from the impending funeral.

"So how do you know Jess?"

"She's Kate's sister-in-law, the one who moved out just before I moved in."

"Oh, she's *that* Jess," Tanya replied. "Well it'll be good to know some people who live in the area. I've already met some people in my block, which means so far, the move is proving to be a good one."

"That's so great," Meg said, and Tanya knew she meant it.

"I'm still kinda pinching myself. Like this morning, I woke up and had coffee in the sunshine on my balcony, overlooking the Thames. It's like I'm on holiday — only, I'm not."

Jess interrupted their conversation, arriving with a slice of salted caramel cake, with two forks.

"There you go," Jess said, placing it on their table. "On the house," she added.

"Free cake — it's going to taste even better," Meg said, grinning. "Did you make this?"

"Of course," Jess replied, as if that were the stupidest question in the world.

Tanya picked up one of the forks Jess had brought and tasted the cake: sweet with a hint of salt, melting chocolate, oozing caramel, creamy filling. Was there anything to dislike? Apparently not.

"I'm single," Tanya said, her tongue still tingling from its recent taste sensation. "Is this cake seeing anyone or can I take it on a date?"

Jess grinned. "She's not a cheap date, but I could ask her."

Tanya licked her lips, scooping a bit more cake onto her fork. "So the place you're opening in Woolwich — will it be like this one?"

Jess nodded. "That's the plan — it's going to be called Porter's, too, and it's going to be my baby. So if you know anyone who needs a job, let me know, I'm looking for staff. And if they can bake, all the better."

"I don't, but I'm sure you'll do well — a good café is what those flats need."

"I hope you're right. Anyway, I better get back," Jess said, jerking her thumb over her shoulder at the queue forming at the counter.

"So do you feel different now you've got your own place?" Meg asked, taking another bite of the cake.

"I do," Tanya replied. "It feels like the right move — like I'm finally a grown-up." She paused. "Not that we weren't grown-up, but you know what I mean."

Meg smiled at her. "I know exactly what you mean."

"I feel so settled, I might even bake some bread."

"That is settled," Meg said, laughing, her blonde hair shorter than when she and Tanya had been together.

Blondes. Huh. Tanya never thought she had a type, but Sophie was blonde-ish.

"You said you met some neighbours, too?" Meg added.

Tanya nodded. "I did. We had a bit of a rocky start, but she helped us move the sofa in." She smiled as she thought about Sophie saving the day with the sofa, stepping in and calmly making sure they didn't get crushed. Something had shifted when they'd chatted on the balcony — that was the friendly moment Tanya had hoped might happen, and perhaps something more than friendship was on the cards.

All Tanya knew was, she hadn't felt such a strong, instant connection to anyone before.

Nothing so visceral, so raw.

Not even when she'd met Meg, and she'd thought that was a thunderbolt. So what did that make Sophie?

"She? Lesbian?" Meg asked, bringing her back to the present.

"Could be," Tanya said, smiling. "Her name's Sophie."

"Sophie — sounds very French and fancy."

Tanya laughed at the similarity of their thoughts on Sophie's name. "That's what I thought, but she's definitely not French."

"Is she fancy?"

Tanya gave Meg a look.

"And she helped you move?"

"She did."

"And you accepted her help?"

Tanya gave Meg a look. "Don't you start. Alice gave me this lecture the other day."

"That's because we know you. How is Alice?" Meg and Alice had always got on; when Tanya and Meg had split, Alice had spent weeks mourning the loss of Meg.

"She's good — she sends her love." Tanya leaned forward. "And she's in love, too — a perky personal trainer called Jake. I like him a lot; he's good for her."

Meg smiled. "That's great news — tell her I said hi." She paused. "Are women still hitting on her, though?"

Tanya laughed out loud. "Every day," she grinned. "Poor old Alice and her faux-lesbian style."

"She's much better than you, Mrs Clean Lines and tailored shirts."

"That's what Alice tells me," Tanya replied. "Anyway, enough about me — how's your lovely wife? Is love still blooming in the Harding-Carter household?"

Meg's smile got broader if that were possible. After all, she was talking about her two greatest passions in life: floristry and Kate — not necessarily in that order. "Certainly is. We're inseminating this week — can you believe it?"

Tanya smiled: Meg was going to have a baby. She tried to picture herself doing that, but her mind drew a blank. "That's amazing, really. How's that going to work with your flower shop?"

Meg shrugged. "We'll worry about that when it happens — but how hard can it be? Millions of parents juggle work and childcare every day, don't they?"

"They do," Tanya replied. "Plus, he or she will have an army of lesbians ready to lend a hand."

"I hope so, Aunty Tanya!"

"Closest I'll ever get to be being an aunty, what with Jonathan buggering off to Dubai forever."

"Have you heard from him lately?" Meg asked.

Tanya shook her head. "Not lately." She paused, remembering again she hadn't told Meg her news. "I need to drop him an email, actually. You just reminded me."

Meg nodded. "And how's your gran doing?"

Tanya took a deep breath and tried to regulate her breathing, but it wasn't easy. Telling Meg wasn't like telling a stranger, because Meg knew Tanya's scars. Meg was the only person Tanya had ever let anywhere near her homelife.

Tanya started to shake her head, the tears bubbling behind her eyes. She went to say something, but her voice was absent, gone.

Meg's face dropped, alarm spreading across her features. "Tanya?" she said. "Is she okay?" Pause. "Has she gone?"

Tanya crumpled then, nodding slowly, the tears beginning to fall. She took a deep breath, and then another, but it was no good, the floodgates had opened. And then Meg's arms were around her, squeezing her, and Meg's voice was in her ear, telling her everything was going to be alright.

Even though they both knew that everything had just collapsed in Tanya's world, and that everything was never going to be quite the same again.

"I'm so sorry. I know what she meant to you, what she meant to everyone. When did it happen?"

"Last month," Tanya said, pulling back, getting a tissue from her bag.

"And you only just told me?" Meg was going to chastise her, but then clearly thought better of it. "Babe, you need to reach out when things like this happen. Your friends are there to help you."

Tanya nodded. "I know," she said. "I just needed some time to process. And to really believe she's gone."

"So have you been to the funeral?"

Tanya blew her nose before she replied, and wiped her

eyes again. "Still waiting on a date — there's a backlog in the area apparently. It's not the time to die in Sturby." She sighed and blew her nose again.

"Have you spoken to your mum?"

Tanya sighed again, shaking her head. "No, you know the score. She'll probably blame me for Gran dying."

Meg snorted. "Don't take any of her shit — because remember, it's her shit, not yours."

"I know," Tanya replied. "I'm going to mentally prepare before going up there. I spoke to Alan, so at least he's there."

"Send him my love," Meg said.

"I will."

"Do you want me to come with you? Moral support and all that?"

Tanya shook her head, despite being touched. The bond between her and Meg was strong; it always would be. Meg had been her first true love.

"That's really lovely of you, but no. This is something I have to do on my own. Face my parents, say goodbye to Gran. I knew it was coming, I just have to be strong."

"You sure?"

Tanya nodded.

"Okay. But ring me, and let me know how it goes. And if you need to talk while you're there, I'm here, okay?"

"I know," Tanya replied.

"There's me going on about birth, and all the while you didn't tell me your gran had died."

Tanya shrugged. "It's the circle of life, isn't it? My gran's gone, but you're planning on a new baby. Life goes on, doesn't it?"

Meg smiled. "It does. But if I can do anything to help — anything at all — just let me know, okay?"

"You could order me a new mother at the parent shop if you like," Tanya replied.

"Is there an app for that?" Meg asked.

Chapter Fifteen

Sophie had forgotten the collapsible doggy water bowl, so she walked Branston back to her block of flats to fetch it. Branston was a snappy mop of a Yorkshire Terrier who thought he was born to take on the world. Sophie wasn't going to be the one to tell him he was only a foot tall, and to stop being so territorial about public pavements.

She rounded the corner into their courtyard, gave Roger a wave and jumped into the lift, pressing the floor 20 button. As the doors closed, Branston squared up to himself in the lift mirror and began to bark at his own reflection. When he moved left, so did his reflection and he barked louder; when he moved right, he stopped, seemingly puzzled.

"Stupid dog," Sophie said, as the lift reached her floor. "It's you, Branston, nobody else." Every time she said the dog's name, she had a hankering for a cheese-and-pickle sandwich.

In response, Branston cocked his head, still thrown.

"Good job you're so cute, isn't it?" Sophie said, leading him out of the lift.

Branston's other less savoury habit, along with challenging every dog that came his way, was peeing in inappropriate places, including on people. His owners had warned Sophie, but so far, he'd resisted peeing on her. However, his reputation went before him, and when other dog owners spotted them out in the park, they gave Branston a wide berth. A dog behaviourist would have a field day.

"No peeing in the flat, okay?" she told him as his paws clip-clopped on the laminate floor in their hallway. She walked through to the lounge, and grabbed the bowl, stuffing it into her backpack. Being able to keep the dogs hydrated was essential in her line of work. She stopped and downed a glass of water herself before leading Branston back to the lift, waiting for it to arrive.

When the doors opened, Tanya was standing inside it, a suitcase by her side, her face drawn. She was dressed in black jeans, black jacket, black boots and black sunglasses. The only thing unblack about her was her hair, which smelt as fresh as it looked. Her expression, while not quite black, was definitely straying into charcoal.

What had gone so wrong with her day to warrant such an outfit, a mood? It was in stark contrast to their last meeting, when Sophie had given her a hand moving and seen the inside of her new flat.

Tanya took a moment to register Sophie was standing in front of her.

Sophie's insides, meanwhile, did a little jig of happiness

— even if Tanya wasn't in the best of moods, it was still good to see her again. She'd been primed and ready to be on her best behaviour whenever it happened.

"Hey! Fancy meeting you here," Sophie said, pulling Branston inside. He assessed Tanya, before starting to bark at his reflection again.

Tanya glanced down, then gave Sophie a weak smile. "Hi," she said, so quietly Sophie almost didn't hear her.

"Going away?" she asked, nodding at Tanya's case. It was black too, hard-shelled and most likely cost more than Sophie's entire wardrobe. She recalled suitcase shopping last summer and being horrified by the prices.

Tanya looked at her case, almost as if she'd forgotten it was there. "Yeah," she replied. "Going home for a few days."

Sophie nodded. "Parental duties?"

Tanya shook her head. "My gran's funeral." Her shoulders slumped as she said it: no wonder she looked so dark and defeated.

Sophie's heart broke just a little when she heard that — she wasn't close to her grandparents, but she understood loss acutely.

She could tell from Tanya's face that her gran wasn't just someone she saw every now and again: her gran had clearly been a major influence on her life, and Sophie wished she could do something to make Tanya feel better.

"Shit, I'm sorry," she said, pulling on Branston's lead as he sniffed Tanya's case. "Were you close?"

Fucking hell, she had verbal diarrhoea. Just shut up, Sophie! What did it matter? The woman was still dead. Now she was the one with bad manners, making Tanya feel worse than she already did.

Tanya gulped, then nodded, taking off her sunglasses. Her eyes were puffy and bloodshot. "We were. She taught me everything. She was the first woman I ever loved."

Sophie was stumped. "Shit, I really am sorry." Should she hug her? Sophie assessed the situation, but then decided against it. After all, she hardly knew her at all, and who even knew if Tanya was the hugging type? She wasn't giving off that air right now. Her body was taut, a mass of sharp angles.

"Where's home?" Sophie asked, popping the silence hanging over them like a weighty balloon.

"The Midlands," Tanya said, screwing up her face.

And then, out of the corner of her eye, Sophie saw Branston raise his right leg: unless she was very mistaken, he was about to perform his party trick.

"Branston, no!" Sophie shouted, but it was too late.

As Tanya widened her eyes in fascination and horror, Branston let out a steady stream of doggy wee onto Tanya's left boot.

Sophie yanked his lead, and he fell off balance, squirting a shaded line of wee up in the air, arcing over Tanya's case and hitting the mirror.

"Shit!" Tanya said, jumping out of the way, as Branston continued to jump around.

"Luckily not, just wee," Sophie replied as the lift reached the ground floor.

Then Branston shook himself, before crouching and lowering his backside towards the floor.

Was he going to poo, too?

Not if Sophie could help it. "Branston, no!" she shouted loudly, pulling him up. He barked, went to squat again, but Sophie managed to stop him. She fished in her backpack and got out a doggy chew and fed it to Branston, which seemed to take his mind off his need to expel anything else from his body.

When she looked up, frazzled, Tanya was shaking her head, a smile on her face. "So how's the dog walking going?" she asked, breaking into a giggle.

Sophie grabbed a pack of tissues from the backpack, and then she was on her haunches, mopping up the wet floor. "It has its ups and downs," she replied, rolling her eyes. However, she was pleased to see Tanya was taking it all in her stride — getting weed on by a dog could have sent her over the edge.

When Sophie had soaked up the liquid, including patting Tanya's shoe dry, she produced a pack of Wet Wipes and mopped Tanya's case, before standing up and offering her a Wet Wipe, too.

Tanya shook her head. "He didn't get me directly — just my shoe. And I'm sure I've had worse than that on a night out in Soho."

Sophie pulled Branston out of the lift, giving him

a stern look. "Apparently he has a habit of doing this. His owners told me it means he likes you, but I'm not sure if that's just a really bad excuse on their part."

Tanya wheeled her case towards the door. "He certainly took my mind off today," she replied. "Perhaps it's just the curse of us in this lift? Maybe we should avoid getting it together from now on."

"Could be tricky, seeing as we live here," Sophie said, still mortified. "I really am sorry. You're bereaved, and my dog wees on you."

Tanya laughed at that. "Brings you back down to earth, doesn't it? Animals are good at that."

"They are," Sophie said. She walked Branston outside so he could finish what he'd started, but now he was outside, he had no interest in expelling anything. Typical.

Tanya assessed her. "You know, his arc of wee got you." She pointed at a wet line on Sophie's trousers. "You want me to hold him while you go and change?" Tanya held out her hand to take his lead. "Consider it my penance for being such an arse to you when we first met. Your dog's weed on me now, so we're sort of even."

Sophie winced: Tanya was being lovely, which made her feel even more guilty for Branston weeing on her. "Are you sure you can hold him? I won't make you late?"

"Yes, it's fine, just go," Tanya told her. "I'm always super-early for trains, it's a fault of mine."

Sophie did as she was told, praying Branston wouldn't attempt any more deposits while she was gone.

She was back in five minutes, with Tanya bent down and chatting to Branston when she returned.

When she saw Sophie, she straightened up and gave her the lead, checking her watch. "I better get going — I have a homestead to get to and a funeral to endure."

Sophie nodded. "I hope the funeral is a fitting send-off for your gran. She sounds like a lovely woman."

Tanya gave a deep sigh. "She was the best. Sadly I can't say the same for her daughter, my mother." She closed her eyes, then took a deep breath. "Wish me luck."

"Good luck," Sophie replied, even though she wasn't sure it was the right sentiment for her gran's funeral. "And Tanya?"

Tanya looked up. "Yes?"

"When you're back, maybe we could grab a drink, and you can fill me in on how it went?" Sophie paused, not stopping to wonder where her courage had come from. This speech was out of the blue, her invitation putting herself out there. If Tanya said no, she might hurl herself off the roof of her life. "And I promise to leave Branston at home," she added.

Tanya laughed gently, and smiled her million dollar smile: it illuminated her face and robbed Sophie of rational thought for a second.

And then her answer spilled from her lips. "I'd like that. In fact, I'll store it up as something to look forward to. It might help me get through the next few days." She smiled a little harder. "See you when I'm back."

Sophie nodded, a stupid grin creasing her face. "You definitely will," she replied.

Chapter Sixteen

Tanya grabbed her suitcase from the luggage rack at the end of the carriage and got off the train. Sturby Central. It still sent a shudder to her heart, even though she was fond of the station's architecture, with its ornate building and long history. Underfoot, the concrete was grey and stained, just like her childhood.

The signs ahead told her of the pies she could enjoy, hand-made at the local bakery, and that took her back to her formative years and the taste of buttery pastry filled with chewy brown meat and veg. She'd loved pies back then, but she never ate them now — she was far too conscious of her figure to do that.

She clicked her way down the stairs, through the dank underpass and out of the station, to the waiting darkness outside. It was 8.30pm, and Tanya walked slowly to the cab rank, queuing for a taxi to take her home.

Home. It'd always seemed like a weird word — she'd never really considered herself to have a home. She had a house where she'd grown up, and where her parents still lived, but she'd never had a home as such.

But now the time had come to go back to that house, to face her parents and to attend her gran's funeral. Her beloved gran who'd succumbed to the cancer that had slowly eaten her from the inside.

A cab arrived and she gave the driver a thin-lipped smile, breathing in the cold air that smelt of disappointment, just like always. The ride home would take her past her old school where she'd stood out for being odd and clever; past the park where she'd tried to fit in on damp evenings, drinking cider in the shelter.

They drove past the pub she'd had her first drink in, now called The Shaggy Dog and not The Red Lion as it had been back in her day. Past the building that had housed the club they used to go to on a Monday night, now a multiplex cinema. Past their old chip shop, which had now branched out to selling pizzas and kebabs as well.

And then, far sooner than she'd have liked, they were turning into her road, and the cab was slowing down, drawing up outside her parents' house. Tanya drew in a deep breath to stop her nerves from jangling. Why had she agreed to stay here tonight?

She suddenly felt very alone, but then an image of Sophie tugging on Branston's lead popped into her head, which caused a smile. Sophie and Branston had at least brought a touch of normality to an otherwise bizarre day. It had been good to chat about where she was going, to crack the surface of her funeral emotions. They were still icy underneath, but Sophie and Branston had made a dent in them, which was something.

The image of Sophie in her jeans and jacket, hair swept to one side, her stunning eyes lingering on Tanya's face was burned into her memory. And had she asked her out on a date as they left? Or had she just been showing concern? Either way, Tanya was keen to get to know Sophie better, because right now, she was the one spot of brightness in her life. Every time she saw Sophie, Tanya felt ten times better.

"That'll be £12.40," the driver told her, turning to give her a toothy grin. His accent was so thick, it curled at the edges. Tanya winced: she knew she was a snob, but she hated her hometown accent.

She paid the driver, put her suitcase on the pavement and slammed the taxi door. The car drove off, which left Tanya staring at the house where her parents would be sitting on their allotted sofas, watching TV, Daily Mail on the coffee table, tutting at anything that didn't conform to their world view.

She couldn't put it off any longer. She clicked up the handle on her wheelie case, took two steps forwards and walked up the garden path.

* * *

When her mum opened the door and saw Tanya, her mouth twitched, her features gritted with disappointment. Her fair hair was tinted golden, her skirt and top painted beige.

"It's you," she said, stepping aside and leaning back into the door, as if physical contact with her daughter might make her a lesbian, too.

"Mum," Tanya replied as she stepped into the mustard-coloured hallway, breathing in the familiar smell of pine-scented air freshener mixed with overcooked meat. Her mum was a great believer in a meat-and-two-veg diet — Tanya's brief flirtation with vegetarianism in her teenage years hadn't gone down well.

Her dad stepped out into the hallway then, saving her and her mum from an awkward scene. She hadn't seen her dad in three years, either. His smile was stilted, sharp angles where there should have been curves.

"Love," he said, extending his hand and letting it rest briefly on Tanya's arm. "Good to see you, despite the circumstances."

Tanya nodded, his words a comfort. "You too, Dad."

"Leave your bags at the bottom of the stairs and come through to the kitchen. I'll put the kettle on," he added, flicking his head to the left.

Her dad looked old — properly old. His skin was wrinkled and sagging, and his hair was now completely grey. He'd always been the oldest dad of her crowd — he was 42 when Tanya was born. Now he was approaching 78, and it showed. Might she be back for his funeral soon, too? And if so, how would she feel?

"How was the train?" he asked, shuffling from the kettle to the dark wooden cupboard, his breathing laboured.

The shuffle was new, too.

"It was fine. Thursday night so it was busy." Tanya still had her coat on, and her mum hadn't followed them through to the kitchen. The air in the kitchen felt lighter because of it. "How are you?"

Three years of nothing and this was the conversation they were having? Tanya's insides churned like a washing machine on fast spin, while her dad poured boiling water into mugs and pretended this scene was normal, everyday.

"Fine, okay. Your gran's passing has been hard on your mum of course, but it's good you came back. Good for her, too, even though she might not say it." He paused, looking Tanya in the eye. "I appreciate it, love. We both do."

If the word bristle hadn't been invented, Tanya would have coined it on the spot. "I came back for Gran."

Her dad didn't say anything in reply, he simply held her gaze and nodded, before getting the milk from the fridge.

"I assume you still take milk? It hasn't gone out of fashion in London, has it?" he said, in an effort to lighten the mood.

Tanya gave him a weak smile. Tonight was going to be just as hard as she thought, perhaps even harder. "Just a touch, thanks."

He joined her at the table, and Tanya let out a sigh, glad to have something to hold in her hands, to fiddle with.

"You're looking well," her dad said. "Job going okay?" He was holding onto his mug as if he were lost at sea and it was the only thing keeping him afloat.

Tanya nodded. "It is. I'm not doing court anymore — I'm working for a city firm doing some legal stuff."

Her dad nodded. "Glad to hear you're doing well. I always knew you would, you've got that determination." He sighed, frowning at her. "Don't be too hard on your mother, she's having a rough time at the moment, what with losing her mum."

Tanya took a deep breath, swallowing down a landmine of emotions. "I know how she feels."

Her dad looked away.

The awkwardness was broken by a yapping sound from the next room. Tanya furrowed her brow and glanced at her dad. "Is that Delilah?" Delilah was her gran's beloved King Charles Spaniel.

Her dad nodded. "She's been living with us since your gran got sick and we've been taking her in for visits." His face softened. "She's a treat to have around, actually. Even your mum thought so till your gran died." He stopped and looked up at the large black-and-white clock ticking on the wall beside the kitchen door.

"But now your gran's gone, she wants to rehome her — says it was only a temporary move while Gran was recovering." He pulled at the skin at the front of his neck — his nervous tick. It was something Tanya remembered him doing quite a bit throughout her childhood. "I tried to talk her round, but you know what she's like," he added in a whisper, glancing over his shoulder.

That lit a fuse in Tanya. They were talking about Delilah, but they might as well have been talking about her life. She hadn't fitted into her mum's vision of family life, so her mum had discarded her, with her dad giving a shrug and passively accepting the decision. And now she was planning to do the same to Delilah?

Her mum couldn't even wait for her gran to be cold in the ground till she made the decision — a decision that took Tanya right back to ten years ago when she'd been cast aside in exactly the same way, apparently surplus to daughter requirements.

"Where's she planning to rehome her?" Tanya asked, her tone like granite, shaking her head. "I used to wonder if she had a heart — I spent my teenage years watching American TV shows, mesmerised by the mums — they smiled, they hugged their kids, they loved them.

"Mum was never like that. She never hugged me, and then she disowned me. And now she's doing the same to Delilah." Rage shot up in her and she knew she had to leave, to get out before she said or did something she might regret. "I shouldn't have said I would stay here, this was a mistake. Nothing's changed."

And it hadn't. Delilah was living proof.

Tanya stood up, and her dad followed suit.

"It's not the same, love, and I am talking to her, trying to get her to come round where you're concerned," he said, reaching out his hand and gripping her arm. "We love you, Tanya, we always have."

Tanya stared at her dad's hand on her. He'd never said that before, told her he loved her.

How she wanted to believe him, she really did, but his words were hollow in the face of her mum's actions — actions he'd supported.

"I'm going to Alan's for the night — he offered, and his place has always felt more like home to me." She swallowed down the tears that were threatening to spill out.

Her dad's grip tightened, his eyes red, pleading. "Please, love," he said. "Don't go. I'd like you to stay. Will you stay, for me?" He paused. "I'll have a word with her, see if she'll talk to you." He cast his gaze to the floor and then back up to look at her. "It's not the way I want it. Please don't go."

Tanya sighed, shaking her head. She leaned forward and kissed him on the cheek, overwhelmed with childhood memories as his familiar scent hit her nose: Old Spice.

"Will you stay?" he asked again, fixing her with his gaze. His eyes were still the same, still watery, uncertain.

Her resolve crumbled. Tanya loved her dad, she always had — she just wished he'd stand up for himself every now and again. Her shoulders dropped and she nodded her head softly. "I'll stay, for you. But I'm not sitting up playing happy families if she won't even be in the same room as me."

Her dad squeezed her arm, a sad smile on his face. He took a deep breath before he replied, pulling on the skin in front of his neck again. "Have you eaten? Let me get you a sandwich and then maybe a glass of whisky? We can toast your gran before you go to bed. How's that?"

Tanya nodded her head. Her dad was trying, in his own small way. She shrugged off her coat and sat down as she heard Delilah bark in the lounge again. Poor Delilah, she had no idea what was coming to her.

Chapter Seventeen

"You sure I can't tempt you to come with me on this job? Your schedule's not booked yet, and I could use an extra pair of hands." Her dad was finishing his tea in his bright kitchen, sunshine splashing in through the skylight.

Sophie smiled at him: he looked happy, which was great to see. "No thank you — I've come to walk Doris, give her a taste of how a professional does it. She's very interested, aren't you, Doris?"

Doris barked, seeing Sophie pick up her lead.

Her dad shook his head. "I dunno, you bring up your kids, and all you want is a little respect and the occasional helping hand. And what do I get? Luke buggers off to Brighton to do designing and whatnot, and you've got no interest in DIY, despite being a lesbian." He rolled his eyes with mock disgust. "I thought that was a banker when you came out."

Sophie laughed. "I know, I'm a DIY disappointment, what can I say?" She paused. "I can give you an hour — the house you're working on is near the park, right?

Did you say you just need help getting stuff into the house?"

He nodded, his smile perked up. "I did."

"Okay — one hour, tops."

He walked over and planted a kiss on her cheek. "You're an angel."

"And you're a manipulator," she replied.

Half an hour later and Sophie was sweating: this was why she also didn't fancy being in the building trade — she wasn't built for lumping stuff around. She walked around to the back of her dad's dusty van and picked up another plank of wood, taking care with the edges. She already had a splinter in her finger and even though she was single, a splintered finger was never a good look.

At that thought, an image of a black-clad Tanya formed in her mind, and her stomach sank. How was she getting on at home, at her gran's funeral? She hoped it wasn't too dreadful.

She'd looked so broken in the lift yesterday, so bereft and worn down by life, and Sophie's heart had ached for her.

If her dad died, she wouldn't know what to do.

Her dad appeared at the back of the van, breaking her thoughts. Small beads of sweat glistened on his brow as he grinned at her. "You see, this is why you wouldn't make it in the building trade — too much daydreaming. Maybe dog-walking is more your thing, you're getting paid to daydream then, aren't you?"

Her dad wiped his brow and fixed her with a look.

"Were you daydreaming about anything? Anyone?" He narrowed his gaze. "Remember, the bad thing about being around your dad is that I've known you since you were born." He tapped her forehead with his index finger. "I know how you think, how you tick. And that look you just had? That was the look that said you're thinking about a girl." He paused. "Am I right?"

Sophie felt her cheeks blossom into redness as she shook her head.

Yes, she had been thinking about a girl. And if she was being honest, Tanya had been on her mind non-stop since their meeting in the lift yesterday, since she'd got to know her that little bit more.

Sophie wished she'd taken her number so she could text her and see how she was, but that might have seemed odd. They were meeting when she was back, and that would have to do. But when they did meet up again, Sophie wanted to ask more questions, get more answers, listen to more words drop from Tanya's lips.

And most of all, she wanted to touch her caramel skin, to run her fingers down her cheek, to soothe her aching heart.

Whoa. She hadn't thought any of that before, and to think it in front of her dad made Sophie blush an even deeper shade of puce.

"I might have met someone new, but it's early days, hardly anything to tell." But even as she said it, she could feel her blood rushing round her body, betraying her calm exterior. Sophie turned away from her dad, the plank of wood covering her blushes. She didn't want to say too much as there wasn't much to tell just yet. For now, she wanted to keep Tanya close to her chest. She smiled at that thought as her mind painted an exquisite image in her brain.

"I'm on a romance sabbatical after Helen, and it's quite nice. I don't have to be on the lookout for love all the time, which was pretty exhausting. Now, I just am." And that part, at least, was true. She turned back to him. "And you know what? I feel quite content."

And as she walked into the house, taking the wood through to the back garden where her dad was going to sand it before turning it into bespoke wardrobes for his client, she knew her words were true. Taking some time for herself had been the right call, as had starting her own business.

In the few weeks since she'd walked out of Helen's life, Sophie had cleansed her from all of her social media, thrown out any keepsakes and dumped all her playlists from Spotify. And now her business was beginning to gain traction, too, with the word getting out.

Her dad followed her through, dumping his wood beside hers. They walked back through the length of the terraced house together to get the final two planks.

"If that's true, that's terrific — I never thought I'd hear you say you were content." His face clouded over. "You haven't been content since your mum left, you haven't stopped moving since." He smiled at her, pushing a hair away from her face. "Maybe now with this business, you can build a life you want, and finally settle into who you want to be. On your own or not." He paused. "Although the way you just spoke about that new woman, your voice had an edge to it. You're excited about her. And that never happened with the last girl."

He gave her a long stare, before grabbing his plank of wood.

For a man, and for a builder, her dad had always surprised her with his powers of perception.

Damn him.

Because Sophie was excited about Tanya, even though she hadn't truly given herself permission to be.

She rolled her eyes, shifting the focus from her as she did. "Stop being such a softie — you're giving the building trade a bad name."

Her dad laughed as they walked back into the house carrying the final two planks. "You should hear some of the conversations down at the timber yard or on projects I've worked on," he said, smiling. "Don't believe builders are hardnuts — we crumble under the slightest pressure."

"Your secret's safe with me," Sophie said, putting down the last plank in the garden. "And if you're so interested in my love life — how about your own? I think you're projecting onto me."

Now it was her dad's turn to look bashful. "I don't know what you mean."

"You're playing golf — there must be tons of women down there looking for an eligible man."

He gave her a more throaty laugh this time. "There are tons of women alright, but most of them bat for your team. None of them would look twice at me."

Sophie grinned. "At least you're getting out there, and my people are a friendly people."

"They are," he said, lining up a plank on his board, sander in hand. "And we've been comparing notes in the 19th hole. There's one woman, Dawn, she's lovely — and it turns out, we have the same taste in women. We've both got a thing for Sarah Lancashire." He shook his head. "She's such a laugh. Me and Mike are playing golf with her and her partner on Thursday — she's also a golf demon."

This was all news to Sophie, who stood in the garden, hand on hip, mouth ajar. "Let me get this straight. My father, who needs to meet a woman asap, is spending his time at the golf club hanging out with lesbians?"

He nodded again. "What can I say? Lesbians love me." He tapped her arm. "Dawn told me I'm a dyke hag."

Sophie shook her head. A dyke hag? Jesus, what was the world coming to when even her dad was talking in these terms. Frankly, she wasn't sure she was ready for such a world. "I'm going to walk Doris now and pretend that never came out of your mouth."

"You're such a prude, you know that?" her dad shouted at her retreating back.

"Bye, Dad," she responded, giving him a wave.

Chapter Eighteen

The funeral lasted 30 minutes, but it had felt like 30 hours to Tanya. She had trouble reconciling the fact her gran was inside that wooden box just in front of them, that she'd never see her again.

All around her, people had sung, prayed and cried — but not Tanya. She'd sat in silence, wishing Alice was there, or Meg, or someone who knew what her gran meant to her. Someone she loved, and who loved her back with no catch. Or even someone like Sophie, who'd come into her life recently and had shown her kindness when Tanya had barely deserved it.

Just someone who knew how much she was going to miss her gran every single day for the rest of her life. Not someone like her mother, who was sitting just down the pew, a veil drawn over her face. Was she crying? What was she thinking? Tanya had no idea.

Tanya took a deep breath, staring down at her black boots, at the scuffed wooden floor of the church. Her gran hadn't even been that religious, hadn't been a regular church-goer, but her parents had insisted this was how she was to be seen out. Tanya was pretty sure her gran would have preferred a 70s disco in her honour.

That thought made her smile, but also made her heart crack that little bit more.

A tear spilled down Tanya's cheek as her gran's face swam into her vision, blurred and smudged with tears.

* * *

Later that day, when most of the guests had gone home and Tanya had helped her dad clear up, her mum retiring to her room with one of her infamous migraines (code for "I can't deal with this emotional situation"), Tanya gave her dad a hug and slipped next door.

Alan welcomed her, putting his arm around her as they walked to the kitchen.

"What can I get you?" he asked. "Cup of tea? Something stronger? Whisky? Gin?"

"A gin would be perfect."

Tanya followed him through to his lounge, all warm and cosy, in stark contrast to her parents' house. And there, lying in front of the fire, was Delilah. She lifted her head when they came into the room, but didn't move — she was far too comfortable for that.

Tanya knelt down and petted her anyway, and the dog smiled up at her as she rubbed her furry brown tummy. "Hey there Delilah, how are you girl? Coping without your mum?"

"She's doing alright — she's been quiet today, but she's

been getting along with Bouncer and Margo, haven't you, girl?" Alan bent down and petted Delilah on the head, and she tilted her neck one way to let him.

A few minutes later Tanya was sat on the cream sofa, a sizeable gin and tonic in her hand. She took a sip, rolling the ice around the glass, sighing as it worked its magic.

"You've no idea how much I needed this," she said, letting out a low sigh.

"I can imagine. I was going to come, but I thought Celia would have appreciated me looking after Delilah more, so I did." Alan hadn't come to the funeral, instead taking care of the dogs. He'd said his goodbyes to Celia the night before, and he'd popped into the wake, too.

"Gran would have thanked you," Tanya replied. "To be honest, I would have rather spent time with the dogs than most of the people there today, and I think Celia would have said the same. But she didn't get the choice." An image of her gran laughing sprang up in her mind and she swallowed down some tears. She hadn't truly cried yet, probably because she was so tightly wound due to spending the day in close proximity with her mother.

Now, for the first time since she'd woken up this morning, Tanya relaxed, her guard down. It was a dangerous state to be in.

"I still can't believe she's gone, you know," she said. "Did you see her in the last few days?"

Alan nodded. "I did, and she was grand. She was resigned, but she told me she'd had a happy life, and she was so proud of you. She loved your visit the other week, too. Didn't stop going on about it."

"I just wish I could have made another," Tanya replied, guilt washing through her. She'd had a meeting about something that had seemed important at the time, but now she realised it meant nothing at all. It was the sort of thing her mother would do, and that thought almost made her retch.

"She understood you had a life; she was just glad you made it to see her as often as you could." Alan leaned forward. "But let's not let the gin get us all maudlin, shall we?"

Tanya rested her head back on the sofa and eyed Delilah. "You know Mum wants rid of Delilah now Gran's gone?"

Alan nodded his head slowly. "Your dad said." He paused. "I would have her, but I've already got two dogs here and I can't really take on a third. I've been asking around but no luck as yet. She's a lovely dog, she deserves a good home."

"I agree — and so would Gran. I would say I can't believe Mum could be so heartless, but I'd be lying."

Alan changed the subject swiftly. "And how's life with you? How's the job and the new flat?"

"The job's going well — boring legal stuff but they pay me a tidy sum," Tanya said. "And the flat's great, I really love it."

"Celia would be thrilled. Two beds or one?"

"Two. It's bigger than most flats I looked at, which is brilliant. There's space for people to come and stay." Tanya gave him a rueful smile. "That's a hint, by the way."

"Duly noted," Alan replied, sitting up straighter in his chair. He studied Tanya for a few moments before continuing. "Bit leftfield, but have you ever thought about taking Delilah?"

Tanya shook her head. "Me?" she said, pointing her index finger to her chest. "I live in London."

Alan gave her a look. "I'm sure they have dogs in London."

"You know what I mean. I work long hours, and I live in a flat. It's hardly conducive to having a dog." She paused. "If I lived in a house and had a garden, maybe."

"You did just say it was a big flat with lots of space. And have you got a park nearby?"

Tanya nodded. "There's a lot of outdoor space as we're by the river. The council are doing it up, trying to make it pedestrian friendly and swanky."

"Well then."

As if knowing she was being talked about, Delilah got up and walked over to the sofa, jumping up and getting comfortable next to Tanya. Her warmth seeped through Tanya's black funeral trousers, and she snaked an arm over the dog, pulling her close.

"Delilah seems to like the idea, though," Alan said, nodding towards the pair of them.

"She does, doesn't she?" Tanya wagged a finger at Alan. "And I know you trained her to jump up beside me as soon as we started chatting. I know your tricks."

Alan held up both hands. "It only occurred to me

today — I just thought I'd mention seeing as I'm desperate to find someone who'll take care of her, now your mum's decided it's a no-go. Shame, as she's taken a real shine to you."

Tanya looked down, running her hand through her soft black and brown fur, and a satisfying glow ran through her. "If the situation was different, I'd do it in a heartbeat. But I just can't, not right now."

But even as she said the words, guilt seeped through her, into her every pore. Her gran's face popped into her head, and she glanced down at Delilah, her cheeks reddening. This was the one thing she could do for her gran now she was gone, yet she was saying no.

Chapter Nineteen

"So what are you going to call it then?" Rachel had just finished doing her yoga session on the lounge floor and was stretching her muscles. Every time she did it, Sophie was impressed all over again.

"You're so damn flexible these days," she said, emptying the dishwasher. "I should probably follow your lead now I have a bit more time on my hands." Because that was another benefit of working from home: she'd lost her commute time. "Maybe I can take up tai-chi or something like that."

"You should do yoga," Rachel said, stretching her hands to the floor as she bent forward. "None of us are getting any younger, and your older self will thank you for it."

"Maybe you're right," Sophie said, putting some bowls on the shelf they lived on. "But before I start a pension plan for my old bones, I have to decide on a name for my new business. I'm putting the site live tonight and I need a name that's not taken. Woolwich Dog Walkers is the current favourite."

Rachel straightened up and gave Sophie a look. "Bit boring, isn't it?"

Sophie smiled. "Yes, but it's a highly searched for term — and if it's what dog walkers are looking for, that means they're going to find me."

"You're a marketing genius."

"I know."

"I still prefer my names."

"But nobody's currently doing many searches for Hot Diggity Dawg and Who Let The Dogs Out."

"That's because people don't know what they want and people are dull."

"I can add in humour once they've found me," Sophie said. "But they've got to find me first."

"I know, and you're right." Rachel sighed. "Woolwich Dog Walkers it is. But don't come crying to me when you're trying to impress women with your business card and they run a mile on account of your lack of creativity." She paused. "Women like Tanya, for instance."

Sophie gave her a look. "If Tanya sees me with a dog, she's unlikely to come anywhere near me after the Branston incident."

"I still love that story — tell me again."

"No," Sophie said, grinning despite herself.

"Have you seen her lately?"

Sophie shook her head: she'd been keeping an eye out for her, but they hadn't run into each other since she left for home. "I think she might still be away. I feel like

I should go round there and see how she is, but I don't want to pry. She seemed upset when I saw her."

"Understandably."

"I know."

"Well, you should go round — it's a neighbourly thing to do." Rachel paused. "And you've got no other reason for doing so whatsoever."

Sophie raised one eyebrow. "What does that mean?"

"You know what it means. You're interested in her."

Sophie squirmed. She still wasn't ready to admit anything to Rachel, because she didn't want to get burned again. Yes, she wanted a girlfriend, and she was attracted to Tanya. But she had no idea where Tanya's head was at, and she didn't want to get her hopes up, only for them to be dashed again. For all she knew, Tanya could be just another Helen. Her stomach flipped at that thought.

Please don't let her be another Helen. Surely the universe couldn't be that unkind, could it?

"She's a good looking woman," Sophie said eventually, trying to make it sound as casual as possible. She even added a shrug just for good measure, but she could tell the way Rachel was looking at her that she wasn't buying it. They'd known each other too long.

"She is," Rachel replied.

"Any lesbian would be interested, don't you think?"

"I'm not."

"Good," Sophie said. "Let's make sure it stays that way, shall we?"

"No, you're not interested in her at all," Rachel grinned, getting up and stretching her whole body up to the ceiling.

"I'm interested in how she's doing, as a friend," Sophie replied, but even she could tell it didn't sound convincing — and that's because it wasn't. Sophie's interest and attraction to Tanya was struggling to break free, but she wasn't letting it. She was sitting on it, constraining it, not giving it the room to breathe. Because if she did that, she wasn't sure what might happen. Or, more importantly, how her emotions would fare. She was only just getting over Helen; she didn't need another knockback.

"Sure you are," Rachel said. "But can I just say, I for one am glad you've dumped Helen and moved on. I thought you might mope like you did over that other girl, but you didn't. I'm impressed."

Sophie puffed out her chest. "I don't mope," she said, putting away the pan they used to boil eggs. They really should just leave it on the hob, seeing as one of them used it every day.

"Much," Rachel told her. "But you haven't with Helen — it's like you were telling the truth when you said you knew it wasn't a forever thing."

"I was," Sophie said. "My ego's still a little dented, but she wasn't my one, was she?"

Rachel raised an eyebrow at that. "And Tanya might be?"

Sophie shook her head, feeling the blood rise in her

cheeks. Damn her inopportune blushing! "I never said that — you're putting words into my mouth. All I'm saying is that I like Tanya. And yes, she's attractive." *Okay, off the scale gorgeous, but she was still keeping a lid on her attraction, remember?* "But it's just friendship for now, and I'm happy to offer it," Sophie said. "She's got a lot on her plate, what with moving and her gran dying."

"But you didn't know her, yet you're drawn to her — I can sense it. And I can sense something's going to happen — and you know my senses are always to be trusted." Rachel was rolling up her yoga mat now, switching off the YouTube yoga video she'd been following.

"I'm not sure they are," Sophie said, walking round to sit on the sofa. Rachel was constantly telling her she was psychic, but so far, the evidence was minimal. However, right at this moment, she wanted to cling to Rachel's belief, because her own confidence that something might happen was pretty flimsy.

If Rachel thought so, maybe it might come true.

"My point is, you haven't made a new friend in a while. I feel change coming on for you, growth. You're open to it as well, which is a new thing for you." Rachel paused. "I think you might almost be ready to do proper adulting: new business, new friendships, and who knows, perhaps new love!"

Sophie gave her a look, even though if she really dug down and let herself feel what she was feeling, she actually agreed with Rachel for once. Rachel was prone to hyperbole, but where Tanya was concerned, hyperbole was something Sophie could absolutely get behind.

If she was honest, she wanted her heart to beat out of her chest, she wanted grand declarations, she wanted the works. She just wasn't sure if her heart would give her permission after their last outing together with Helen.

Chapter Twenty

Tanya was glad it was the weekend: getting through this week had been horrific. She simply couldn't get the image of her gran's coffin being lowered into the ground out of her mind, and she kept waking up at 4am, dazed, numb, broken. She wasn't crying, though — somehow, she couldn't. Her body was simply leaden, a dead weight, and she was hardly eating either. Her clothes hung limply on her tall frame, and nothing felt right, normal. Because it wasn't.

In a way, she wanted desperation to come and swallow her whole, just so she could grasp a solid feeling and hold it in her arms, rocking back and forth. She'd put up with the futility if she could just feel something pure. At the moment, it was as if she was an empty vessel, her emotions having jumped overboard.

And then sometimes, like yesterday at lunch with her boss, she'd forget she should be sad and find herself laughing at a joke — and then feeling guilty for that. She couldn't win.

This morning, she'd woken up and smelt her gran:

vanilla, lilies, roses. She was right there, the fragrance of her soft, delicate skin lingering in Tanya's nostrils.

Tanya could have sworn she was stroking her cheek, whispering Delilah's name in her ear.

She knew it wasn't real — she didn't believe in ghosts. Unless Alice's predictions for her having a haunted flat were about to come true.

However, it had been enough to make Tanya run out of the flat in a funk, and now she was sat on a bench looking over the Thames. So much for enjoying her weekend mornings on her balcony.

This morning was clear after a week of unsettled weather. It was 9.30am and the river was low, the tide out. Brown and green marks covered the river walls, and tug boats bobbed lightly on the river's surface, their chains sticking out of the shallow waters.

Over on the far side, Tanya spotted some eager rowers lowering their boat into the water, their wellies standing at the top of the shore, their lycra gear clinging to their slim bodies. She'd dated a rower once, she remembered how fit they were, and also how much they drank. She glanced to her left and spied the Woolwich ferry gliding across the short river span, taking cars and passengers to the other side: even though it was early, there was already a queue of cars building on the north side.

The world continued to turn, even though hers had tilted. What should she do to rectify it, get it back on an even keel? She still wasn't sure.

A dog barking interrupted her thoughts and Tanya glanced to her right. A massive dog was bowling down the path, its owner struggling to get a hold of its leash. The dog looked like a massive teddy bear on furry stilts, and he was high on life, clearly revelling in the Saturday morning sunshine. The same couldn't be said for its owner.

It was only when the owner came into clearer view that Tanya realised it wasn't the owner: it was Sophie, looking hot, bothered and a touch frazzled.

Tanya waved as she got closer, the dog calming down as it neared her and Tanya stroked it, receiving a warm lick on her hands in return.

It was strange how the world worked, wasn't it? Tanya had grown up with dogs, but when she'd moved out of home all those years ago, she'd left them behind, too. But now, dogs were in her life constantly thanks to her recent move and her meeting with Sophie.

And then there was Delilah. Could she cope with a dog? It seemed like what Alan said was right: people did have them in London.

Sophie was soon pulling up at her bench, taking a swig from the water bottle in her hand. She was dressed in shorts and a T-shirt, with Aviator shades on her face, her hair dappled with sunshine. Tanya smiled: Sophie was the coolest dog walker around.

"Hey you," Sophie said, coming to a halt and yanking on the dog's leash. "Smudge, what did I just say, stop being such a big puppy," she said, with a grin. She leaned down and rubbed the dog's belly. "I swear, he could get away with anything, look at him."

"He could," Tanya agreed, as Smudge panted, his long, pink tongue hanging out of his mouth, his teeth glinting in the morning sunshine. "Nobody would ever think you'd do anyone any harm, would they?" She paused. "What breed is he? I'm assuming not just 'teddy bear'?"

"He's an Airedale — and he's only a year old. By the time he's grown, his owners might be able to ride him to work."

"It'd save on tube fares."

Sophie grinned. "I walk Smudge every day — he needs the exercise. But sometimes, I think it's more him taking me for a walk than the other way around."

"I didn't like to say," Tanya replied. She also didn't like to say how much she'd enjoyed Sophie being dragged towards her, her shorts showing just enough leg to pique Tanya's interest, her T-shirt revealing surprisingly tanned arms for this time of year. In fact, this was one of those moments where Tanya had realised she was smiling, but she let herself — her gran wouldn't mind her smiling at Sophie, a ray of Technicolor sunshine in a life that had suddenly been cast into black and white since her gran's death.

Sophie sat on the bench next to her, pulling Smudge between them, rubbing his fur to keep him amused. "So how are you? How did the funeral go?"

Tanya saw last week whizz through her mind: her mum's face, her dad's faltering voice, Alan's warm hug, her gran's coffin, Delilah's pleading eyes. She blew out a breath and tried to erase it all from her memory, instead nodding her head, staring over the water.

"It was... okay. We saw her off, my parents were the same." She shrugged her shoulders, patting Smudge as she did. "But I have a dilemma." She turned to face Sophie, trying not to stare at her full lips.

"When my gran died, she left her dog. My parents have been looking after her, but now they want to give her away — they're good at that. So the question is, should I take the dog? Do I have the right lifestyle for it? I always thought I might get a dog somewhere down the line, but maybe when I'd moved out of London, when I had a partner. But now, it's kind of in front of me and I have to make a decision."

"What type of dog is it?"

"She's a King Charles Spaniel, brown and black." Tanya smiled thinking about Delilah. "She's got a lovely temperament, too."

"All dogs learn things from their owners. Sounds like your gran's dog mimics her. What's she called?"

"Delilah."

"Good name."

"It is, isn't it? My gran always gave her dogs good names. She called her daughter Ann, which was a puzzle, but her dogs always got the glamour: Marilyn, Sasha and then Delilah. She loved Delilah so much, she was so worried what was going to happen to her. When my parents took her, I think she finally let go, knowing she was okay. She's turning in her grave now."

Tanya gave a sigh and rubbed her palms down her face. When she looked back up, Sophie had taken off her shades and was looking at her with such a soft gaze, Tanya wilted under it. Her stomach flip-flopped under its concentrated heat, so much so, she had to look away.

Tanya was spinning so many plates that if someone was kind to her, she might collapse. And if the kindness was shown by this particular woman who Tanya couldn't stop edging towards on the bench, the plates might smash into smithereens.

"What do you think you should do?" Sophie asked.

Smudge gave a bark then. "Smudge has an opinion."

"I bet he does," Tanya said, glancing over at the dog, trying to regulate her breathing. "You think I should take her, boy? Do you?"

Smudge gave another bark, moving his legs in a little doggy dance.

"I don't know really," Tanya said, addressing Sophie once more. That gaze was still on her, and she was basking in its intensity.

"My heart says yes, my head says no. I work long hours, I like to go out. I'm not sure I'm ready for the commitment." But when the words came out, Tanya knew they were only half-true. That was what her head told her to say, but was it what she felt?

Sophie nodded. "But you might surprise yourself. And I could help — I could walk her and look in on her if you needed it."

"I would," Tanya replied. "It's just... I feel like I'm not ready yet. I've just started again, and taking on a heartbroken dog wasn't in the picture." And it hadn't been: but this was Delilah, not just a dog. "And I always thought that when I got a dog, I'd have a partner to share it with." She let her mind jump forward to her, Delilah and a partner round the fire.

Only, the partner looked very familiar. Tanya shook her head, erasing the image.

"Sometimes life accelerates faster than you want it to," Sophie said. "What happens if you don't take her?"

"She goes to a dog's home to be rehoused, hopefully."

"And how would that sit with you?"

Smudge barked and Sophie stood up. "You want to walk and talk?"

Tanya nodded, thinking about Delilah going to another home. When she truly considered it, her heart ached, her body dragged that little bit more. Even thinking about it left her winded.

"I'd be devastated," she said.

And that was the first time she'd admitted it out loud.

The first time she'd admitted it to someone else, and now it couldn't be taken back.

Tanya wasn't 100 per cent sure she could offer Delilah what she needed, but she hated the thought of someone else even trying. Delilah was family, and Tanya couldn't turn her back on her.

Sophie said nothing as they walked on, and that response spoke volumes.

"I've got to take her, haven't I?" Tanya said eventually.

Sophie shook her head. "Only if you want to." She paused. "But in matters like this, it usually turns out if you follow your heart, you end up happier."

Tanya glanced at Sophie and smiled, as her stomach did a small somersault of its own. Sophie had a way of calming Tanya down, making her see things clearly. Sophie was a calming influence in her life that she so needed, someone to make her pause, reflect, think about what she wanted. She trusted Sophie somehow, even though she was new. But perhaps her being new in Tanya's life was a blessing. She didn't know about her past; Sophie was simply judging Tanya on what she could see.

Tanya really hoped she liked what she saw.

"I know you're right," Tanya said. "Thanks for listening to me: I was tying myself in knots on my own. But when I said it out loud, the conclusion was staring me in the face." She smiled. "I can be stubborn, sometimes."

"Can't we all," Sophie said, pulling on Smudge's lead as he stopped to sniff something less than savoury on the pavement. "So shall I put you down for some dog walking sessions, then?"

Tanya shook her head. "We'll see. I might be able to

handle it myself, I don't want to confuse her. Plus, I only just decided I'm taking her for good."

But in the back of her mind, she could hear Alice and Meg telling her to accept help when it was offered, to not try to do everything on her own. It was an old habit, and it wasn't dying easily.

Plus, one upside of that help that was staring her in the face was she'd get to see Sophie more, and that had to be a win, right? If Tanya had a tail, it would be wagging right now, just like Smudge's was.

"Having said that, there's a high possibility I will need help," she replied, turning her body towards Sophie and holding out her hand. "So shall we shake on that? There being a high possibility?"

Sophie took her hand in hers, her fingers warm on Tanya's skin. A jolt of electricity radiated between them, causing a flush to travel down the length of Tanya's body, through her groin, ending in her little toe. She flicked her eyes to Sophie and their gaze met, held in place like a sudden shard of a new reality, a moment in time.

Tanya held on, not wanting to let go. Somehow, Sophie had found a way past Tanya's walls, and even though she hadn't spilled her family history to her in full, she'd opened up far more than she had to anyone else, and that wasn't lost on her. She let her eyes settle on Sophie's full lips once more, glistening in the morning sun. She knew she was staring, but she didn't care. Tanya licked her lips as she moved her gaze upwards and locked it with Sophie's once more.

And that's when she saw the burning desire reflected right back at her, turning Tanya's breathing shaky. Could it be that Sophie was feeling something for Tanya, too? Might there be a chance that when the dust on Tanya's life had settled, there might be something to pull from the wreckage?

Sophie dropped her hand first, but not her eyes, her stare penetrating to Tanya's very core.

If this was what it felt like just staring at her, she couldn't even imagine what it might be like to kiss.

Okay, that was a slight lie: Tanya could well imagine what that might be like. In fact, it was all her mind was thinking about right now, pressing her lips to Sophie's, tasting her for the very first time.

Smudge's barking broke the moment and Tanya jumped: she'd been far away in the land of make believe, but she had faith that sometimes, fairy tales did come true. Sophie was fussing with Smudge, pulling him back to her and away from a nearby snarling dog; what breed, Tanya couldn't be sure.

When Sophie turned to look back, Tanya sent her best seductive smile in her direction, every bone in her body wanting to lean forward, take Sophie in her arms and kiss her.

Seeing her look, Sophie stopped in her tracks, her cheeks visibly colouring.

Was Tanya that transparent? Could Sophie read minds? Embarrassed, Tanya looked away, as did Sophie.

The pair walked on for a few seconds in silence, Tanya staring at the river, Sophie patting Smudge before clearing her throat.

"So I'll clear a space in my schedule. I'm getting booked up, plus I took on a part-time job in a new café that's opening up, too. Suddenly, from being destitute, my prospects are getting brighter."

Tanya risked a shy smile her way. "Great to hear," she said, enjoying the way Sophie's face lit up when she smiled. Sophie seemed genuine; there was nothing fake about her. And after dating a million bankers with their buttoned-up lives and high expectations, that was a breath of fresh air.

"Plus, we still have to arrange that drink you promised me," Sophie added. "Maybe after you've sorted Delilah?"

Tanya nodded. "That sounds perfect."

Chapter Twenty-One

"It's not the worst idea in the world. You love dogs — you always said you wanted to get one when you were older."

"I did," Tanya said.

"Well, this is the opportunity. You're getting older every day, and Delilah needs you." Alice was eating something on the other end of the phone, which Tanya hated.

"It's just come a bit early, but sometimes life throws these things at you — or at least that's what Sophie told me yesterday"

"The Lift Woman," Alice replied.

Tanya could almost hear her eyebrow raise on the other end of the line. "That's the one. She's a dog walker and said she'd help out." Tanya paused. "You think this is the right thing to do?"

"I do — and you do, too." She paused. "Is Sophie single?"

"I'm not sure — I think so."

"Then please find out. I could see there was something in our brief moment together."

"It was called gratitude for her not letting the sofa fall on your face."

"Ha ha."

"I'm still hesitant about having a dog in a flat. What if she jumps off the balcony?"

"Keep the door shut. Plus, I don't think King Charles Spaniels are known for their gymnastic prowess." Alice paused. "You know what else? I honestly think this would be good for you. You're starting a new phase of your life alone—"

"—thanks for the reminder—"

"—and having a pet would be soothing for you. It's a well known fact that dogs relieve loneliness and lower stress. Getting a pet would be brilliant for that."

Tanya thought about it. She knew what Alice was saying was correct. Plus, Delilah was family.

"Anyway, I'm not second guessing it. I've made up my mind. Now for the big question. Can you come with me to get the dog?"

"Of course. When were you thinking?"

"One weekend soon — I'm not sure, I'll have to call my mum to check she's not shipping her off any minute now."

"And I get to meet the evil Ann one more time. Do you think she'll speak to me this time?"

"Doubtful, she probably thinks we just took a little time off from shagging and corrupting the world to come and get the dog."

"She's not far wrong," Alice laughed. "Apart from the shagging bit." She paused. "Well let me know when you have a date, but I'll absolutely come — this is a big thing you're doing."

"It is," Tanya replied, taking a deep breath.

"And you know what your homework is?"

"No?"

"To watch as much Dog Whisperer with Cesar Millan as you possibly can."

"Who the hell is Cesar Millan?" Tanya asked, perplexed.

Alice tutted down the phone. "Oh, you have so much to learn."

Chapter Twenty-Two

Tanya sat in her flat, drumming her fingers on the sofa. Her index finger hovered over the number, but she was having trouble swiping.

Just swipe left, Tanya. As she was gearing up to it, she thought of Marilyn, her gran's golden Labrador who'd been around when she was growing up. Her gran had loved that dog and, in turn, so had Tanya. She still remembered his smell, his face when he saw her, and the way he followed Gran around the house in his later years. Maybe Delilah would do that to her, too.

"Hello?"

Damn, it was her mum.

"Hi Mum, it's Tanya." Tanya thought she might be sick with nerves, but she swallowed them down.

"Oh," was her mum's reply.

Then there was a long pause before she said anything else.

"Did you leave something behind?"

Tears pricked the back of Tanya's eyes, but she took a deep breath. "In a way, yes." Tanya could list so many things, but Delilah was top of them.

"Send your dad an email and I'll get him to package it up and send it on."

Was she preparing to put the phone down? Tanya wasn't going to let it happen.

"It's not going to fit in an envelope, Mum," she said, hearing an intake of breath at the other end of the line at the mention of her name.

Did she care, deep down? Was her heart beating as fast as Tanya's, too? Tanya knew it was nonsense to ask as she'd just deny it: her mother was all stiff upper lip, canned emotions.

"I'm calling because I want to take Delilah. Dad said you wanted to get rid of her, but I don't think that's what Gran would have wanted. So I'm going to collect her and bring her to live with me."

"But you live in London. You can't keep a dog in a flat in London."

Her mum's voice had got higher, and shockingly, Tanya heard herself in it. Hadn't this been her argument to Alan when he first mentioned it?

The last thing in the world she wanted to be when she grew up was her mother.

"I can, and plenty of people do. Anyway, I'm not calling to discuss the merits of this, I'm calling to let you know. I'll come and get her at the weekend, so hang on to her till then."

There was a pause on the end of the line. "She's being picked up on Friday."

Tanya's breathing stilled. "By who?"

"The Dog's Trust. I spoke to a lovely woman there last week, and she says Delilah will be housed in no time at all. King Charles Spaniels are popular, apparently, and being she's only four, she'll be gone in no time." Her mum paused. "And I have to say, going to a lovely family who've got the time to love her will be far better for her than being cooped up in a flat in London, living with… *you*."

She spat the last word, and Tanya was taken back to all the times her mum had said similar things to her in the past. That she wasn't worthy. That nobody would ever love her. That she was destined to lead a miserable and lonely life.

But then Tanya had a lightbulb moment: her mum was describing her own life, *not* Tanya's. All those harsh words her mum had spoken to her: she was projecting, trying to keep Tanya down and not let her fly.

With that thorny revelation, Tanya was still angry, but also a little bit sad on her mum's behalf. Sad for her life, for living in such a small space, for rejecting so much of what might have made her happy.

"Delilah is coming to live with me, so please call back the woman you spoke to at the Dog's Trust and tell her Delilah has a better offer. I'm sure she'll be thrilled." Tanya paused. "And Delilah will have a great life with me, because she'll be wanted, loved, and be allowed to be exactly who she is."

"She's a dog, Tanya," her mum said, almost snorting with derision.

"She's an individual," Tanya replied, knowing she wasn't talking about Delilah at all, now. This call had run its course. "I'll be up on Saturday, so please make sure Delilah is there. I'll see you then."

Tanya clicked the red button and then stared at her phone like it was a bomb and might explode any minute. Only, it'd already done that. She leaned her head back into the sofa's soft leather.

Then she opened them sharpish.

Her mum would do anything to spite her, which meant the chances were, she would give Delilah to the Dog's Trust just because. All of which meant, she needed to act, and do it soon.

Tanya picked up her phone again and clicked the first speed dial button it had. Alice answered in two rings.

"What's up, sugarpuff?"

"I've just called my mother and she says she's giving Delilah to the Dog's Trust on Friday."

Alice exhaled loudly down the line. "What the fuck? After you told her you wanted to have Delilah?"

"That is exactly the reason she would do it — she insinuated I'd be corrupting Delilah, like I was going to make her gay."

"Oh for heaven's sake — she's tipped into lunatic territory."

"All those stories I've told you, I wasn't joking."

Tanya smiled sadly: no, her whole life had been one long tickertape parade of nasty where her mum was concerned. She'd never been good enough before she came out, and thereafter Tanya was never going to be anything but her disappointing lesbian daughter. Nothing she said or did would ever eclipse that.

"I don't know what to say."

"It's not so much what you can say, it's what you can do. I'm going to drive up to Sturby tonight after work to pick Delilah up, then come straight back."

"Will your mum let you in?"

"If she won't, my dad will. Plus, I'll call ahead and make sure our neighbour Alan is there — that way, at least I know he'll open the door."

"I can't do today — I've got parent-teacher interviews tonight and tomorrow," Alice said. "Is there anyone else who could go with you?"

Tanya's spirits, which had been soaring, plummeted immediately. This was her standing up to her mother and taking back control, in a way she never had when she was in her 20s. Back then, she'd been happy to listen and take the blows. But now, that wasn't the case.

Her mum wasn't going to get life all her own way for once, especially not where Delilah was concerned. But doing it on her own? She could if she needed to, but having her best friend alongside her would have made it far easier.

Perhaps she'd just have to be brave and go it alone — it was very short notice, she knew that.

"Don't worry, I knew it was a long shot — and Alan will be there to take care of me. I'll go on my own."

"You want to borrow our car?"

"No, I'll hire one from the car club."

"Okay," Alice said. "Call me when you get there and let me know how everything's going. I'll be rooting for you as I fill in some bored parents about their offspring's achievements or otherwise."

"Thanks," Tanya said. "I better go."

"It's going to be fine — and just think of the happy dog you'll have at the end of it."

"I hope so," Tanya replied.

She clicked off, then scrolled through to Alan's number and hit the green button.

This was Operation Delilah and there was no time to lose.

Chapter Twenty-Three

Tanya stepped out of the lift and into the block's foyer: it was a steely morning outside that matched her mood. If she was picking up Delilah solo later, she needed coffee, but the phone call to her mum had made her late leaving her flat. Should she run to the station to make up a couple of minutes? Maybe.

She was just about to race off when she looked up and nearly bowled into Sophie. Again.

Luckily, Sophie stepped out of the way at the last moment, avoiding a head-on collision. "Whoa — where's the fire?" she said, holding up both hands. She had a set of keys dangling from one finger, a rucksack on her back. Next to Sophie was Jess from the café — they seemed to know each other.

"Hey Tanya, how are you?" Jess said, not waiting for an answer. "I gotta run, got a delivery coming — so you'll be able to do a few shifts at the café to start off?" Jess said to Sophie.

Sophie nodded. "Yeah, happy to help out till my dog walking takes off. I'll call you."

"Great — see you soon!" Jess ran off, leaving Sophie and Tanya staring at each other.

"I walk her dog, Spinach," Sophie said, answering a question Tanya hadn't verbalised. "She just dropped off the keys to their flat to pick her up later. Dog-walking perk: you get to be nosy." Sophie grinned, but then cocked her head. "You don't look happy. What's up?"

"I'm late for work and I've already had a terrible morning." Tanya didn't have time to stand around gassing, even though she could already feel a sense of calm descending now Sophie was here.

"Why's that?" Sophie asked, her stunning blue eyes full of genuine concern.

So much so, it floored Tanya, making her slow down. She could be a couple of minutes late, the world wasn't about to cave in.

"I called my mum this morning to let her know I was coming to get Delilah — my gran's dog? She told me she'd rather give her away." Tanya pursed her lips. "Anyway, the upshot is I'm going to drive up to Sturby to get her, before my mother gets rid of her."

"That's rough," Sophie replied, frowning. "When are you going?"

Tanya checked her watch. "I'm going to try to get off work early, so I'm hoping to leave around four." She nodded towards the station. "So I really better get going."

Sophie pursed her lips before speaking. "If you need company, I'm happy to come along for the ride."

That made Tanya stop: she'd dearly love some company, but was she prepared to take Sophie with her, bring her into the lion's den? More to the point, was she prepared to make the journey with Sophie, knowing she fancied her? If anything were to happen between them, she didn't want it to have any connection to her home. London was where Tanya's heart was, not at some random address 150 miles away.

"I couldn't put that on you," Tanya said, shaking her head. There were so many reasons, but one of them was Sophie's lips that she was looking at right now. They didn't belong anywhere near Sturby.

Sophie reached out a hand, laying it on Tanya's arm.

A quiver ran through her, and when she looked up, she knew Sophie had felt it, too.

"I wouldn't offer if I didn't mean it," Sophie said, not letting go. "This sounds like a big deal, and maybe you could use some backup. Plus, I'm good with dogs."

Tanya desperately wanted to say yes, but she liked to keep her family separate from all other parts of her life: she found it always worked out far better that way.

But then she heard Alice in her head: "Stop trying to do everything yourself. Accept people's help when it's offered." She was only just learning to do that with her friends. Was Sophie a friend now? Or was she shifting into something else, something more than that?

"You're very kind, but you've probably got dogs to walk. I don't want to get in the way of that either."

Sophie shook her head. "Tomorrow morning I'm free. So long as we're back here for 2pm, I'm at your disposal." She paused, looking Tanya directly in the eye. "Just think about it. I'm offering and I think you'd like to say yes. So I'll be ready in my flat at 4pm and if you change your mind, just knock on the door, okay?"

Tanya nodded her head slowly. "Okay. And I'm planning to do the journey there and back today."

"Even better. Plus, I can help out driving, too. Think about it."

Tanya checked her watch again, then gave Sophie a curt nod. "I will." She paused. "And thank you."

Sophie held Tanya's gaze, her tongue licking her lips. "No problem," she said, before turning and walking into their building.

Tanya's whole body flushed with warmth, the heat hurtling up her body and tickling her ears. She wasn't sure what had just passed between them, but it was something.

She checked her watch again. It was still the same time it had been ten seconds ago.

Chapter Twenty-Four

"So tell me again what's going on." Rachel was ladling cake mix into a tin, before tapping it gently on the side. Apparently, that removed the air bubbles and that was important.

"I'm going to Sturby with Tanya to pick up her gran's dog."

"Her dead gran?"

Sophie winced: it was the truth, but Rachel's phrasing was a little stark. "Yes, the dead one."

"Why are you going?"

"Because she needs someone to go with her, and we've chatted lately. Her parents aren't the most supportive, so I thought it'd be a nice thing to do."

"For the girl you've got a crush on."

"It's not a crush. I like her as a person."

"Wow — way more serious than a crush."

"Shuddup." Sophie paused. "By the way, did I tell you I got a part-time job through one of my dog walkers? She's opening that café round the corner next week and you're looking at her new part-time assistant."

"What about dog walking?"

"I'm still doing that — I just thought I could do this as well, fit it in around the dog walking. A bit of variety might be nice." Sophie stroked her chin. "And you know, she said she wanted someone with baking experience. Maybe you could make cakes for her, too."

"I have a full-time job, in case you hadn't noticed."

"I know — but this could be some extra on the side income. Plus, she's a lesbian, so it's for the sisterhood."

"Well, if it's for the sisterhood, how can I say no?" Rachel said, slotting her cakes in the oven. "So this is why you're sitting like this on the sofa, then?"

"Like what?" Sophie said, sitting up to her full passport height and smoothing down her hair.

"Like that," Rachel said, pointing. "You're wearing your favourite jeans and you've got mascara on. I always know you're interested when the mascara comes out. Plus, you're sitting funny."

"I don't want to crease my shirt before she gets here, I only just ironed it."

"I rest my case. What time's she turning up?"

"She might not at all: it was a loose arrangement."

Rachel frowned. "And what are you going to do if she doesn't show?"

"I'm going to slump on the sofa and not worry about creasing my shirt."

A knock on the front door interrupted their chat, and Sophie jumped up, her blood pulsing in her veins.

From being relatively calm, she was suddenly all manner of flustered.

"Are you going to answer that? I don't think it's for me," Rachel said eventually.

Sophie nodded, striding towards the front door with faux confidence. She'd hoped Tanya would show, but now it looked like she had, suddenly the thought of three hours in a car with her was fraught with danger.

She liked Tanya, that much was clear, and she didn't want to put her off before anything had even happened. Could she trust herself not to say anything idiotic during their journey? She guessed she'd just have to draw on all her 30 years of life experience to find out.

Sophie opened the door and Tanya was stood there, a small black bag hanging from her shoulder. She was dressed in jeans, a blue sweatshirt and a pensive smile, and she dragged a hand through her chestnut hair before she spoke. Even though her movements were hesitant, Sophie's heart wasn't. It sprang to life when it saw Tanya, unfurling 'Sophie Likes Tanya!' banners across its front.

Sophie tried to ignore her heart flutters, instead giving Tanya an encouraging smile.

"Hi," Tanya said, looking down, then back up. "I wondered if your offer still stood? I can promise you service station meals and free rein on my iPod if it does." She paused. "So does it?"

Sophie nodded. "Of course," she said, her heart dancing a happy jig in her chest. "Give me two seconds to grab my bag and I'll be right with you. You want to come in?"

Tanya shook her head. "I have to go and get the car from its bay — I've just hired it for today. Shall I meet you outside in ten minutes?"

Sophie nodded again. "Sure. See you then."

Chapter Twenty-Five

"So when did you develop such a big taste for Coldplay?" Sophie asked, scrolling through Tanya's streaming playlists.

"Coldplay are one of the most misunderstood bands of their generation," Tanya said, glancing over at Sophie. "I didn't pick you as a Coldplay hater." She tutted. "Anything else I should know?"

"I wear glasses," Sophie said, pushing her black frames up her nose.

"I guessed that one," Tanya said with a grin. "And tell me, do you wear contact lenses, too?"

Sophie shook her head: it wasn't the first time she'd been asked that. "Sometimes," she said. "Why?"

Tanya didn't look at her, just stared straight ahead. "No reason, just your eyes. They're a startling colour."

Her words rolled through Sophie like a warm breeze and she tried hard to keep still in her seat, to act like that comment meant nothing. But it did: Tanya had noticed her eyes.

Tanya had thought about her eyes.

"It's my natural colour, no tinted lenses," Sophie said. "And I smoke too, although I am trying to give up."

Tanya grimaced. "A smoker — how retro of you."

"I like to keep it real," Sophie replied, still scrolling through Tanya's playlists. She liked how easy they were chatting so far — it wasn't forced at all, it was just natural. Being in Tanya's rented white Peugeot felt right, like this was where she was destined to be at this moment in time.

And Tanya had noticed her eyes.

"But you didn't answer my Coldplay question."

"Coldplay are like Marmite, so I'm not going to convince you. Choose something you like and I'll put up with it — that was the deal."

"Shall we just put the radio on for now, let the music guide us?"

"Sure," Tanya said, laughing. "Let's let the music gods decide."

Sophie pressed the tuning button until it fell on the latest Beyoncé track. Satisfied, she sat back as the countryside surrounding the M1 flew past them at speed. So far, despite it being rush hour, the traffic hadn't been too bad. Tanya was convinced it was going to be terrible once they tried to join the M6, but both of them were enjoying the novelty of being in a car and on the road, so they weren't too concerned. With Beyoncé singing to them, what could go wrong?

"So, are your parents still together?" Sophie asked, licking her lips. So far, they'd talked about their respective careers and living in London, along with world politics and a shared love of One Direction. But the topic that was screaming to be chatted about hadn't been brought up — until now.

"They are," Tanya replied, her shoulders hunching slightly.

Sophie guessed there was a reason she didn't often bring this subject up. "And do you get home much? I'm getting the feeling you don't."

Tanya gripped the steering wheel that little bit tighter, her knuckles whitening, her face growing pensive.

"I went up to visit my gran when she was around." She paused. "Let's just say, my parents and I had a difference of opinion. I told them I was a lesbian, and my mother told me I couldn't possibly be. We still haven't come to a conclusion we both agree on."

Sophie sucked air through her teeth. "That's tough."

Tanya shrugged, checking her mirror before easing into the fast lane.

"I live with it. My gran was the one shining light in my life, she never judged, she took it all in her stride. But now she's gone." Tanya shook her head. "And I'm getting her dog." She paused. "There's Alan, too. He's my parents' neighbour and he's brilliant." Tanya smiled for the first time in a while. "I love Alan — when I was little, I used to wish I could live with him, that he was my real dad."

"But your dad's still alive?" Sophie asked.

Tanya sighed. "He is, yes. He tries his best, but he's no match for my mother." Tanya paused. "Anyway, enough about me," she said. "Tell me about your family, let's get off my dismal tale."

Sophie winced, seeing red flashing lights ahead. "Looks like we might have a little time to chat," she said, as Tanya sat up straighter, bringing the car to a stop at the back of the queue.

"I hope it's just roadworks and nothing more," Tanya said. "I've spent my life driving up and down this stretch of road, and half of that has been stuck in traffic."

"Fingers crossed," Sophie replied, stretching her seatbelt which was cutting into her shoulder. "Anyway, my family. My dad's called Nick and he's great. He's a builder, a gentle giant. When I told him I was gay, he took it in his stride, and now he's making lesbian friends at his local golf club."

Tanya's face told Sophie she couldn't quite believe what she'd just heard.

"I know," Sophie said, laughing. "He's a modern man and a model dad — I love him to pieces."

"Wow, I'm envious," Tanya said.

Sophie grinned. "He's pretty awesome. Which he needs to be, to make up for my mother, who's a train wreck."

"Oh really? We both have mother issues?"

Now it was Sophie's turn to snort. "That's one way to put it." She'd tried hard to understand her mum over the years, to not let her behaviour affect her life, but it hadn't been easy. "Let's just say she was last seen living in Portugal, desperately trying to locate her maternal instinct."

"Perhaps your mum and mine missed that class at school."

"Maybe they did."

"So does she still live in Portugal?"

Sophie nodded. "Yep — she left my dad a few years ago and now lives with her new Portuguese boyfriend, Rui. Sun, sea, sangria, no kids. All the time I was growing up, our mum seemed puzzled, like she couldn't believe this was her life. I swear, that was her face every morning as Dad got our breakfast ready: it was like she was always saying, 'Am I living someone else's life? Is this mine? It's not what I ordered — can I send it back?'."

"I've had that thought more than once," Tanya replied.

"I think everyone has — but it's a bit more troubling when it involves your kids."

The car was silent for a moment as they both digested Sophie's words — silent apart from the DJ on the radio. When he announced he was going to play a classic Abba track next, Sophie's stomach fell. She hoped it wasn't the track she still couldn't listen to. No such luck. When the opening bars of Mamma Mia blasted their way into the car, nausea rose in her throat, just like always.

She reached out and changed the station as if it meant nothing at all. She knew she should have got over this by now, but there was something about this one aspect of her mum leaving that hadn't shifted, no matter what she did.

When the digital dial hit some old-school Fleetwood Mac, Sophie took her finger away.

"You're not a fan of Abba either? First Coldplay, now Abba?" Tanya said, smiling. "This friendship might have stalled before it's even begun."

Sophie's stomach knotted, her emotions tight inside her. However, she carried on speaking. It wasn't her usual course when it came to her mum, but clearly Tanya had that effect on her, making her want to open up.

Still, it wasn't easy to articulate because Sophie never had before. Not to anyone. Not even her dad. She'd kept this particular wound for herself, nursing it all alone.

Until now.

"The day Mum left, it was a Friday," Sophie began, looking down at her hands, a tremble passing through her. "We were meant to be going to see Mamma Mia in the West End the next day, but we never did."

Sophie shook her head. "I remember it so clearly, sitting on my bed and staring at the tickets. I'd just finished university, and I was stunned. I still can't listen to Mamma Mia without being taken straight back to that day. Abba gives me the chills. How weird is that? I'm terrible going to weddings. I spend half the disco in a corner grinding my teeth."

Sophie glanced at Tanya, her heart thumping, her ears turning pink. She'd never said that aloud to herself before, never mind to anyone else. "I really wanted to go to the show, too. My brother's the same."

Just thinking about it, Sophie could still taste the disappointment as fresh as if it were yesterday. Eight years had gone by, but her mum's timing still stung. Couldn't they have had just one more afternoon together as a proper family?

Tanya shifted in her seat before replying. "I think you're allowed to have an Abba aversion when you've got a good reason," she said. "Although you're missing out on some fabulous tracks." Tanya paused, looking over at Sophie. "And are you still in contact?"

Sophie nodded. "We are — she's happier living away from us, and we've all adapted, some of us better than others. I've been over to see her, and we Skype. But it's affected my relationships: if you can get up and walk out of a romantic union you said you were committed to, just like that... It's made me doubt them all. But my brother gets on with his life, and even my dad's talking about dating again, so perhaps it's time I gave it a go, too."

When she glanced up at the mirror in the sun visor, she could see part of her mum staring back at her. It was happening more and more as she got older, this eerie resemblance in her reflection.

"For what it's worth, it seems like you're doing fine to me," Tanya said, with a smile. "But you know what they say — you can't choose your family."

Sophie shook her head: she knew that only too well.

"You can't: families are like a postcode lottery, aren't they? But I wouldn't be without them. I still love them, even if some of them drive me mad. So anyway, that's my story: my mum's done a bunk, and my dad's still here, living with Doris."

"Your step-mum?"

Sophie smiled. "No, she's our dog — and the most reliable female I've ever known. Which tells you all you need to know about my relationship history." That sentence was truer than Sophie cared to admit.

Tanya's laughter boomed in the car. "Well, I'm sure I could challenge you on that." She paused. "What's your brother called?"

"Luke. He lives in Brighton with his wife, Sky. I see him irregularly, when he's not DJing or designing or whatever else hip shit he does. I think my dad always had visions of running a business and training Luke up as his apprentice, but he was never interested."

Sophie pursed her lips. "Sometimes, it feels like I'm an only child, because Luke always flits in and out of our lives as he wants to. It's always on his terms, and I'm the one who was left to check up on dad once Luke met his wife." She sighed. "I'm probably painting a bad picture of him. I've seen more of him recently, but you know — families."

"Sounds familiar."

"How so?"

"I have a Luke — but he's called Jonathan. He also

couldn't wait to flee our parents' dysfunctional home, although in retrospect, he was smarter than me. Jonathan made sure the distance was significant, not just Sturby to London. He lives in Dubai."

"He wasn't doing it half-arsed."

"Nope." Tanya eased the car forward a few feet, before stopping again.

In the car beside them, a man was singing along to some music, banging his hands on the steering wheel as he reached a critical point. Sophie smiled: she loved doing that herself.

"He's really going for it," Tanya said, noticing too.

"He is."

"Maybe we should put some upbeat music on to take our mind off our family woes," Tanya continued. "It seems like everyone has a tale to tell."

Sophie shrugged. "Everybody's family is a bit weird, isn't it? We all think we're the weirdest, but we're not."

Her gaze lingered on Tanya as she turned back to the traffic, the car edging forward a fraction more under her guidance. She had a strong chin, high cheekbones, and her lustrous hair caressed her cheeks and ended on her shoulder.

However, more than her physical attributes, Sophie was drawn to her forthright nature and her humour. It wasn't every day she met someone she connected with this well: as she kept having to remind herself, they didn't really know each other — yet here they were, comparing family skeletons. It had been so long since Sophie had met anybody she wanted to do that with — so *very long* — and every inch of her was singing with happiness. She loved the connection they were building, the shared glances and memories, the laughs. It warmed her from the inside, making her woozy with possibility, with what might happen next.

"So how will your parents take you turning up tonight?" Sophie flexed her fingers as she asked: her pinky had gone to sleep.

"My dad will be jittery, my mum will be stony and impassively aggressive. Just the usual."

"At least you know what to expect. My mum always blew hot and cold with affection: as I've got older, I've realised she's just uncomfortable in her own skin, nothing to do with me. But it took a fair few years to work that out."

"I think my mum's uncomfortable in her own skin, in her lounge, in her country and in the world. The best solution would be to put her in a cave and leave her there. I told Alan to slip something into her tea and put us all out of our misery, but he refused. Spoilsport."

"I'm looking forward to meeting Alan," Sophie said with a grin.

"He's the best."

"Is he married?" Sophie asked, her interest piqued. She loved getting to know about other people's families: she was nosy by nature, which was why dog walking suited her.

Tanya shook her head. "He's not. He lived with Uncle Rod for a while, but then Uncle Rod died. Alan's been alone since then, just him and his beloved dogs."

Sophie raised both eyebrows. "Uncle Rod?" she said, her tone rising. "So he's one of us?"

"I don't follow," Tanya replied, her gaze falling on Sophie briefly.

Sophie smiled. "I assume Alan and Rod were an item?"

Tanya gripped the wheel tighter, looking straight ahead, but Sophie could hear her teeth grinding, her jaw clicking.

They were approaching the flashing lights now, a mix of red and blue, and Sophie could see there had been an accident: a Renault Clio had hit a Ford Fiesta in the driver's side, glass and debris sparkling on the road. Two ambulances were present, along with two police cars. Tanya manoeuvred the car round the traffic cones that were zoning off the road.

"I hope nobody was injured, but it looks bad."

"It does," Tanya replied. "And about Alan — I don't think him and Rod were an item. They were just friends."

Sophie sat up straight, her face a question mark. "Really? How long did they live together?"

"About ten years."

"And have you ever asked him?"

Tanya shook her head. "No, but I heard my parents talking about it once, and that's what they said. And Alan didn't seem that upset when Rod died — I mean, not unduly…" She tailed off, putting her foot down on the accelerator as the road suddenly opened up after the accident. It took a few more seconds before the blocks fell into place.

"Shit, Alan's gay, isn't he?" Tanya said eventually, shaking her head. "Why did I never ask whether or not Alan was gay?"

"Because you believed what you'd been told? How old were you when Rod died?" Sophie asked.

"About 15."

Sophie shook her head. "You were young, you weren't to know."

But Tanya was still shaking her head. "But I could have been there for him. I could have helped, been more sympathetic." She thumped the steering wheel as she drove.

Sophie's muscles tightened as the mood in the car changed. Had she said the wrong thing as she'd been fearing before she left? She hadn't meant to upset Tanya. She reached over and placed a hand on Tanya's arm, and a spark shot through her as she did.

Tanya jumped, too.

They both stared at each other for a moment, before Tanya turned her eyes back to the road.

Sophie took away her hand, not sure what to say next.

"You didn't know, and I'm sure Alan doesn't hold it against you." Sophie paused. "And maybe they were just friends. *Really* good friends." Sophie tried to suppress a laugh, but it didn't work. Instead she began spluttering like an old water faucet.

And at the sound of that, Tanya smiled and joined in as well.

Once Sophie had permission to laugh, the floodgates opened. The car's air lightened, now filled with gales of laughter.

"What a plonker," Tanya said, shaking her head when she got her breath back. "I know enough couples who've been described as 'just good friends' to know what it means. I guess Alan just never struck me as being really gay — he's not a stereotype."

"And you are?" Sophie said, wiping her eyes, recovering. With her long hair and perfect make-up, Sophie would be hard-pressed to pick Tanya as gay in a line-up.

"I guess not. Unless you take me on at pool. Then I'm a demon," Tanya replied, grinning. "Shit, I need to speak to Alan."

"You do," Sophie said. "But first, we need to get to Sturby and rescue Delilah from your mother's evil clutches." She paused: had she said too much? "Am I allowed to say that, even though I've never met her? Is it too soon to be making jokes about your mum?"

Tanya chuckled. "My mother gave up the right to be protected by me the day she disowned me and threw me out of the house. Call her what you want, I don't give a damn."

"Duly noted."

They passed a sign with a list of towns on it: Sturby wasn't one of them.

"How far are we now?" Sophie asked. She really needed a cigarette, but she didn't want Tanya to know that. Plus, this enforced will power was good for her. At least, Rachel would say so.

"Still a good hour, so let me know if you need the loo. There's a service station in about five miles, but then you'll have to hold it in for a good while. So speak now."

"I'm good, I can wait," she said. "Besides, I'm looking forward to getting to Sturby — I've never been before."

Tanya snorted at that. "You're about to find out why."

Chapter Twenty-Six

That last hour turned into a couple when they ran into another accident on the M6: the final ten miles had taken nearly 90 minutes. Under normal circumstances, Tanya might have succumbed to road rage, but Sophie was a calming presence, making light of the situation and chatting away, like they'd known each other for years.

Whisper it, but she'd even enjoyed the journey. Six hours in a car with someone definitely gives you clues as to whether or not you're compatible. If they hadn't got on, the drive would have been interminable. As it was, the hours had flown by and Tanya was surprised to find she felt almost relaxed as she pulled up — even though they were a couple of hours behind schedule.

"Here we are, home sweet home." Tanya parked in front of her parent's house and tugged on the handbrake, risking a glance at Sophie.

What was she thinking? How did her home town present to someone who'd never seen it before? Tanya was well aware of what she saw — more to the point, how it made her *feel*. Every time she came back, it was

181

like she was visiting a past version of herself, and she knew she had to change that. Because Tanya wasn't that person anymore.

"You okay?" Sophie said, as if sensing the internal dialogue going on with Tanya.

Tanya nodded, clearing her throat. "As I'll ever be." She checked her watch. "But it's ten o'clock — Mum's not going to be in the best mood to see me at this time." She paused. "Let's go to see Alan first."

Sophie nodded and got out of the car, performing a full body stretch as she did. When she looked over at Tanya, she gave her a thumbs-up, which made Tanya grin. Having backup at home was a welcome change.

She strode up Alan's path, making sure Sophie was behind her. When she rang his bell, he didn't take long to answer. And if Alan was surprised Tanya had brought a friend, he didn't show it.

"Come in, come in!" he said, smiling at them both, as Bouncer and Margo yapped at their heels. "You're later than you thought. Are you thinking of going next door now?"

Tanya nodded, checking her watch again even though she already knew the time. "We have to — I've only rented the car till tomorrow morning, and I have to be at work then, too." She sighed. "We got caught up in two accidents, hence the time."

"At least you weren't in them," Alan said, holding out a hand to Sophie. "I'm Alan, by the way."

Sophie shook his hand, showing off the gorgeous smile that Tanya was already becoming accustomed to. "Sophie. Nice to meet you."

"You, too," Alan replied, before turning back to Tanya. "But seriously — why don't you stay the night and go next door in the morning? Your mum will be more receptive and it'll be better for Delilah, too. She'll be in her bed by now."

Tanya stopped at that. She'd been so set on getting Delilah and heading home, she hadn't considered the dog's routine. She glanced at Sophie, trying to ask how she felt. Was staying the night okay with her?

Sophie seemed to get the message. "I don't have clients till 2pm tomorrow, so I don't mind," she said, shaking her head. "So long as we leave early, it's fine." She paused. "And it'll probably be better for us, too, as well as Delilah. Do you really fancy driving back again after the journey we just had?"

Tanya shook her head. "It's not top of my list."

"That's settled, then," Alan said. "I already made up the guest room, so now I'll make a cup of tea."

Tanya ushered the dogs and Sophie into the lounge, and they sat, listening to the sound of Alan getting mugs, milk and spoons ready.

"Are you sure you're okay to stay?" Tanya asked.

Sophie nodded. "Yes, it's fine. Plus, it means I get to know Alan, doesn't it? I can see what you mean — I wouldn't necessarily have picked him as gay." She paused, giving the living room a once over. "But he does have a woman's touch. I don't know many straight men who have candles in the fireplace or this many flowers around. My dad definitely doesn't."

"I'd almost forgotten that bit after getting here so late. Must ask Alan if he's gay. So many loose ends to tie up."

But that wasn't the most pressing thing on Tanya's mind at the moment: that honour went to their sleeping arrangements for the night.

Tanya had stayed with Alan numerous times, and she knew he had three bedrooms: his own, the spare room and his office. All of which meant she and Sophie were destined to share a bed — but she wasn't going to think about that now.

"Did I hear my name being mentioned?" Alan asked, coming in with a tray of tea and biscuits. The tray was vintage kitsch, with floral decor along with a chintzy gold rim and handles.

Sophie gave Tanya a 'told you so' look, which Tanya steadfastly ignored.

Yes, she saw the signs now she was looking.

"I was just telling Sophie I didn't know what I'd do without you," Tanya replied with a smile.

"The feeling's mutual," Alan said, pouring out the tea, before handing round the biscuits. "So, how do you two know each other?"

Tanya sat up straight: how did they know each other? She'd crashed into Sophie, nearly crushed her with a sofa, and they'd spoken a couple of times. The more time she spent with her, the more she liked her, but what did that make them?

Tanya spluttered. "We, er… we kinda just met randomly," she began, her cheeks colouring.

"What Tanya's trying to say is we live in the same building and we kept running into each other. We got chatting, and I'm a dog walker, so I offered to help her out on her dog rescue mission."

Sophie said all of this so smoothly, it was almost as if it had been rehearsed.

Not for the first time today, Tanya was so grateful Sophie was there.

"Splendid idea," Alan said. "Many hands make light work and all of that." He leaned forward and smiled at Sophie. "It's so lovely to meet you. I've only met a handful of Tanya's friends; she likes to keep London and Sturby very separate."

"Can you blame me?" Tanya said.

Alan shook his head. "No, but it means I get shut out, too."

"Well you should come to London," Sophie said. "Shouldn't he, Tanya? We could show you around town."

"I'd love to come — we've been talking about it long enough, haven't we? I was meant to bring your gran, but that never happened."

Tanya let that comment roll through her like a strong gale, but she didn't let it flatten her. Her gran was gone, but Alan was still here, and she was going to get to know him better in whatever time they had left.

"All the more reason for you to come now, Sophie's right. Let's put a date in the diary before we leave."

Alan smiled. "Okay. Let me see who can look after these two characters," he said, pointing at Margo and Bouncer, "and then we'll talk." He paused. "One thing about staying tonight — it's in the spare room, which is one bed. I mean, it's king-sized, but still just one." He paused. "Is that okay? Or I can make up the sofa if you'd prefer?"

Tanya glanced over at Sophie: the thought of sharing a bed with Sophie, king-sized or otherwise, made her half-giddy, half-pensive. She didn't know where they stood yet, and she certainly didn't want to have that chat today — not with everything else going on. But she couldn't say any of that to Sophie, especially not with Alan staring at them.

"I'm okay with it if you are?" Tanya said, a cough working its way out of her mouth. She cleared her throat, feeling her cheeks burn. "But also, I'm equally happy to sleep on the sofa." She didn't want Sophie to feel like she had to share a bed.

But Sophie was already shaking her head. "That's fine," she said, looking down at the carpet, then back up at Tanya.

Was it Tanya's imagination, or had Sophie's cheeks turned a shade darker, too? Thinking about sharing a bed with Sophie made Tanya aware she needed to regulate her breathing, and fast.

Her mind suddenly presented a vivid sketch of what Sophie might look like naked: this was a new departure. She broke out in a cold sweat as the sketch came to life: Sophie naked, reclining, beckoning her closer with her index finger. And that's when her clit joined in on the act, perking up and sending shockwaves right through her.

Tanya styled it out, focusing on Alan and the knit of his charcoal woollen cardigan, which was suddenly super-interesting to her. Alan liked to knit, and she wondered if he'd knitted it himself.

Shit, the signs really were there, weren't they?

"That's settled, then," Alan said, rubbing his hands together. "Shall we have a nightcap before we retire?"

Tanya didn't know much, but she knew a drink sounded like a godsend.

Chapter Twenty-Seven

"Are you sure about this?" Tanya said, glancing down at the towels, spare T-shirts and toothbrushes Alan had left on the white duvet. "I'm happy to take the sofa if you prefer."

Sophie glanced up, stroking her cheek as she did. "I can keep control of myself if you can," she said, with a tiny smile, before holding up one of Alan's T-shirts. It had the words 'I Love British Rail' written on it, and it was about ten sizes too big for Sophie. "Although now I've seen the T-shirts we're sleeping in, it might be more of a struggle."

Tanya chuckled, holding up her own to read it, before bending over laughing.

"What?" Sophie said. "What does yours say?"

Tanya took a little time to recover, swallowing down her snorts before replying. "I can't," she said, shaking her head. Tanya flopped down on the bed, before handing the T-shirt to Sophie.

Sophie held it up, before grinning hard. On the front of Tanya's faded pink T-shirt were the words 'Gay Men's Chorus'.

"I don't know, do you really think he's gay?" Sophie said, before laying down next to Tanya, the T-shirt still clasped in her hands. She was laughing so hard and then trying not to laugh at the same time, and the bed was shaking.

"I know, I'm a terrible surrogate daughter," Tanya said, when she could breathe again.

"You are," Sophie replied. But she was smiling, too, because laying there next to Tanya felt calming, right. Tanya's warmth was buzzing from her, and Alan's welcome was all around.

Sophie had been fearing the worst — and she knew that was still to come — but she was glad for Tanya that she had a place to come, a place of love and shelter. Everybody needed that. And she was glad she was able to experience it with her, to see a different side to Tanya. Because everyone became a different person when they went home, and Tanya clearly saw Alan's house as just that.

"You want to use the bathroom first?" Tanya grazed Sophie's arm, breaking her thoughts. Her touch made Sophie's breath catch in her throat, but she rolled off the bed as if nothing had happened. Yes, the situation was escalating, she knew that, but she wasn't ready to deal with it just yet.

However, when she looked at Tanya and saw her eyes, as dark and swirling as galaxies, she knew she'd felt it, too. That indiscernible thing she couldn't quite put her finger on.

The kernel of an idea, the seed of what might be.

And now they had to share a bed together. One big bed with them both just in T-shirts and knickers: naked legs, arms and faces, and lips within kissing distance. Lips that Sophie had been assessing the entire drive here, and now, they were hot and close.

How was she going to get through this without expiring? How was she going to be under the same duvet without pinning Tanya down? She'd just have to work out a way. Because she was here to be Tanya's support, she knew that, and the last thing Tanya needed was a distraction from the main point of being here: namely, rescuing Delilah.

And yes, being in the same bed together was a huge distraction, but Sophie was an adult, so she could deal with it.

Despite the fact her heart was beating like a kick drum.

Her phone went, interrupting the moment. She snatched it up from her bedside table, frowning. "It's a London number, but I don't recognise it," she said, swiping the green button right. "Hello?"

It was a client, a man called Tim. Apparently, his girlfriend was away with work, and he'd left his bag in the pub with his keys in it. Tim was slurring his words and hoping Sophie would come to his rescue.

"Sorry Tim, I'm in the Midlands, I can't help you out," Sophie said, shaking her head at Tanya. "Best thing to do would be to break a window or go and stay with a friend — whichever's easiest." She paused. "Good luck!"

Sophie quit the call and put her phone back on the bedside table. "I don't know what these people did before they had me walking their dogs. I've only got eight clients and three of them have called me having locked themselves out, wanting the key they gave me." She paused. "Seriously, put one under the mat or something."

Tanya grinned at her. "You do have that look about you — the one that says you'll rescue someone in distress." She paused, locking her gaze with Sophie's. "You're doing it for me right now," she added, her voice an octave lower, her cheeks showing a slight flush.

Sophie's clit pulsed when Tanya spoke, and she looked down, just as they heard Alan come out of the bathroom. She went to speak, but her breath stuttered even as she tried to regain control of it.

"I'll be quick," Sophie said, walking round the bed and reaching for the door.

Once inside the bathroom, she slid the lock across and sat down on the loo, her heart still doing press-ups, her head in a spin.

What was it Rachel had said? That when she eventually let her guard down and started to like someone, it was going to floor her? If her body was saying anything to her, then this was that moment.

She needed to calm down, process and try not to hump Tanya in her sleep. She took a deep breath in, then out, and tried not to focus on how Tanya's long legs had looked on the bed, how her hair had splayed on her pillow.

She shook her head, imagining somewhere else. Somewhere like Tanya's flat. And then she imagined Tanya pushing her down on top of her wooden dining table, spreading her legs and…

Sophie shook her head harder this time.

Fucking hell, she was doomed, wasn't she?

Chapter Twenty-Eight

Tanya walked back into Alan's guest room, where Sophie was already under the covers, her head poking out. "Hey," she said.

She looked adorable, and that's when Tanya knew this might be more tricky than she'd first thought. Adorable? When she started thinking things like that, she knew a line had been crossed in her head. And then it was only a matter of time before it was crossed in real life.

But this situation wasn't typical. If Tanya thought someone was cute in real life, she'd chat them up, with the hope of getting them into bed. This situation was far from normal, because Sophie was already in her bed. However, what they'd shared today was different: Tanya was on unfamiliar turf, with a whole new set of rules.

Sophie was different, and she didn't want to bugger up their emerging friendship — wherever that ended up. Sophie had said she could control herself: Tanya just hoped she could promise the same.

"Hey," she replied, getting into bed and laying still, just like she used to when she was younger and playing sleeping lions. If she moved, she might touch Sophie, and she didn't want to run the risk. As she lay still, she was aware both of their breathing was a little laboured.

"Did you notice the massive Abba collection in the lounge?" Sophie asked, staring at the ceiling.

"I would have stopped him if he tried to put it on, don't worry," Tanya replied. "And anyway, that doesn't mean he's gay, that just means he's got great musical taste."

"What about the lavender handwash in the bathroom?" Sophie said, turning her head to Tanya. "Exhibit number 243 in the Alan Is Gay show."

Tanya smiled, turning her head to Sophie. "Okay, you win. Can we change the record now?"

"I just like teasing you," Sophie replied, before locking eyes with Tanya. "About Alan," she added quickly, turning to stare at the ceiling.

Tanya gulped. Sophie had said the word 'teasing' while they were laying in bed. Suddenly, her mind pressed play on its very own mini-series named Sophie, formed of small vignettes: Sophie smiling on her balcony; laughing in her car; blushing in Alan's bed.

It wasn't helping, and Tanya tried to shut it down before it got out of control. She was in charge of her own mind and actions: at least, she hoped she was.

Her phone bleeped on the side and she rolled over, picking it up. It was a text from Alice, asking how the rescue had gone. She put the phone back on the bedside table and switched it to silent.

"Everything okay?" Sophie asked.

Tanya nodded. "Yes, fine."

Sophie waited a couple of seconds before continuing. "You know, if you'd told me a few weeks ago, when you landed on me in a lift, that I'd be lying in a strange bed with you in a Gay Men's Chorus T-shirt, I wouldn't have believed you."

Tanya grinned, turning her head. "Was it the T-shirt that took the scenario too far?"

Sophie smiled. "Absolutely." She paused. "I thought you were so rude at first, you know. Terrible manners, and I think manners are underrated."

"I can't say I blame you," Tanya replied. "Our first few meetings weren't stellar."

"No," Sophie said, a smile in her voice. "But you've hauled yourself back, and now, here we are."

"So what do you think of me now?" Tanya asked.

* * *

Sophie took a deep breath, turning her head so their faces were inches from each other on their pillows, so close she could see the baby-fine hair above Tanya's upper lip.

"Now," she said, finding Tanya's gaze. "Now I just think you've got terrible taste in music and awful gaydar."

Tanya grinned at Sophie. "I'll give you the second one," she said. "But my musical taste is good. Come over for dinner at my flat and I'll prove it to you."

Sophie swallowed down hard, her whole body whirring to life: Tanya was proposing a proper date, and she hoped this one might actually happen.

"I'd love to come over for dinner," Sophie said, before pausing. Some of Tanya's hair was falling on her face and straying into her eye. Her natural instinct was to reach out and push it away, but her hand was paralysed.

She was in bed with Tanya, in Alan's house, so her natural instincts had to be curbed. She'd promised.

"And what about me? What did you think about me at first and now?" Sophie studied Tanya's face as she answered. Her skin looked so soft, and she had the faintest of laughter lines around her mouth and her eyes.

Those laughter lines became more pronounced as Tanya smiled. "I thought you were amazingly cute when you were vexed at me in the lift," she said. "And how could I miss your eyes? I couldn't stop staring."

That wasn't the answer she'd been expecting: honest, forthright, daring. Sophie's heart boomed when she heard it.

"But I was in the wrong, so you were right to be vexed," Tanya continued. "I owe you a bottle of wine as an apology. I was going to bring one round, but with gran dying, I forgot. Sorry."

Sophie blinked. "You're forgiven."

"Thanks," Tanya said, before continuing. "And then, when I saw you and you helped us move, I thought you were pretty heroic to stop us getting crushed by my sofa. Although when your dog peed on my foot, that was a bit much."

Sophie allowed a grin to punctuate her face. "Not my dog. And in my defence, it was my second time out with him — I can't untrain bad habits that quickly."

"Bad Branston."

"You remember his name, I'm impressed."

"He made an impression," Tanya replied, her tongue stroking her top lip, which distracted Sophie. "A bit like you. I was unlikely to forget you." Tanya paused. "Not when you saved the day, and especially not when you're so beautiful, too." As the words tumbled out of her mouth, Tanya's face froze, along with her breath.

Sophie's brain went into lockdown, too. Did Tanya really just say she was beautiful?

She wasn't sure how to respond, so she simply gawped at Tanya, her mouth slightly ajar. "You think I'm beautiful?" she said eventually, her eyes never leaving Tanya.

She hadn't expected that. She knew there was something between them, but for Tanya to say that? It made Sophie's head spin that little bit more. Tanya was being brave, putting herself out there, jumping without a safety net. It was something Sophie had to get better at, and her heart's response was to break into applause.

Sophie could learn a lot from Tanya. And right now, she wanted to drape herself over her and soak up everything she could.

Tanya simply nodded, slowly, carefully, as if she did it any harder her pillow might break in two.

Sophie reached out her hand now, sweeping Tanya's fringe from her face, leaving the tips of her fingers to skate across Tanya's left cheek. As she touched her, she heard Tanya's breath hitch, suspended in time.

And then her eyes were on Tanya's mouth, with a laser focus, willing her lips closer to her own. Should she close the space between them? Was this a good idea with everything that was to come tomorrow?

It was probably the worst time to start anything, she knew that.

However, the decision was taken out of her hands as a banging on the door interrupted the moment.

They sprang apart, both of them sitting up. Sophie's stomach fell to the floor as her mouth filled with saliva. She couldn't hear anything but her heartbeat in her ears and the deafening anxiety plastered on Tanya's face.

"I'm just going to bed, girls. Have you got everything you need?" Alan's voice was low and thick through the bedroom door.

Tanya's face was bright red next to her, clashing with her pink T-shirt. "Yes thanks, Alan. We're all good. See you in the morning!"

"Righteo!" he said. "Sleep well."

"You, too," Tanya replied, holding her breath.

Sophie heard Alan's footsteps retreating, then his bedroom door shutting.

She sat still, the only sound their breathing.

Then she felt Tanya slide down inside the covers again, and she followed, both staring at the ceiling.

The tension hovered over them like a mosquito, buzzing on a low setting all around.

"I guess we should get some sleep. We've got a big day tomorrow and an early start," Tanya said, her voice a whisper.

Sophie nodded her head, a cocktail of disappointment and understanding pooling in her stomach. There was nothing she'd like more right now than to kiss Tanya into next week and to feel her body next to hers, on top of hers, under hers. But she knew this wasn't the right time

"We should," Sophie concurred, sadness enveloping her weak smile. They had all the time in the world to explore what might become of them, and tonight wasn't that night. "But can I make one request?"

Tanya nodded. "Sure."

"Can we make a note to discuss you calling me beautiful sometime in the very near future?" As Sophie spoke, a wry smile tugged on her lips.

When she turned her head left, Tanya was reflecting her smile. "We certainly can," Tanya replied. "I've got a lot to say on the matter."

Then Tanya rolled over and grabbed her phone. "You okay if I set the alarm for 7am? That way, I can go next door and we can get away early."

"Whatever you need," Sophie said. "You should get

some sleep — you're going to need to be alert for the dog heist."

Tanya set her alarm, then lay back down again. "Don't say that. I'll have nightmares about it."

Sophie smiled. "It's going to be fine — I'm here to back you up, as is Alan." Then she slipped her hand under the cover and found Tanya's hand there. She took it in her own and squeezed it tight, not letting it go. "And you won't have nightmares," she said. "I've got you."

Chapter Twenty-Nine

Tanya woke up the next morning to the sound of an unfamiliar toilet flushing. She took a few moments to process where she was before reaching over for her phone: 6:55, five minutes before her alarm. When she turned to her right, Sophie was still sound asleep, her hair ruffled, completely relaxed.

Waking up with someone in her bed was a feeling Tanya had forgotten, and it felt good.

With Sophie, it felt right.

She was in deeper than she'd first thought.

The urge to lean over and kiss Sophie's cheek was almost too strong, but she held back. Tanya should kiss her lips before she kissed her cheek, and she hoped that would happen sooner rather than later.

She slipped out of bed, clambered into her jeans and tiptoed down the stairs. She found Alan in the kitchen in a purple velour dressing gown with matching slippers: exhibit 244. She suppressed a grin as she gave him a hug.

"Morning," she said, smiling. "When did you turn into Sturby's answer to Hugh Hefner?"

"Christmas," Alan replied, matter-of-factly. "Little present to myself, seeing as nobody else is going to buy me anything."

A stab of guilt hit Tanya in the gut. Every year, Alan sent Tanya a gift voucher for John Lewis, but she only gave him a gift when she saw him over the holidays, which hadn't been all that often. She made a mental note to change that from now on.

"Sleep well?"

She nodded. "Surprisingly well, thanks."

He paused, moving his head sideways. "And Sophie seems lovely."

Tanya grinned: she couldn't help it. "She is."

"How long have you been…" Alan asked, leaving the end of the sentence open.

"We're just friends," Tanya said, blushing despite herself.

Alan gave her a nod, but the look on his face told her he didn't believe her.

Tanya flashed back to last night when they'd so nearly crossed the line from friends to more. Then she scrubbed it from her mind. She had bigger things to worry about right now.

"I need to get next door." She checked her watch: 7:12. "Mum will be up, won't she?"

Alan nodded. "She's a 6am woman, rain or shine," he said, walking over to the kettle. "Can I interest you in a tea or coffee before you go?"

Tanya shook her head. "I want to get this over with as soon as possible, and then we need to get going. Wish me luck."

"You'll be fine," he said. "And remember, she's more scared than you."

Tanya nodded and walked towards the front door.

Chapter Thirty

Her mum's face curdled when she opened the door, as if Tanya had just soured her day. "What are you doing here?" she asked, arms folded across her chest. "It's not even 7.30."

"I've come to get Delilah, I told you." Tanya's voice came out soft, but confident.

"And I told you she was going to the Dog's Trust on Friday."

"Which is why I'm here now," Tanya said, putting a foot on her parents' doorstep. Her mum still hadn't invited her in. "Can I come in?"

Her mum bristled, but stepped back: she was choosing her battles.

Once inside, her dad walked through from the kitchen with a tray of tea: he stopped in his tracks when he saw her, panic flitting across his face. "Tanya!" he said, unsure of his next move, or those of his daughter. "What are you doing here?"

Tanya sighed: some kind of welcome would be nice rather than getting grilled on her motives for being there.

She was their daughter, she shouldn't need a reason to
be there.

"I'm here for Delilah," Tanya said. "And it would be
nice if someone could ask how I am rather than what the
hell I'm doing here."

She walked into the lounge and waited for her parents
to follow. With the curtains open, the lounge looked
brighter than it had on her previous visit, but it still held
the fusty air Tanya had become accustomed to throughout
her childhood. Even at this early time in the morning,
the house was boiling, heat pumping out of the radiators.
The grey carpet was new, though: plush underfoot,
vacuumed daily.

Delilah was sitting on the rug in the lounge, playing
with a toy bone. Tanya squatted down to pet her, and
Delilah licked her hand.

"Hello girl, how are you?"

"Did you just drive up this morning?" her dad asked,
putting the tray down on the green fabric pouffe that
matched the avocado sofa.

Tanya nodded: she didn't want to drop Alan in it.
"I've come for Delilah and I can't stay long as I've got to
get back. So can you get her stuff together, please — bed,
toys, food."

When Tanya looked over at her mum, her lips were
pursed and she was almost squinting at Tanya.

Tanya braced for her mum's opening salvo, and it
duly arrived. "I don't think it's good for Delilah to go

with you. Now Mum's gone, she needs love and stability. She doesn't need the life you lead."

Tanya had heard it all before, but her mum's ignorance still took her breath away.

"I agree Delilah needs love and support, and it should come from within the family. And seeing as you're kicking her out, I'm taking her." Tanya paused, drawing herself up to her full 5ft 9, which was still dwarfed by her mum. "It's what Gran would have wanted."

Her mum made a spluttering sound, glaring at Tanya. "She didn't know what she wanted. She was an old woman, taken in by your smile. She wasn't to be trusted by the end."

Tanya kept her cool, but it wasn't easy. She wanted to reach out and slap her mother for speaking ill of the dead.

"Gran was ill, not stupid," Tanya replied, her voice see-sawing, despite her intentions. "She knew exactly what she wanted and who she loved, and she loved me. And she would have wanted Delilah with me."

Tanya caught her breath, wondering whether she might throw up. Being in this house did odd things to her. But she wasn't backing down, and she was holding her mum's gaze.

"How dare you speak to me like that." She glanced behind Tanya, looking at her husband. "Aren't you going to back me up, Graham?"

Her dad cleared his throat. "I think Tanya should take her," he said, looking over briefly towards his wife, then down at the floor. "Delilah will be well loved and looked after, and it's what Celia would have wanted."

Tanya was stunned, turning to her dad, mouth ajar. For once in her life, her dad was backing her up. She wanted to hug him, but now wasn't the time. Her mum wasn't done, Tanya knew her too well.

Sure enough, when Tanya turned back, the older woman's face was clouded over. "I might have known you'd say that. You always take her side, always have. Ever since she was born, she's been the first woman you think of, not me. But you dreamed of walking her down the aisle and that's never going to happen, is it?"

Tanya shot her gaze to her dad, then her mum, then back. This was new, this sparring. Was her mum jealous of her? Is that what this had been about all her life?

"It might happen, actually," Tanya heard herself say, stepping back into the crossfire. "I don't know if you heard, but marriage equality is a thing now." She paused, glaring at her mum. "They must have written about it in the Daily Mail at some point, saying how disgusting it was. I'm sure you might even have written them a letter pointing that out."

Her mum scoffed. "It's not proper marriage though, is it?" She stared at her husband, but when Tanya swivelled her head towards him, he was looking away, not meeting either woman's gaze.

"And I don't believe a word of it," her mum continued. "Marriage is something you can only dream of. Yes, they might have told the world that deviance should be celebrated, but do you even have someone to marry?"

Tanya recoiled, as if her mum had just caught her with a right hook, square on the jaw. The gloves were off, her mum was fighting with bare knuckles.

Tanya didn't *exactly* have someone to marry, no, but it was *possible* in today's world. She could meet someone any day — in fact she might have already done so, although even she would concede that might be racing a little too far ahead.

She and Sophie hadn't even kissed yet, after all.

Tanya wanted to tell her mum she was wrong, to shut her mouth.

But she couldn't, because her mum was right.

Tanya didn't have anyone to marry, and she hadn't ever come close in her 36 years on the planet. And she'd lain awake more nights than she'd care to admit wondering why that was.

Her mum saw the weakness and came in for the kill. "For all your high and mighty ways, thinking you're better than us living in London, when you close the door at night, you're alone."

Left hook.

"You think you're so different from me, but you're not: you're just like me."

Upper cut.

"You don't suffer fools gladly and you have high standards that people struggle to live up to — and that's no bad thing. And you don't let people in easily, which is

208

good, because people will run all over you. I taught you something, at least."

Tanya hit the canvas with her mum's final triple-salvo. *Knockout.*

Her mum wrinkled her nose, before glancing down at Delilah. "Take her — she needs a home and you need the company. Because your sort never prosper, they're never happy. You've chosen this life, and it's a lonely life — just be aware of that."

Her mum crossed her arms over her chest again, as if punctuating her diatribe with a full stop.

Tanya's head was spinning. She wasn't sure where to start or what to say to any of that. She just looked from her mum, to her dad, to Delilah, then back. Yes, what her mum had said had cut her. Yes, it was cruel beyond belief. But was it true? Was Tanya just like her mum, pushing people away, standing in judgement?

"You know what," she said, picking Delilah up and edging towards the door. "I'm nothing like you. I have friends, I have a life, I let love in. And Delilah is going to have a great life with me. So you can spout your hate-speak all you like, but it's not going to work."

She took hold of the door handle, her spirit drained. It was going to take all her efforts to summon the strength to get out of this house and the negative force field around it, but she was determined.

"You could have had it all, Mum," Tanya added. "But you chose to have nothing."

With that, Tanya snatched open the door to the lounge and almost fell into the hallway, gasping for air. Delilah began to bark in her arms, but Tanya just headed for the front door — the sooner she got out of there, the better.

"Tanya!" her dad said. "Let me get her bed and everything."

Tanya turned back to him, her face bricked with sorrow. "I'll buy new ones, Dad. I have to get going." And with that, she scrabbled for the front door latch, yanking it open and stepping out into the new day that was still only a few hours old.

She bent over, swallowing down deep gulps of fresh air. Delilah was wriggling in her arms, but all Tanya could hear were her mum's words echoing round her head. "Just like me", "don't suffer fools", "high standards", "unlovable".

She was nothing like her mum, *nothing*. She'd made sure of that, building a life of her own far away from this street, this town.

Tanya was her own woman, and nothing like the bitter person on the other side of the door.

Wasn't she?

Chapter Thirty-One

The drive home was tense, particularly because the rain had been lashing down for most of it. Tanya had sworn all the way down the M6 as she'd careered through the side-spray of lorry after lorry.

Sophie had sat wincing in the backseat with Delilah, who was thankfully behaving brilliantly.

Prepared after a couple of weeks of dog walking, she'd brought along a water bowl and treats for Delilah for the journey. When she'd produced them, Tanya had given her a weak smile and a muttered thanks, but nothing more.

In fact, ever since she'd come back from her parents' house, Tanya had been a shadow of herself, even with Alan. When she'd uttered words, they'd been staccato, like a machine gun. When she'd moved, she'd done so in slow motion, as if under water. The only thing that had sparked her to life were the lorries.

They'd stopped at a service station so Delilah could wee on some manicured grass, and Sophie could smoke two cigarettes. On the drive there, Sophie had been happily chatting the whole way, so her lack of cigarettes hadn't bothered her. On the drive back, she could have mainlined the entire packet. Nobody bought food, because nobody had an appetite.

The M6 had slipped by and Tanya's head was still set firmly forward, no glances in the rear-view mirror coming Sophie's way. And now they were just an hour or so from home, it was as if yesterday and last night had never happened. As if this whole trip were a mirage.

But Sophie knew it wasn't.

When she'd woken up at three o'clock this morning, she and Tanya had still been holding hands: she smiled at the memory. She could get used to holding Tanya's hand, but who knew when it would happen again? Now wasn't the time to ask.

Chapter Thirty-Two

They got home just before midday, the drive back proving far smoother for traffic, if not for conversation. Tanya parked the rental car and got out, grabbing her bag from the front seat. They didn't have a lead for Delilah, so Sophie scooped her up in her arms and carried her to their building.

Tanya said nothing, her mind clearly elsewhere.

They got in the lift and smiled at each other, Tanya stabbing her floor's button and leaning back on the mirrored wall.

"So, are you going to work this afternoon?" Sophie asked.

Tanya shook her head. "I'll do some work from home, get Delilah settled." She paused. "I think I'm going to have to do that quite a lot until I get a routine down." She closed her eyes. "This isn't going to be easy to work out, is it?"

Sophie gave her a warm, encouraging smile. "I can help, like I said." And she wanted to. She wanted to make this as easy as possible for Tanya, because she saw how much it mattered. Whatever had happened this morning, getting Delilah settled and happy would go some way to making Tanya feel better, she was sure of it.

Tanya hesitated, but Sophie reached over and touched her arm. "And before you refuse, let me help you. I'd like to," she said, giving her arm a little squeeze.

As soon as Sophie touched her, Tanya's breath stilled. Sophie understood, because hers did, too. It felt daring to touch her, to hold her. And despite the fact this was hardly the romantic clinch of the century, she hoped that might come later. One thing was for sure: Sophie didn't want to let go.

Last night and what they'd shared was still very much in her mind; and standing in this lift together, on the brink of something she couldn't quite put a name to, felt like fate. Like this was what was meant to happen all along. Like this lift was meant to be a catalyst to their future: it was where they'd first had a close encounter, and here they were again.

Sophie knew what had nearly happened last night, and she wanted to explore it further. To that end, she decided to be bold; to go beyond the usual. She didn't want there to be any doubt about her intentions, her desires.

Stealing herself, her chest rising and falling just that little bit faster, she reached out with her hand and brushed Tanya's face with the tips of her fingers. "Whatever happened this morning, it's going to be okay. You're going to make a go of this," Sophie said in a low voice, leaning in.

"I hope so," Tanya replied, her caramel skin smooth, her scent enticing. And yes, she might have been distant in the car journey home, but when Tanya locked eyes with her again, Sophie held her gaze, leaning in a little further.

"It will — you can do this and I can help you." Sophie licked her lips, watching Tanya watching her.

She was close enough now she could feel Tanya's breath on her, smell her coconut lip balm.

Her lips glistened in front of Sophie like a shiny prize.

"You've been so much help already," Tanya said, not taking her eyes from Sophie's lips, her focus fixed, her voice hoarse. "I don't know what I would have done without you there. It was such a help, you'll never know."

Sophie's heart was thumping in her chest, beating so wildly she could only take tiny sips of breath. She reached up with her hand one more time, slipping it into Tanya's silky hair, guiding her lips towards her.

"I just did what anyone who cared would have done," she replied, never taking her eyes from Tanya's mouth.

No more words were needed as Sophie took a final step into her space, before pressing her lips to Tanya's, desire exploding in her like a grenade. They'd nearly kissed the previous evening, but they'd been halted by Alan and circumstance. But now, they were fusing together as one, with desire lighting up her body in blinding white. She wanted this more than she knew — her lips didn't lie, and neither did her body.

Tanya's lips on hers were soft and insistent; if Tanya

had trouble opening up with words, her lips were telling Sophie everything she needed to know. This kiss was connecting to a place deep inside Sophie, one she hadn't visited for some time.

As she sank into it, her fingers gripping Tanya's hair, she was grinning inside, knowing how right this felt. Knowing this could be the start of something. Knowing that if this was how their first kiss went, she couldn't wait for more.

Sophie's fingers were back on Tanya's face now, drawing her closer. She slipped her tongue into Tanya's mouth and groaned as she felt her warmth, her heart pulsing anew. Her fingertips skated inside Tanya's jacket, her breath catching as their breasts touched.

And then the ping of the lift crashed their party.

"Floor 30," the announcer said, and Sophie opened her eyes around the same time as Tanya. She pulled back and they both stood staring at each other, breathless, eyes wide. Sophie's brain scrambled for something to say, but she came up with nothing.

Instead, she looked down and saw that Delilah had walked out of the lift and into the hallway. Tanya followed her eyeline and was the first to react, running out of the lift.

"Delilah!" she shouted, as the dog waddled down the hall, her brown and black bottom swaying. "Here, girl!" Tanya said, bending down and scooping her up. "First thing today is shopping for a dog lead." She smiled at

Sophie, the tension between them still palpable, but now it had another layer altogether.

"Shall I come in with you?" Sophie asked. Her skin was flushed and she was out of breath as the lift doors closed behind her. She didn't put her hand on the button to hold it. She had no idea where she was or what day it was.

All she could see and hear was Tanya, but she had a feeling she was about to be thrust rudely back into reality.

As if on cue, Tanya shook her head. "I know you've got clients this afternoon, so you better get on," she said, avoiding Sophie's gaze. "Plus, I need to get her a lead and get her settled in." She looked down at the carpet, and then back up to Sophie. Her face was flushed pink, a different shade to when they'd got in the lift.

"But thank you so much for coming with me." She took a deep breath, as Delilah turned to look at Sophie, too. "I'm beyond grateful."

"No problem," Sophie said, swallowing down all the questions that were bubbling up to the surface.

What just happened? What happens next? What did that kiss mean to her? But Tanya wasn't ready to deal with any of those; she was too distracted by Delilah.

Instead, she put a hand on Tanya's arm again — and when she did, Tanya stopped.

They shared a look, her body still pounding with desire, and for a second, neither of them spoke.

Eventually, Sophie cleared her throat. "And I meant

what I said — I can dog walk, dog sit, whatever you need, you know where I am." She paused. "I know you've got a lot on your plate, but I'm here for Delilah and for you, okay?"

Tanya bit her lip at that, then nodded her head. "Sure, thanks," she said, flicking her head left. "You better get the lift before someone else calls it."

Sophie nodded and hit the button. "See you soon," she said, before patting Delilah's head. "See you soon, too, Delilah!"

The lift door sprang open and she hesitated, before walking into it.

Tanya raised a hand towards Sophie and her gaze burnt a hole in Sophie's heart.

Sophie was still staring when the lift doors slammed shut.

* * *

Tanya made herself a cup of coffee and sat on the balcony with Delilah on her lap. Weirdly, Delilah was having no trouble settling into her new surroundings — it was Tanya who was the stumbling block.

She stared out across the river, watching a barge rumble up the grey waters. That's what she'd always done with her life: moved on, made progress. And she'd been doing that just fine until this morning.

No, she was still doing that just fine, dammit. Her mother was not going to throw her off course again, even if

Tanya had recognised a flicker of truth in what she'd said. That she was like her, that she didn't suffer fools gladly. Could it be that no matter how many miles Tanya put in between herself and her mother, she still managed to leave her mark, to sneak into Tanya's life and have an effect?

"What do you think, Delilah?" Tanya asked, ruffling Delilah under her neck. "Did the wicked witch have any effect on you while you were there? Or are you actually a lesbian and glad to escape her clutches, too?"

In response, Delilah let out a little sneeze.

Tanya grinned. "I'll take that as a yes, then."

And what about Sophie? Gorgeous, warm Sophie.

She'd been distant with her on the drive home, she knew that. Sophie had helped her out, come all the way home with her, and she wouldn't wish that on her worst enemy. She'd been brilliant today, too, not pressing her, making sure Delilah was fine in the car.

And then they'd kissed in the lift, and Tanya could still feel the impression on her lips. They were still hot, alive. She touched her lips with her fingertips and allowed herself a smile.

Make no mistake, that was a dynamite kiss and one she'd be more than happy to repeat, again and again. She was still shaky from it, from the whole day. This was a Wednesday she wasn't going to forget in a hurry.

Should she have invited Sophie in for a coffee? Or to just kiss some more? Because that would have been okay, too.

No, there was too much going on in her head to have Sophie here as well. And she didn't want to scar anything that happened with Sophie with the mess of her mother.

Plus, Delilah had to come first today.

Tanya's mind wandered backwards to this morning, to the scene in her parents' lounge. She'd always known something like that would happen again, there was an inevitability about it. Her mum was always spoiling for a fight, and she knew just where to hurt Tanya: go for the jugular and tell her she was just like her. That wound was still fresh, open to the elements.

Was there any truth in it? Was that why she hadn't been able to hold down a relationship? Meg had been her closest attempt, but that had disintegrated, and now Meg had found true love with Kate. But Tanya was still alone.

Was it because she was like her mum? Steely, aloof, impenetrable? Maybe that was why she was feared and respected at work in equal measure. Why she only had a couple of close friends, because most people fell at the first hurdle of friendship.

She sighed and glanced down at Delilah.

"Am I like her, girl? You'd tell me if I was, wouldn't you?"

Delilah cocked her head in answer.

Chapter Thirty-Three

"I thought you were giving up smoking?" her dad said as Sophie stood on his back doorstep, blowing smoke out onto his garden. He'd done a nice job of it and the flowers were blooming.

"Your camellia are looking nice," she told him, not turning her head.

"Don't try to change the subject," he replied.

Sophie turned, giving him a sigh. "I was, till this woman I was interested in didn't call me. Then I took it up again."

Her dad shook his head, shifting in his dining chair, tapping the screen of his iPad as he did. "You can't fall back on smoking every time something goes wrong for you. That's not how it works."

"It's how it works right now," Sophie said, sighing. Yes, Tanya was going through a lot of stuff, but she'd at least expected a call to help with Delilah. She'd offered to help, but Tanya seemed to have a hard time accepting it.

She heard her dad chuckle at the table. "It's at times like this you remind me of your mother," he said.

Sophie almost choked on her cigarette, before blowing the smoke away. "That's a low blow. I came round here for solace — you're normally good at that."

Her dad smiled at her as she stubbed her cigarette out under foot. "Your mum used to stand on that very step moaning at me, blowing her smoke out the door. Sometimes, it's uncanny."

Sophie finished her cigarette and sat opposite him, slumping on the table. "Great — now not only am I unable to keep a woman, I'm like my mother. Any other gems you want to add while we're here?"

"Your mother had her good points, too. They're just harder to remember." He reached across and squeezed Sophie's shoulder as she sat up. "It was her dramatic side that drew me to her, so it's not a bad thing." He paused. "Whereas the smoking is a bad thing."

Sophie held up her hands. "I'm giving up from this moment on. I can't take you and Rachel moaning at me."

"Good — I've still got that Allen Carr book here somewhere. Worked for me, you can take it with you."

"I will," Sophie said. She took a sip from the mug of tea sitting in front of her.

"So what's gone on with this woman then?" her dad asked, shutting the paper, giving her his full attention. He was freshly showered and smelt like men's toiletry products: musky and soapy.

"It's nothing. Just that woman I told you about. I thought there was something there, but maybe I misread it."

"The one you mentioned the other week?"

Sophie nodded.

"So what's the problem?"

Sophie sighed, getting up to get a drink of water — it was hot today, and her cigarette had left her with a furry mouth. "She's just... dealing with a lot of stuff." She shrugged. "Maybe she just needs a little more time."

"You can't push these things — if it's meant to be, it's meant to be," her dad replied. "But you like her?"

Sophie leaned against his kitchen counter, nodding. "I really do." She paused, looking down at his slate grey tiles, cool under her feet. "She feels... different. When I'm with her, I feel different."

She wasn't explaining it very well, she knew that. Then again, that's because she wasn't sure what there was to explain — their whole relationship so far had been short and studded with emotion. And now, it had just stopped.

However, Sophie kept replaying their kiss over and over again in her head. The heat. The intensity. How good it had felt. If Sophie closed her eyes and really concentrated, she could still taste Tanya on her tongue. But she had no idea if Tanya had been replaying their kiss, too, because she hadn't heard from her.

That kiss in the lift, and then, nothing. It was hard to take, especially when Tanya felt like she could be the gateway to something Sophie had never had: a proper, full-on relationship. Sophie had never been in love, never given herself fully. But she craved it; sweet Jesus, she craved it now.

Tanya had unlocked something deep inside her, and it wasn't just physical: it was intense, smouldering emotion, something Sophie had always shied away from. She'd been preparing to fall and for Tanya to catch her.

However, Tanya was now nowhere to be seen.

"Different is good," her dad said, holding her gaze. "And this woman, you think she'll get over her stuff and realise what she's found?"

Sophie smiled: trust her dad to see her as the prize catch. He hadn't met Tanya yet.

She shrugged. "I hope so. I mean, I think she will, but who knows?" She bit her lip, sitting back down at the table. "But I really hope the answer's yes."

More than anything in the world, she hoped Tanya would come around. Because if she didn't, Sophie might retreat even further into her shell, and she didn't want to do that. She'd let some light in where it had never been, and she'd been warmed by it. Retreating now simply wasn't an option.

"Well, keep me posted on your potential love match, because I want my baby girl smiling, not pouting," he said, putting a hand to her chin. "And if you do that, I promise to keep you posted on mine." Her dad gave her a grin when he said that.

"Sorry?" Sophie said, furrowing her brow. "You've got a potential love match?"

Her dad nodded, a broad grin populating his face. "I do," he said.

Sophie slapped the table, temporarily distracted from her love woes. "Who, what, why, when, how?"

Her dad laughed at that. "Remember Dawn, the woman I was telling you about from the golf club?"

Sophie nodded. "I remember," she said, sitting up straighter in her chair.

"Well," her dad replied, spreading his palms on the table as he spoke. "She's having a dinner party next week and she's setting me up with one of her straight friends." He paused, for maximum effect. "So it's going to be me, this woman and four lesbians." His smile got even bigger if that was possible. "You officially have a dyke hag for a father."

Sophie blinked rapidly at that news, before snorting with laughter. "You're going on a date? With four lesbians?" She paused, taking his news in. "Anything else I should know? Will you be coming to Pride this year, too? Will you be on a golfing float with a rainbow flag?"

"No plans as yet, but don't rule it out," her dad said. He was enjoying this, she could tell. "So wish me luck — this woman is a teacher who needs some new wardrobes in her bedroom. So if nothing else, I might get a job out of it."

"I'm speechless," Sophie said, grinning. "But I'm happy. A dinner date! You haven't been on one of those in years."

"I know," he said, blushing. "But I really like Dawn, so I trust her judgment. And who knows? It might come to nothing or it might be the start of something."

Sophie nodded. She hadn't had to think of her dad with anybody new, because it hadn't come up before. But he deserved this after everything he'd been through. "I'm happy for you," she said, squeezing his hand.

"So if your old man can score a date, then I'm sure you can, too — the power of positive thinking." He motioned between them with his index finger. "Us Londons are hot right now. How can women resist?"

Sophie gave him a smile. She had to hope her dad was right, but it didn't change the fact that Tanya hadn't called.

Chapter Thirty-Four

It was Saturday, four days since Tanya had returned from Sturby, and her mum's words had left her battered and bruised. She'd taken the rest of the week off work in a bid to settle Delilah and it had worked, the pooch acclimatising to her new situation well. She still followed Tanya around, keeping her close, but she'd stopped barking when Tanya left a room, and had only weed inside once.

If only Tanya could settle down and stop having nightmares, life would be sweet.

Meg was on her balcony, admiring the view. After a few moments, she strolled back into the flat, where Tanya was making coffee.

"So this is lovely, you've done well," she said, taking a seat at Tanya's dining table. "This new?" Meg ran a hand over the table's solid wooden top.

Tanya nodded. "Came with the flat. You think it looks good there?"

"It's the perfect spot, looking over the river." She smiled up at Tanya. "This new start is going to be great for you."

"I hope so," Tanya replied, bringing over the coffee, Delilah at her feet. In the corner of the room stood a number of boxes Meg had been storing, rescued from her loft. Tanya was interested to see what was in them, as she seriously couldn't remember.

"So you said you took some time off this week? This is so not like you," Meg said, interrupting her thoughts.

"I had no choice — I couldn't leave her this week," Tanya said, rubbing Delilah's neck just the way she liked it. "Plus, it's been such a whirlwind what with moving and Gran dying, it's nice just to have some time at home to get used to the place myself."

"I can understand that. When I moved into Kate's place, it took a while for it to feel like home." Meg paused. "It's still not exactly 'our place', but Kate's done her best to make it so. But you don't have that issue — this is a blank canvas, you can make it your own." Meg paused.

"And if you need help with Delilah, you should get in touch with Jess's dog walker — I think she lives round here. Her name's Sophie — I can get her number if you like."

Tanya felt her face turn crimson as she studiously avoided Meg's gaze. "We've already met," she mumbled, burying her face in her coffee.

"So don't be a martyr, call her. What did we say about you accepting help? Jess says she's great, and I believe her."

"She came to get Delilah with me," Tanya blurted out.

"What?" Meg asked, furrowing her brow.

"Sophie — she came to get Delilah with me. Alice was going to come, but she couldn't make it, and I've met Sophie a couple of times and she kindly stepped in."

"So let me get this straight — Sophie, who you've just met, travelled up to Sturby with you and met your mother. I was going out with you for four years and that never happened."

"She didn't meet my mother — I wouldn't wish that on anyone. We stayed at Alan's and she kept me company on the drive there and back."

Meg raised one eyebrow. "You slept at Alan's? In the spare room?"

Tanya nodded, blushing despite herself. Memories of that lift kiss assaulted her mind, as they had been doing intermittently over the past four days. And every time they did, she felt the heat like it had just happened, like Sophie was standing over her, her lips about to close in on hers.

She wanted to go back for more, but she wasn't sure she was fit for purpose.

Not if any part of what her mum had said was true.

"Yes, but nothing happened," she replied, her skin prickling as she spoke. "We shared a bed, that's all."

Meg leaned back in her chair, regarding Tanya. "That's all?! You don't share beds with people you're not interested in. Especially not Alan's spare bed."

"Nothing happened!"

"Yet." Meg studied Tanya's face. "You're blushing, and you seem flustered. Nothing happened at all? Not even a brush of your hand over her thigh? A meeting of your lips? I went out with you remember, I know what you're like when you meet someone." Meg smiled. "Subtlety isn't your style."

Tanya smiled at that. "I like to let people know where they stand," she said. "And nothing happened, like I said." She paused. "But we did kiss in the lift when we got home."

"What! You've waited this long to tell me! And what happened then? When you kissed? Have you seen her since?"

Tanya shook her head. "Er, no."

"Why not? You're not normally shy in coming forward."

"You make me sound like a nightmare."

"Nonsense — you know what you want and go for it. It's a quality I've always admired in you, even though it annoyed the hell out of me at times." Meg gave her a smile Tanya recognised from their time together.

"It's just — she's seen me — all of me. There's no show with her. She's kinda different." Tanya paused. "I mean, nothing's happened, and yet she was there when Gran died, and she's visited my home. Nobody else has done that. It's like she knows all my secrets before we've even started."

"And that's a bad thing? If she knows it all and she's still here, that's a plus point, isn't it?"

Tanya nodded her head slowly. "And then there's my mum."

"How is Ann?" Meg's voice was laden with sarcasm.

Tanya responded in kind. "She sends her love," she replied, rolling her eyes. "Ann told me I'm just like her — and it got me thinking. Am I? Is that why no other relationship has worked for me?" She bit her lip, addressing Meg directly. "Be honest, am I a nightmare to be in a relationship with?"

Meg shook her head. "No, I've told you before. I loved you — I still love you a little. You were a great girlfriend; we just weren't meant to be." Meg laid a hand on her arm and it soothed her.

"Really? It wasn't because I was closed off? Because I wasn't open to what you wanted and I didn't want to compromise?" Tanya almost didn't want to hear the answer, but she knew she had to.

Meg hesitated before she spoke, and Tanya felt sick. But then Meg shook her head. "You know, you could say those things about anybody in *any* relationship — otherwise, we'd still be together, wouldn't we? Everyone's a little selfish when it comes down to it, and you were no more closed or stubborn than me or anyone else I've gone out with. Like I said, we just weren't meant to be.

"Everyone deals with those issues; it's how you work them out that counts. Don't listen to what your mum says — that woman's never made any sense. Why would she start now?" Meg smiled at that. "Honestly, you were a great girlfriend. You were just a nightmare ex-girlfriend at first." She let out a chuckle at that. "But you're the perfect ex now — two years later and living apart."

Tanya blushed at the recollection of that particular time in their lives when they lived together as exes. She hadn't been the kindest. "Sorry," she said.

Meg shook her head, smiling. "This isn't about us — it's about you. And you told me you're ready to get back into the game again, and Sophie sounds like she's already got under your skin. And she could help you with Delilah, too. I don't see a problem. You've got your flaws, but we all have. I say go for it — you've got nothing to lose."

Tanya nodded. "When you put it like that, it sounds easy."

"So you'll call her? At least for help with Delilah, because it sounds like you could use it."

Tanya released a slow breath. "We'll see."

Meg frowned, regarding her. "Whoever would have thought, two years ago when we were at loggerheads, that we'd be here now? Me married, sitting here telling you off for not going after someone." She smiled. "Slow, steady, careful. This is a whole new side of you." She paused. "And how are you feeling after your gran? Are you coping?"

Tanya nodded. "I forget, and then I remember — it comes over me in waves. But there's been so much else going on, I haven't really had time to sit down and grieve. I'm sure it'll happen." She glanced down at Delilah. "But having her here makes me feel likes Gran's still around, so that's something."

Chapter Thirty-Five

Sophie walked into the pub by the river, appropriately named The Water Loft. It had a boat theme, with oars, sails, ship's wheels and life buoys mounted on the walls. It had been built to service their flats, so it still had that new sheen about it, the floors not yet dulled by the incessant foot traffic of time. She checked her watch, then glanced around, seeing if she could spot Jess or Lucy — and her gaze fell upon them when she saw Jess's hand in the air.

She grinned and waved back, approaching the table with a jaunt in her step — she was looking forward to a drink after the week she'd had. When Jess had called to suggest it, she'd jumped at the chance.

That is, until she saw who else was sat there.

Not just Lucy, but also Tanya, looking just as attractive as she remembered.

Sophie stopped just short of the table, her face frozen in a half-smile. She wasn't displeased to see Tanya, far from it. But it'd been a few days since Sturby, since that kiss in the lift. She had no idea where they stood, or how Tanya felt.

All she knew was this was not what she'd been expecting tonight, her emotions gridlocked inside. She'd wanted to see Tanya again, of course she had, but these weren't exactly the circumstances she'd imagined.

Was Tanya going to clam up, or bolt? Had she known Sophie was going to be here, too? By the part-surprised, part-flummoxed look on her face, Sophie guessed the answer was no.

"Great to see you!" Jess said, giving Sophie a hug. "This is my partner, Lucy," she added, introducing the cute pixie-haired woman beside her, who was wearing dark sunglasses and a black leather jacket, together with a movie-star dimple.

Sophie shook hands with Lucy, but her mind was elsewhere.

"And I hope you don't mind, but I invited Tanya as well — I think you've already met."

Jess gestured towards Tanya, who was now giving Sophie an awkward smile. "Hi Sophie," Tanya said, her laser-like stare giving Sophie no choice but to meet her gaze.

When she did, Sophie came alive, her heart stuttering, her lips remembering. "Hi," she said, not sure what to do with her arms, her legs, her entire body.

If in doubt, talk about dogs: it was a ploy she was becoming used to with owners. "How's Delilah doing?"

"She's good — she's asleep under the table, miraculously," Tanya said, motioning downwards with her hand.

Sophie bent down and smiled at Delilah, curled up at

Tanya's feet. It seemed like they were getting on just fine. She sat down on the seat next to Tanya, her breathing unsteady as their proximity increased.

"And how are you getting on?" Sophie asked, recalling the bed they'd shared, followed by their explosive kiss.

Calm, that's what this situation called for, but it had deserted her right now.

"Much better for seeing you," Tanya whispered.

Jess leaned down, interrupting. "What can I get you to drink?" she asked Sophie.

Sophie glanced at Tanya, her eyes smiling. "I'll have whatever she's having."

Chapter Thirty-Six

"She doesn't look very happy with you," Sophie said, as they strolled out of the pub.

"You wouldn't be either if I'd just woken you up after you'd been sparked out on the floor for the past couple of hours," Tanya replied. "It's a form of doggy torture — making her walk home." She glanced down at Delilah. "Look at her little wobbly legs."

Sophie grinned. "She'll live," she said, threading her arm through Tanya's.

They were back to where they'd left off, back on an even keel, and Tanya was thrilled. She knew they had a connection, she still remembered their trip to Sturby. It had been special, despite everything else that surrounded it. And now they'd reunited, Tanya hoped she knew where tonight was heading.

When Sophie had walked into the pub tonight, she'd held her breath for a few seconds, wondering how she was going to be. But having Jess and Lucy there smoothed the waters, and it'd felt right to have her sitting by her side. Towards the end of the night, after Sophie's third beer, Sophie had even put a hand on her arm when she was telling a story.

And that's when Tanya knew that things might just be okay.

They arrived back at their building, with Tanya holding the big glass door open for Sophie.

"Your manners have certainly improved since the first time we met," Sophie said, glancing up at her. "Then you were barging into me. Whereas tonight, you bought all my drinks and now you're holding doors open."

"It's the least I owe you after this week," Tanya replied.

"So long as you're not going to run off now, you don't owe me anything." Sophie's gaze met Tanya's as she spoke, her words laced with trepidation.

Tanya shook her head: that was the last thing in the world she planned to do tonight. "No running off, I promise," she said.

Sophie nodded her head as they waited for the lift, her tongue wetting her bottom lip. "Okay, then."

The lift arrived and they both got in hesitantly, Tanya pressing the button for her floor. Now Sophie was back in her life, she wanted to keep her there, get to know her better. Starting right now, back in this lift.

Today was Sunday, but their kiss seemed like a lifetime ago. However, Tanya still recalled how she'd felt, what she'd desired — and the same desire was back today. When she looked up, Sophie's gaze was burning into her.

"So this lift," Sophie said, clearing her throat. "It does things to me, where you're concerned." She took a step forward into Tanya's space. "What about you?"

What did being in such a confined space with Sophie do to Tanya? She could write a thesis on it. Being so close and *not* kissing her was making every nerve ending tingle with excitement, making her clit pulse.

"Being this close to you is driving me wild," Tanya said, her voice glazed with want. "I know we've a lot to iron out, but you think we can shelve it for tonight?"

"I think that can be arranged," Sophie replied, flicking her gaze up to meet Tanya's fully. "So what's going to happen tonight? Is there going to be more kissing?"

Heat flooded Tanya's entire body: she felt wet with it. "I certainly hope so. I might be a little disappointed if there wasn't. It's kind of a tradition now, isn't it?"

Sophie's mouth turned up at the sides. "Kind of," she agreed, nodding her head.

Delilah's bark interrupted them, and then they were at floor 20, the lift announcer bringing their journey to a close a lot sooner than Tanya wanted. The doors sprung open and panic flooded Tanya's body: she didn't want this to end, but she didn't want to assume. She guessed she could ask, but her normal brashness deserted her when she was with this Sophie.

With Sophie, despite herself, Tanya was a different woman all together, no matter what she tried. But far from being scared, she was revelling in it: Tanya was learning new things about herself every moment they spent together, and she hoped that wasn't about to end.

"Are you getting off here?" Tanya asked, her voice crackling with emotion.

Dear god, she hoped not. She wanted to spend all night with Sophie, undressing her slowly, getting to know her body intimately, licking her all over, drowning in her beauty.

Sophie smiled at her, and her smile lit up the lift. "I was hoping to be getting off at floor 30," Sophie said. "Perhaps in more ways than one."

Tanya took a moment to process her words, before desire flooded her body, her mouth going dry. Sophie had just told her she wanted exactly the same as she did, and that was enough to make Tanya leap forward and stab the lift button. "Well in that case, let's get to floor 30, shall we?"

The doors slid closed and as the lift whizzed upwards, she simply stared at Sophie, but didn't move forward. Because she didn't need to snatch a kiss in the lift: today, Sophie's kisses had been promised to her, in multiples she hoped.

They stumbled out of the lift, hand in hand, until Tanya had to break their hold to get her keys from her bag. At her feet, Delilah was sniffing at the skirting boards in the hallway, seemingly oblivious to the sexual tension in the air.

And it wasn't just in the air: Tanya could feel it in her blood and on her scalp; it was coating her from head to toe. When their lips actually connected, she wasn't going to be responsible for her actions.

Once inside, Tanya let Delilah off her leash and she wandered across the lounge to her water bowl. They watched her, glad of an excuse to focus on something else rather than the electricity in the air. But when Tanya turned her head and caught Sophie's heated stare, she couldn't hold back any longer.

And neither could Sophie. "If we don't kiss soon, I might expire," Sophie said, closing the distance between them and backing Tanya up against her lounge wall.

Tanya's mouth curled into a smile. "I don't want to be responsible for that," she just about managed to get out, as Sophie's lips travelled to hers, stopping her certain expiration in the simplest way possible.

Tanya recalled her lips from before, but this time, as they slipped over hers, she was able to revel in them: to appreciate them on a whole new level. Their warmth, their welcome, their touch. She hadn't had a kiss like this in quite some time, and when she tried to make sense of it, her mind refused, instructing her not to over-analyse.

Instead, it demanded she enjoy the moment for what it was: a dynamite kiss from a hot woman.

Tanya obeyed.

Then Sophie's mouth was travelling: her hot breath on Tanya's cheek, then her jaw, then her neck. Her tongue flicked, her teeth nipped. A rush between Tanya's legs told her if this was a game, Sophie was winning.

And then Sophie's mouth came back up and crushed against Tanya's, followed by Sophie's tongue parting Tanya's lips and sliding into her mouth and ohmyfuckinghell.

Tanya lost all power of rational thought, as if she'd just slipped on a banana skin and lost control of the emotion tray she'd been carefully balancing. Now, her emotions were all thrown into the air, and it was lust that landed first, sprawling all over her, covering her body with a lazy grin. And when Sophie's hand landed on her left breast, Tanya was pretty sure that lust was controlling Sophie, too.

She was just sinking into Sophie a little more when a phone ringing cut through the air, shattering both their senses and causing Sophie to pull back, her face ruffled, her eyes half-closed.

"That's my phone," she said, reaching for her back pocket.

"Leave it," Tanya replied, moving her lips closer to Sophie's once more. Heat was pouring off her and Tanya wasn't sure where she stopped and Sophie started. She didn't want anything to come between them now, not when it had taken this long for them to get here.

Sophie checked the screen, then winced slightly. "It's Lucy. What on earth is Lucy calling me for? We only left them ten minutes ago." She was out of breath as she spoke, flicking her gaze to Tanya, then giving her a quick, juicy kiss. The ringing was only getting louder in the comparative silence of Tanya's flat.

"Hold that thought," Sophie said, with a wicked grin. "Whatever you're thinking, hold that exact thought."

Sophie swiped the call and began speaking to Lucy: Tanya hoped it was going to be quick.

Hold that thought? Sophie, naked, pinned against her, Tanya fucking her wildly. Okay, she could hang onto that one, it was pretty vivid in her mind. And not only in her mind but also in her body. Tanya could feel how wet she was already, and all she wanted to do was get naked and come together with Sophie. Again and again and again.

However, she had a feeling she might have to be patient.

"Uh-huh," Sophie said, wincing. "You're there now?" She shrugged at Tanya, trying not to sound winded down the phone. "Sure," she said. "I'll be there in ten minutes." Pause. "No, no problem at all."

Sophie slotted her phone into her pocket. "I have good news and bad news," she said, turning up one corner of her mouth. "The good news is, this doesn't end here."

Sophie put her index finger on Tanya's lips and Tanya melted on the spot. Then she opened her mouth slightly and sucked the tip of Sophie's finger into her warmth.

Sophie let out a small moan, which sent a mini-flood of happiness right to Tanya's groin. She let her mind wander forward to sucking the rest of Sophie, and then she had to stop.

There was bad news to hear, first.

"And the bad?"

Sophie gave her a rueful smile. "The bad news is Lucy

and Jess don't have their keys. They've locked themselves out and it's down to the dog walker to save the day."

"Really?" Tanya said, her libido throwing itself onto the floor and starting to wail. "I'm going to kill them."

Sophie laughed. "And our friendship was going so well, too."

Tanya kissed her lips, then pulled back, regret coating her body. "So long as we can carry this on when we get back? You promise?"

"I don't have any other plans," Sophie replied, kissing her lips again. "Besides, you taste delicious — why wouldn't I come back for more?"

Tanya gave her a resigned sigh: it was Jess and Lucy after all, they couldn't really do anything else. "Okay. But I'm coming with you, just to make sure you return."

"Look on it as an extended form of really weird foreplay," Sophie said, holding out her hand. "Shall we?"

Chapter Thirty-Seven

They turned up at Jess and Lucy's flat 15 minutes later, Delilah on her lead, Tanya and Sophie hand in hand. Jess and Lucy were sitting on the sofa inside the lobby of their apartment block, their dog, Spinach, on Jess's lap. As they heard their footsteps approach, Lucy looked up.

"Hey!" she said, her gaze taking in their joined hands. "I only expected Sophie," she said, a puzzled look on her face. "Did I interrupt something?" she asked, scrabbling to her feet as Sophie held out her keys.

"Let's just say, your phone call was at a slightly inopportune time. We've got some unfinished business, haven't we?" Sophie said, grinning at Tanya.

Tanya nodded, not quite knowing where to look.

"But never let it be said I leave a damsel in distress, because I don't," Sophie added.

Lucy blushed, shaking her head. "You should put it on your business cards. I'll pay for a new print run." She took the keys. "But thank you, you're a life-saver." She paused, regarding the pair with a grin. "You want us to take Delilah overnight so you can have some space alone?"

Sophie glanced at Tanya, who shook her head. "No thanks, she needs routine and stability right now. We'll just have to wait for her to go to sleep."

"Sleeping pill for Delilah it is," Jess said, putting an arm around Lucy. "We'll let you get off — take that however you want it," she added with a wink, before dragging Lucy by the hand towards their corridor.

They almost ran back to Tanya's flat, tearing through the concrete jungle of Woolwich, across the main road and into the lift. This time they didn't stand on ceremony, hitting floor 30 and sinking into each other. When they reached Tanya's flat, her keys were already in her hand, and she tugged Sophie through the door with purpose.

Yes, she knew how this was going to go.

She was 36 years old after all; she'd been here before.

But yet, somehow, she hadn't. With Sophie, everything was new, including Tanya.

Her thoughts stopped as Sophie reached up and pulled Tanya to her. "You know I said earlier that if you didn't kiss me, I might die?"

Tanya nodded.

"Well now, if we don't get naked very soon, the same might happen," Sophie told her, staring at her with hungry eyes. "I've wanted you since the moment we met."

Tanya said nothing, simply pulled Sophie down the hallway and into the master suite.

* * *

Now she was in the bedroom with Tanya, Sophie hoped this was the start of something real: a story they'd begun writing a few weeks ago, one Sophie's pen had been poised over for so long.

Now, as Tanya raised her arms and stripped off her top, the nib was being pressed to the paper and the ink was beginning to flow. A little like Sophie's emotions and everything inside her.

"You're beautiful," Tanya said, her eyes roaming Sophie's naked skin as she slipped off her white bra. "But I already told you that at Alan's house."

Sophie pulled back, eyeing her. "We never did talk about that, did we?" she said, breathless.

"You want to now?"

Sophie shook her head, grinning. "God, no," she said, taking off her glasses and pressing her lips to Tanya's, her whole body pulsing with promise. She loved this part: the anticipation, the heart-shaking desire, the knowledge that anything was possible.

As Sophie slipped off Tanya's top and bra, feeling Tanya's hot mouth encase her nipple, she wiped her mind clean of everything she'd learned before. Because Tanya wasn't like the other girls she'd met — Tanya had let her in, been raw and bruised.

Tonight, Sophie was going to make sure the bruises healed.

Tanya unbuttoned her jeans, her warm hands pulling down Sophie's zip, easing the denim over her thighs.

Just that slight touch made Sophie pulse anew. "I want you so much," she said, having no control over the words coming out of her mouth. However, she didn't care if she sounded trite, because she wasn't trying to be cool. She was living in the moment, with surety pulsing through her veins. As she parted her legs beneath Tanya, Sophie's whole body smouldered in the charcoal of the day.

Tanya's hand was on her breast, then her hip, before settling between her legs. And as her fingers swept through Sophie's soft hair and touched her lips, Sophie's brain flicked through her album of top life moments, making way for this one.

She took a mental snapshot, looking up into Tanya's green eyes that were fixed on her: this was their moment, their time to shine.

Tanya's fingers circled her clit, and Sophie's whole body shuddered, her world tinted red with delight. When Tanya slipped two fingers inside her, Sophie saw bright lights even though her eyes had flickered shut, the pulse of her heart thick in her ears. She threw her head back and drowned in the moment's sweetness: it tasted of honeycomb and molasses, and Sophie simply couldn't get enough. Two becoming one was sweeter than she could have imagined.

She pushed her legs open wider, and Tanya ground into her, Sophie's body responding in kind. Their breasts were pressed together, just like their lips, and Tanya's hand inside her was the most natural pose in the world: she never wanted it to end.

But if it had to, Sophie was leaving on a high. And so, as Tanya thrust into her, Sophie ground her teeth together, her ears filled with a rushing sound, her body alive like it hadn't been in ages. She was holding nothing back with Tanya, and her actions were reciprocated. And when Tanya slid out, connecting with her clit, then back into her pussy, something deep down inside began to pulse, and within minutes, the fire in Sophie's heart had taken control.

As her orgasm ripped through her, she came in an explosion of heat and juice, crying out, biting down on her lip, her hips and heart bucking like never before. And when she opened her eyes, the crazy parade of lust still rattling through her very core, she saw nothing but Tanya on top of her, under her, enveloping her.

Sophie wanted to pause, rewind, replay. She wanted to give Tanya her own DVD to watch back, too.

She reversed their positions, rolling Tanya under her with ease, her body long and lithe beneath her. Tanya didn't put up a fight, her face baked red, her skin hot to the touch — just like the heat inside Sophie. Her body was still pulsing with pleasure as she slid down Tanya.

"My turn now," she said, before pausing, holding the moment in her hands, cradling it, loving it. "By the way, that was incredible. You were incredible."

Tanya let a lazy grin wander across her face. "I could say the same to you."

Sophie put a finger to her lips.

Tanya's breasts were fuller than she'd imagined, and they were glorious in her hands. As she swept her tongue around Tanya's swollen nipples, she could feel Tanya spark beneath her, could feel that spark replicated within herself. She placed a line of kisses all the way from Tanya's neck to her navel, as if leaving a trail to follow back later. Then finally, Sophie's mouth came to rest just where she wanted it: between Tanya's thighs.

She looked up and caught Tanya's gaze, fully focused on her, Tanya's tongue licking the corners of her mouth.

"Oh god," Tanya said, and Sophie felt her whole body shudder as she hovered over Tanya's pussy, blowing hot breath into her. This was her chance to show Tanya what she meant to her; to demonstrate that when she looked at her, something deep inside Sophie went boom, sending shockwaves to her very soul.

As Sophie dipped her head, flicked out her tongue and drank Tanya in, her lover moaned, making Sophie smile into her. She'd waited so long to taste her, and Tanya was everything she wanted and more. As Sophie began to push Tanya over the edge, letting her tongue roam free, she let go of everything that had held them back to now.

All the diversions, all the obstacles.

Sophie pushed it all aside for this one moment, instead sinking into the moment, into Tanya. Right now, she was a VIP in Tanya's exclusive club: she was the only guest on the list and she was coming in.

Tanya groaned some more as Sophie added one finger, then two, before letting her tongue swoop through Tanya's flowing juices, dancing on Tanya's clit and Sophie's heart. She and Tanya were off the scale.

Within moments, she felt her lover's body shake: Sophie wasn't surprised, because she was shaking, too. Their momentum was unstoppable, as were the feelings cascading through her right now.

Eventually, Tanya crumbled, releasing all her emotion, clamping down on Sophie's fingers as an earthquake rocked her body. Sophie didn't let up, lapping her lover until she felt Tanya's hands in her hair, telling her she could take no more. She stopped and crawled up Tanya's miles of skin, retracing her kisses from earlier. Sophie's chin glistened, as did her heart.

Tanya looked at her, then shook her head. "Fuck me," she said, then laughed. "It always amazes me how sex renders you completely bereft of language."

"You just said the word bereft, so I don't think you're doing too badly." Sophie kissed her again. "Whereas the only words going through my mind are wow, clit, pussy and shall we do it again." She grinned. "What do you say, once more with feeling?"

Tanya let out a throaty laugh. "Can I get my breath back first?" she asked, smiling.

Sophie ground her body into her, a smile invading her face, too. "Okay then, but only because I like you." And then she gazed at Tanya, a slow, steady gaze. "Because I really do like you," she said, again seemingly having no control of what was coming out of her mouth.

But Tanya didn't flinch; she simply nodded her head, her eyes cloudy with desire. "I kinda like you, too."

Chapter Thirty-Eight

They fell asleep in a tangle of limbs just after 3am, and Tanya felt more content than she had in ages. They'd clicked in a way she'd only dreamed of, leaving her wanting to get to know Sophie more.

But Tanya wasn't feeling content when she woke up with sweat pooling all over her body at 5.30am, with Sophie snoring softly beside her. In contrast, Tanya's heart was trampling through her body as she clutched her hands to her chest and tried to calm down. As normal, it was all her mother's fault.

She'd had the dream about her mother again. And in her dream, Sophie and her gran had been standing beside her mother, agreeing with everything she said. That Tanya wasn't capable of proper love without judgement. That Tanya would never settle for anything less than perfection. That nobody would ever measure up to her exacting standards.

And now Tanya was lying in bed, wishing this dream would go away — it was the third time she'd had it this week, although Sophie judging her too was a new addition.

She reached out and clasped one of the bars of her iron bed's headboard, glancing at Sophie who looked angelic next to her. Was she up for this? Was Tanya to be trusted with her own heart, as well as Sophie's?

She crept silently out of her bed, careful not to wake Sophie or Delilah who was curled up in her blanket, and tiptoed into the living room. There, she poured herself a glass of water from the tap and sat on her sofa, shivering as the chilled liquid filled her.

Was she like her mother? Was she doomed to a loveless life? She hadn't thought so earlier on, when she and Sophie had sketched out their love, a blank sheet of paper suddenly filled with curves and shapes, shading and perspective. But the dream had been so vivid, and her mum's face and resulting bile so realistic, she was finding it hard to shake.

Day to day, Tanya got on with her life so well, sailing through her career, surrounded by a handful of good friends and colleagues. She didn't think about her parents often, and when she did, she made a concerted effort to push them to the back of her mind, because what good could come of them?

However, ever since she'd come back from Sturby, doubt had drizzled inside her — the worst kind of internal weather — her entire body sluggish and drawn. She should be upbeat and dancing after the night she'd had, but this was one persistent narrative that wouldn't go away: *you're turning into your mother.* And, like clockwork, almost every night since she'd returned, the dream had come. Even Sophie hadn't been able to stop it.

She looked up as a gentle padding broke her thoughts: Delilah was up and out of her bed, as if sensing Tanya's turmoil. She'd heard dogs were good at that, and here it was in action. Delilah waddled over to her bowl, gulping down some water before sidling over to Tanya.

"Hey, girl," Tanya whispered as she picked Delilah up and hugged her close: still sleepy, she was happy to oblige as Tanya's very own hot water bottle. It was soothing, seeing as every part of her was wracked with self-doubt. And she hated that it had happened on the night Sophie was here.

She drank a little more water, then made a pact with herself.

She wouldn't bow to this dream, or its resulting feelings. She and Sophie had shared something special, and she was going to go back to sleep and wake up happier.

With Sophie in her bed, the chances were high.

Chapter Thirty-Nine

A while later, Sophie stirred. She eased open her eyes and rolled over, letting a slow smile spread across her face as she recalled the previous evening. She was in Tanya's bed, and their first time together had been everything she hoped for, and more.

However, now she was in bed alone — as it was a work day, she guessed Tanya was in the shower. She stretched out in the bed, flexing her calves and her toes. She was aching all over, but in such a decadent way, she couldn't be happier. Tanya had been spectacular.

She checked her watch and saw it was just after 8am. Shit: her first dog walk was in an hour, and she had to get home and change first. But not without a kiss from Tanya first.

She hopped out of bed, grinning at her nakedness, slung on yesterday's clothes and yanked open the door.

As she walked into the lounge, Delilah ran over, barking. Sophie bent down and gave her some love, before catching the back of Tanya on her balcony. She walked out into the morning sunshine and put an arm around her new lover, her hand grazing Tanya's breast, her lips kissing her cheek. Tanya gripped her coffee a little bit tighter on contact, before turning.

Sophie paused: what was with her tight smile? Perhaps Tanya just wasn't a morning person.

Undeterred, Sophie kissed her lips and they didn't lie. Tanya might be off somewhere in her head, but Sophie was sure Tanya's body was responding to her just like it had yesterday. Her lips were still delicious, tasting of promise and coffee.

"Morning," she said, smiling at Tanya.

"Hey."

"How'd you sleep?"

"Patchy."

"Really? I slept like a log."

"I noticed."

"You wore me out," Sophie said. Every muscle in her body was telling her so, with a satisfied grin. Nights like last night were ones Sophie would like to slot into her calendar on a regular basis.

Nights like last night made her feel alive.

But she wasn't sure Tanya felt the same, because there was that tight smile again.

Sophie took in the scene below, the river sparkling in the early morning sun. But despite that, she couldn't help picking up a slightly chilly air on the balcony. What had she missed?

When she'd fallen asleep last night, limbs entwined,

Sophie would have put big money on them waking up all smiles. But Tanya had changed the rules overnight, and now she was sitting on her idyllic balcony like she'd just lost her house on the roulette wheel.

Sophie swallowed, her earlier elation now laced with fear. Had she done something wrong? Was she the only one to think their time together had been the start of something? She was beginning to have that nagging dread, just like she'd had with Helen. And if that was the case, she was going to bolt first, before she was kicked out of another flat before 9am.

Again.

"Everything okay?" she asked, sitting down on the chair beside Tanya, taking her hand and kissing it.

Tanya nodded slowly, not turning her head. "Yeah, fine. I just had a weird dream. It woke me up, then I went back to sleep, only to have it again." Tanya shivered as she spoke. "It's left me feeling a bit weird, sorry. And I've got a really busy day today." She let go of Sophie's hand, turning her body towards her. "But I am pleased to see you." She looked into Sophie's eyes. "I had a fabulous time last night."

"I did, too," Sophie replied, relief seeping through her. Tanya had a bad dream and no sleep — she could deal with that. Plus, she did have to get going. "I have to scoot — my first client's at 9am and then I'm meeting Jess at the café to help her this week." She paused. "You want me to pop in to check on Delilah today?"

Tanya shook her head. "Maybe, I'll let you know. I'm working from home, but then I need to work out my schedule." She gave Sophie a weak smile, then turned her gaze to the horizon. "Sorry, I'm just a bit… freaked out. It's not to do with you, honest."

Sophie didn't want to press her anymore; she seemed upset. But was this really to do with a dream and nothing to do with her, with last night? Sophie had woken up this morning like a Disney cartoon bird: she'd wanted to whistle and dance. Now, if she were that same bird, she was in an angry farmer's sightline, just about to be shot.

"Okay, just drop me a text. I can drop in whenever, you know that." She paused, turning up the flirt in her voice, rippling it with honey. "Because you know what? I've got a lot of time for Delilah, and her owner." Sophie reached for Tanya's hand again.

Tanya glanced at her, then at their joined hands, before looking away, dropping their contact.

Shit, not even her flirtatious tone was working. Sophie checked her watch again: she didn't have time to analyse.

She got up, but when she turned back, Sophie swore she saw a hint of regret in Tanya's deep green eyes — why that was, she couldn't be sure. She swallowed down a 6ft tall sigh, instead putting on a chirpy smile.

"You want a coffee before you go?" Tanya asked, jumping up and walking ahead of her into the lounge.

No smile. No kiss. No nothing.

Sophie was stumped. "No, I better get going." She paused, staring at Tanya's back. "I'll see you soon?"

Tanya turned and nodded her head. "I'll call you," she said, her eyes dead, her smile flattened into dust.

But Sophie wasn't leaving it like that. She stepped forward and pressed her lips to Tanya's, and just like that, the electricity was turned on again. No matter what was going on with Tanya this morning, she was going to make sure she left her with something to remind her of them. It seemed to work: as Sophie pulled away, Tanya's breath quickened on her lips.

"Make sure you do," Sophie said, adding a final kiss before squeezing Tanya's hand.

She got out of the flat and pressed the lift, taking it all the way down to the ground floor. Then she walked towards the river, lighting up a cigarette as she went.

Without Tanya in her life, she'd have kicked this habit for good by now. She'd read the Allen Carr book like her dad told her, but she reckoned Allen must have been in a settled relationship, or single. Tanya was playing havoc with her willpower in more ways than one.

She took a long, deep drag on her cigarette and walked over to the river wall, clambering onto it and leaning back into the morning sun. She stretched, feeling all her muscles clench, then relax. Then she let go of the sigh she'd been storing, shaking her head at the sky, looking back up to their building.

Since meeting Tanya, Sophie had been on a rollercoaster

ride of emotions. And now she'd added red-hot sex into the equation, it wasn't about to get any easier, was it?

Sophie was just about holding it together, but she already knew she was in trouble.

Her heart was falling into Tanya's hands, and there was nothing she could do about it.

Chapter Forty

Tanya got in from work that night at 6pm, having been called into the office for an emergency meeting — just what she hadn't needed on top of everything else. She'd snapped at her colleagues and her boss had asked if she was okay — that's when she knew her open wound was bleeding into every part of her life.

She had to find a way to fix it, but who to talk to? She was at a loss. She needed someone who knew her and her parents, someone who could be objective. She'd even thought about calling Jonathan, but had stopped when she picked up the phone. She'd tried Alice, but got her answerphone. Maybe Alan was the answer. She threw her keys on their hook by the door as that answer hit her. Yes, she should talk to Alan.

Delilah was already at her feet, yapping as she did. Tanya bent down and petted her — and then spied a present Delilah had left for her on the lounge floor, just by the patio doors. A reminder to Tanya she didn't like being left alone.

"Delilah!" Tanya said, her voice stern, storming over to the kitchen to get a poop bag and some detergent. She cleaned it up, with Delilah around her feet, but then she felt instantly guilty. It wasn't Delilah's fault, it was hers. Tanya got down on her haunches and made a fuss of her dog, but Delilah still looked hurt. "I'm sorry, I shouldn't have shouted," Tanya said, kissing the top of her head.

Her week was shaping up to be busy, which meant she was going to have to sort out a plan for Delilah. Which meant she needed to speak to Sophie.

Sophie. Just the thought of her made Tanya's blood pump faster, but also made her cover her face with her hands. Was Sophie still speaking to her after she'd been so rude this morning? She guessed she'd find out. Today wasn't getting any easier, was it?

Perhaps a walk would make her feel better. Tanya went into the bedroom to get out of her work gear, and was instantly hit by images from last night: Sophie naked, Sophie coming, Sophie inside her. She needed to talk to Sophie. She slipped on her jeans and a sweatshirt, then put the lead on a delighted Delilah and strode out of the flat, slamming the door behind her.

Tanya swung around onto the wide grey path that ran along the Thames, the Woolwich ferry behind her, the rows of new flats lined up to her right, shivering in the evening wind. At her feet, Delilah trotted along obediently, and that at least made Tanya smile. No matter what was going on in her life, she was beginning to see how dogs kept you grounded, gave you some perspective. She was grateful to Delilah for that.

Her thoughts were broken by a growling nearby, followed by a yelp from Delilah. Tanya's features froze as she looked down, to see a grey-and-white dog named Barney baring its teeth at Delilah. She'd asked the owner its breed before, but the owner hadn't been sure — only to say that somewhere along the line, a German shepherd had been involved.

Tanya pulled Delilah's lead and she jumped right, as Barney followed.

Fear bubbled up and lodged itself in Tanya's throat. This was one aspect of dog owning she was yet to get used to: dealing with other dogs and their owners. She bent down to pick Delilah up, just as Barney growled again.

Tanya straightened up and gave his owner a stern glare. "Hey," Tanya said, addressing the woman. "You need to keep a tighter hold of your dog — it's not the first time he's come for Delilah."

In response, she got a perky smile from the woman, who was wearing tailored jeans and a blazer, along with a my-dog-is-a-saint attitude.

"Barney wouldn't do that. Look at him, the face of an angel." The woman was showing her full set of teeth, just like her dog. "He's just being friendly, aren't you, Barney?"

As if to prove just how friendly he was, Barney bared his teeth and growled again, reminding Tanya of the creatures from Gremlins when they'd been fed after midnight. "Delilah's got enough friends, thanks, so just watch your dog."

The woman rolled her eyes at Tanya, bent down to pet Barney and dragged him away, much to Barney's disgust.

Tanya waited until they were well ahead before she put Delilah down. So much for the therapeutic power of walking.

A podcast — maybe that could brighten her mood. She rooted in her bag for her phone, then walked a few paces slower, head down, scrolling through her podcast menu. Tanya rounded a corner heading towards the local park, not looking up, and walked smack into another person.

"For fuck's sake," Tanya muttered, "watch where you're going." It was only when she looked up she saw the other person was Sophie, with Branston at her feet. Tanya closed her eyes: she was being rude again, wasn't she?

"You want to try that again?" Sophie said, narrowing her eyes. "Only, I'd say you walked into me, not the other way around."

Tanya's breathing stalled as she focused on Sophie's stunning eyes and full lips — lips she'd kissed only hours ago. But now, crossing the few inches and doing so would seem like madness. She knew she should have texted her today, to follow up their night and sort Delilah, but the hours had just slipped by. And now, here they were, having an altercation on a pavement.

Tanya shook her head in apology, but that only

seemed to anger Sophie more. "I didn't see it was you," Tanya said. *That hadn't come out right.* "I'm sorry, I'm just having a terrible day, like you wouldn't believe."

But as soon as she said it, she knew it was the wrong thing.

"You're having a terrible day?" Sophie said, her tone disbelieving. "Thanks very much. Your day started with me in your bed, or have you forgotten that bit? You seemed to have this morning." Sophie shook her head, sighing. "I've been giving you the benefit of the doubt for quite a while now, but do you deserve it?"

Tanya opened her mouth to speak, but nothing came out. Her mind was turning cartwheels of all the possible things she could say, but it couldn't settle on one answer. It just seemed to go round and round like the worst Waltzer ride in the world.

"Seeing as you seem mute, let me fill in the gaps," Sophie continued, pushing her shoulders back, her chest out. Like she was preparing for battle. "I expected more from you, after everything. And maybe I was naive, but I did," she said. "I thought we had something, especially after last night. And then you just brush me off this morning, and I let you because you're going through a lot, I know that.

"But I need something from you, Tanya. I'm putting my heart on the line here, and I just need you to say you are, too, and that you want me in your life. Because you're blowing hot and cold and I'm not sure how long

I can take this." Sophie stopped, her gaze gripping Tanya, hands on her hips.

She'd never looked more brave, decisive or sexy, but Tanya's mouth was dry, her mind blank. But she had to say something, she owed it to Sophie.

Tanya looked up and saw such hurt in Sophie's eyes, and she was responsible. That killed her. She cleared her throat and stood up taller. "We *do* have something, we really do. And I know I'm in the wrong here, but you just have to give me some time to work out my shit. And it is *my* shit, I know that. But please don't throw in the towel, I couldn't take it."

Was that enough? Tanya had no idea, but right now, it was all she could give. She had to slay the demons of her home town first, before she could fully embrace a girl called London.

Sophie shook her head gently, letting out a sigh. "I can't just walk away when I'm already involved, can I?"

She sounded so defeated, Tanya wanted to take her in her arms — but she was frozen to the spot.

"If you'd just let me help you, maybe we could work it out together." She paused. "But make up your mind soon, because I won't wait around forever."

"I know," Tanya replied.

And she did.

She had to get home and call Alan.

Chapter Forty-One

Sophie pulled back her right fist, then let fly, her gloved punch hitting the pad plumb centre.

Behind it, Rachel stood firm, bouncing on the balls of her feet.

Sophie took aim at the right pad and slammed her left fist into it with a satisfying thud. On nights like tonight, she loved boxing. She could punch these pads forever.

"I mean, who the fuck does she think she is?" Sophie asked, pounding her right fist into the pad again.

Rachel smiled at her friend, arms up. "I should send Tanya my bill at the end of this if my wrists have stress injuries."

"You should," Sophie replied, slamming her left fist down, shrieking as she did. There were only two other people in the gym at the bottom of their building, but neither of them looked up. Boxing and shrieking were happy bedfellows.

"I mean, we have a night of *fantastic* sex — off-the-charts great — and then she acts like she does today. Aloof." *Punch*. "Incommunicative." *Punch*. "Fucking rude, frankly." *Slam*.

Rachel took it all in her stride. "Fantastic sex. I remember that, in the dim, distant past," she replied. "And then this morning she just threw you out?"

Sophie put her gloves down for a moment, picking up her water bottle. This was thirsty work. "More or less," she replied. "I mean, she wasn't exactly rolling out the red carpet."

"Sounds worryingly familiar," Rachel said. "You wanna swap over?"

Sophie nodded. "Sure," she said, taking off her red gloves and putting on the blue boxing pads. Now it was Rachel's turn to get out her frustration.

"I swear, though, she was there with me, every step of the way last night. It wasn't just a solo show, and she wasn't faking it." Sophie paused. "I know faking when I see it, believe me."

"You do?"

Sophie nodded. "I've done it enough times."

"You have?"

"Will you stop answering questions with questions."

"I can't help it." Rachel paused, before throwing her first punch.

Sophie absorbed it, springing to life to take the next one.

"So she wasn't faking it, but this morning she wasn't so keen."

Sophie nodded. "Correct." *Punch.* "And then she just ran into me a few hours ago — swearing at me when it was her fault by the way. She's so infuriating." *Punch, shimmy.* "I mean, she's good-looking, she's funny and don't get me started on the sex."

Rachel threw another punch, rolling her eyes. "Don't worry, I won't," she replied.

Sophie smiled. "Yet she's also crippled by her past, and seems to think she's the only person to ever deal with that. I mean, haven't we all at some point?" *Punch.* "Apart from you with your chocolate-box family," she said, smiling at Rachel.

Rachel gave her an extra-hard punch for that. "Leave my parents out of this. I can't take the blame for their happy marriage, so don't make me."

That made Sophie laugh for the first time today. "Oh, I dunno — I just want a straightforward woman. Is that so hard to find?"

Rachel snorted at that, throwing a one-two combo. "If you meet her, can you see if she's got a twin sister, please?"

Sophie snorted some more. "I know, I know." She paused, putting the pads down and getting more water. "She's going through a lot, I know that. Her gran meant the world to her." She paused. "But we'd just had the *best sex ever.*"

Rachel laughed again. "So what it comes down to is your ego is a little bruised," she said, before sucking on her water bottle and catching her breath. "I'd say, cut her some slack, then go and talk to her. She seemed sane and reasonable, unlike the normal ones you usually go out with."

"She is a bit rude at times. This afternoon reminded me

of that — like her problems are the biggest." Sophie bit her top lip. "My worry is I'm falling for the wrong woman." She sighed. "I didn't think I was, but maybe my gauge is all out of whack. And I didn't like her attitude today; it reminded me of when we met."

Rachel put up her gloves and Sophie did the same with her pads. They were silent for a few moments as they practised their one-two-jab routine, ten times, as instructed by Alice's boyfriend, Jake. Once done, they swapped over again, both out of breath.

"And did you just say you were falling for her?" Rachel asked, one eyebrow hoisted high on her forehead.

Sophie gave a defeated sigh. "You knew that already — you knew before I did. I just wish Tanya could see it and throw me a bone."

Rachel put up her pads and they worked through their routine, this time with Sophie doing the punching.

"Imagine that's her head if that makes you feel better," Rachel said from behind the pads.

Sophie stopped punching when she said that. "I don't want to punch her in the head," she said, throwing off her gloves and sighing. "I just want to put my arms around her and tell her everything's going to be okay."

"Despite her bad manners?" Rachel said, as they both slumped down to the floor, their backs against the mercifully cold gym wall.

"Yep, despite that," Sophie said.

"You have got it bad."

"I know."

Rachel nudged her then, grinning as she took another slug of water. "And is it like I said? Is she all you're thinking about?"

"Every hour of every day."

"Poor you," Rachel replied.

"I spoke to my dad earlier, and even he had a successful date this weekend. This has to go well, otherwise I'm the only single London in town. And my work's suffering, too — I've been walking dogs off pavements and dropping poo bags all day, and it's all her fault."

Rachel took a deep breath in before she replied. "I wouldn't worry, I think your love jar has happiness written on the label. I had a vision that you and Tanya would be together, and they don't call me Mystic Rachel for nothing."

Sophie laughed for the second time that day. "Who calls you Mystic Rachel?"

"Well, I do now," Rachel said with a grin.

Sophie's phone rattled with activity. She picked it up and saw two texts: one from Helen and one from Tanya. Sophie's emotions reacted in precise opposition, causing her to sit up straight, then slump in confusion.

"You okay?" Rachel asked.

Sophie shook her head. She held her breath, clicking on the text from Helen: she snorted as she scanned it. Then she quickly read the text from Tanya, feeling guilty she hadn't done that first.

That one put a smile on her face.

"Would you believe, I just got two texts, one from Tanya and one from Helen?"

Rachel rubbed her hands together. "Sounds juicy."

"Helen's just sent me a text asking for a booty call — she's split up with her girlfriend and wants to know if I'm free." Sophie shook her head. "Honestly, the cheek."

Rachel raised an eyebrow. "Well you did run every time she clicked her fingers for three months. You can't blame her for trying."

Sophie ignored that comment. "Whereas the text from Tanya is asking if I can call in on Delilah tomorrow and walk her."

"So she is still in contact."

"About the dog," Sophie replied.

"Nothing about you and last night?"

"She's put one kiss at the end."

"A kiss is good!" Rachel said, wiping her brow. "Now you have to follow that up and talk to her, get this straightened out, okay? Do it for me, because my wrists can't take another session like this."

Chapter Forty-Two

Two days later, Tanya had just got back from Delilah's evening walk when her phone rang. It was Alan.

"Hey," he said, his voice calming as always. "Just returning your calls, sorry it's taken so long. How are you? How's Delilah?"

"She's fine, only weeing occasionally indoors now."

Alan chuckled. "The perils of being a parent." He paused. "And you?"

"I'm fine," she lied, her voice flat. "I've tried you the last two nights — where have you been? I was getting worried."

"I've been at choir rehearsals," he replied. "We've got a show this weekend."

That took Tanya back to Alan's house, to his Gay Men's Chorus T-shirt — and she realised they still hadn't had *the* conversation. The one about Alan being gay.

Tanya paused. "About that," she began, then stuttered. Yes, she was gay, but she was still shy about asking this question. Still, it was a distraction from what she *really* needed to talk about, wasn't it?

"About what?" he asked, clearing his throat. "My choir?"

Tanya took a deep breath, her heart pounding in her chest. "Partly," she said. "And also about Uncle Rod."

"What about him?" Alan asked, his voice quieter now, more subdued.

Tanya continued. "There's no easy way of asking this." Pause. "Were you together?" Her cheeks burned as she said it. If she was wrong, she was stupid; but if she was right, she was a fool.

On the other end of the line, she swore she heard Alan smile. "Of course we were," he said. "For 12 glorious years, darling Rod. I still miss him every day, too." He cleared his throat. "First Rod, now Celia."

A tidal wave of emotions rushed through her when she heard the truth: relief, pride, embarrassment, sadness. Rod had been the love of Alan's life, but now he was gone — and Tanya had never even realised.

"And your choir is the Gay Men's Chorus?" she asked, feeling lightheaded with relief.

"It is — you should come and see us sometime."

"I will," Tanya said, shaking her head. "Why did you never tell me?" Pause. "And why did I never know? I feel like such an idiot. Here's you supporting my life, when I was no comfort to you when yours fell apart." She paused, running through all the times Alan and Rod had been there for her. "I'm so sorry he's gone — I loved Rod, too."

"And he loved you," Alan replied. "And why would

I tell you? If you'd ever asked, I would, I wasn't ashamed. But you were young, and your mum preferred to ignore it. If she acknowledged it, she wouldn't have been able to be my friend, and she needed me — she knew that."

"So Mum knew?" Tanya couldn't help her voice turning up at the end. How could her mum have known Alan was gay, yet still have been his friend? She couldn't quite wrap her head around that. Or perhaps it was okay for her friends, but not for her flesh and blood?

"I assume so, how could she not? Rod and I were together for 12 years. We watched you and Jonathan grow up, we never hid it. I mean, we didn't kiss each other in front of people, because nobody does that in Sturby. You keep yourself to yourself, and we knew things would be hard if we didn't." He paused. "It was a different time then, the expectations were different. Although, if he were alive today, I don't think we'd do much different now."

Tanya still couldn't quite get her head around this revelation. "One thing, though: how did I never know? And why didn't you give me a clip round the ear and let me know?" She laughed at her last comment. But really, how dumb and self-absorbed had she been?

"Jonathan asked me once, and I told him."

"Jonathan?" Now she was really shamed. Her brother knew and she didn't?

Alan nodded. "He asked me a few years ago when he came back to visit your parents. He didn't stay long, like always." Alan paused. "But the thing was, Rod died when you were 15. You didn't ask, and I didn't tell. We all lost him, we all mourned."

"But he was your partner," Tanya replied.

"And these things happen."

Did such stoicism come with age, or was that just Alan's way? Tanya would love to know.

"Did he die of cancer, like you said?" Tanya held her breath, waiting for the answer.

There was a beat before Alan answered. "No, it was AIDS."

She shuddered at the words she hadn't wanted to hear, before fear wrapped her in its tight embrace. "And you — are you okay?" She couldn't take Alan dying, too.

Alan laughed at that. "Don't worry, I'm not going to drop dead any minute," he said, blowing his nose. Was he crying? If Tanya had made him cry, she felt doubly bad.

"I'm fine, I'm not even positive. Apparently some people are immune to the virus, and I'm one of the lucky ones. Unfortunately, Rod wasn't, and he was born just too early to benefit from the drugs that could have kept him alive." Alan let out a long breath. "It's just one of those things. I watched many of my friends die."

Tanya wished she was having this conversation with him in person so she could reach out and hug him. Sadness washed over her for the loss of Rod and all of Alan's friends. "I'm so sorry," she said.

Alan blew his nose again before continuing. "We had

12 great years together, that's the main thing. He was the love of my life, and some people never find that. It's what I focus on when I feel sad."

"And Mum's never asked you about him?"

"Your mother is a strange creature, as I'm sure you know. She clings on to her beliefs, but she's not religious, she's just proud. She can't get over herself, and your dad does nothing to balance her out, so she gets away with it." He sighed. "But I've seen a softer side to her when we chat."

"But you think she knows about you?"

"Being gay? Absolutely. But the thing is, I never told her, and neither did anyone else. And if she doesn't know, she's happy to live in her ignorance." He paused. "With you, you told her. It's a different time, and people are more out now — and your mum doesn't know how to deal with that, so she buries her emotions and shuts down. I'm not saying it's right, it's just what she does."

"So because I was honest, she can't cope?"

She heard him snort softly. "That's about the size of it. I'm not saying it makes sense, but it does in your mum's head." He paused. "Your gran used to worry terribly about her — she wanted her to be happy. She wasn't worried about you because you'd found your path." Pause. "Sorry if that's not what you wanted to hear."

Tanya rubbed her cheek: it wasn't as if she hadn't known already. "It's not as if it's a surprise," she said softly. "And by the way, I'm thrilled you're gay," she said, changing the subject swiftly. And she was, more than she could have possibly anticipated.

"The feeling's mutual," he said. "When you came out, I almost cried with joy. But then your mum did what she did and I hardly ever saw you. You've no idea how sad that made me."

"I'm so sorry, but I promise to make it up to you," she said. "I want to come and see Gran's grave soon, and I want to bring Delilah, too."

"She'd love that," he said. "And you're welcome to stay over, too. Assuming you won't be staying with your parents."

Tanya spluttered at that. "I don't think that's going to happen. Mum was quite nasty to me on Wednesday, said some things I haven't been able to get off my mind."

"Sorry to hear that."

"She told me I was just like her, that I didn't suffer fools gladly and didn't let people in." Tanya paused, letting the familiar sinking feeling settle in her stomach. "The trouble is, I know there's a bit of truth in that. I can be prickly and I don't let people in." She paused. "You've known me since I was born. What do you think? Do you think I'm like her? Do you think I'm unlovable?"

"Of course I don't," he said, after what seemed like an eternity. "Your mum's got issues and they're her own. She sees you've made a different life for yourself and she lashes out at that. You've done something she might have liked to do: you've got out in the world, made something of yourself. But she won't admit that, so instead she just criticises you." Alan paused before continuing.

"But here's the trick — don't take it to heart. I'm not saying you're perfect, nobody is, but you've blossomed into a beautiful young woman with a big heart, and Sophie would be lucky to have you, don't you forget it."

Tanya's breathing stalled. Was Sophie even still interested in her? She hoped so. But if Alan knew everything, he wouldn't be saying she was lucky. Tanya was damn sure Sophie wasn't saying that right now.

"And I know you'll probably still question it, still think your mum's right, but she's not. Of course you've got some of her traits — it's inevitable, she's your mother. My mum was always critical of stuff, and I've worked hard to ensure I'm not that way — but naturally, I am."

"I'd never say that about you," Tanya said — it was the last thing she expected to come out of Alan's mouth. He was always Mr Positive, despite everything.

"That's because I'm aware of it, and I work hard to make sure it doesn't come true." He paused. "If you're worried you don't let people in like your mum, that you're too judgemental, do something about it. Make a change, turn it around. But one thing I will say is you're not her — you're very much you, and that's the key thing. And Tanya Grant is someone I know and love. And I'm sure Sophie will, too."

Warmth flooded Tanya for the first time that week. "You've no idea how much I needed to hear that," Tanya said. She cleared her throat, swallowing down the emotion that was bubbling to the surface. "And how did you know about me and Sophie?"

Alan chuckled. "I've got eyes."

"But nothing had happened when we stayed," Tanya replied.

"But it has now?"

Tanya nodded. "Yes, it has now. But I'm not sure if I might have messed it up already."

"Tanya, I saw the way you both interacted, the way you looked at each other. And believe me when I say, it'd take a nuclear bomb to get Sophie unstuck from you." He paused. "You reminded me of how I used to look at Rod, for all those years." He sighed, before rallying. "What would your gran say?"

Tanya pictured her wily gran in her mind, remembering the tears she'd shed on the balcony for her that very morning. Deep down, she knew her dream was telling her lies: her gran hadn't agreed with Mum when she was alive, so why would she start in death?

"Gran would tell me to stop being such a clot and go after what I wanted." Saying it out loud, it sounded easy.

"Well, then," Alan said. "Whatever's happened with Sophie, go over there and fix it. Do something big, something that'll let her know what she means to you. Don't let pride stand in your way." He paused. "Do it, and prove how unlike your mum you really are."

Chapter Forty-Three

"Hello?"

Tanya's stomach dropped: her palms were sweaty and nothing had even been said yet.

"Hey Sophie, it's Tanya."

"I know, I have your number in my phone."

"Right," Tanya replied. Of course she did.

The hairs on the back of her neck stood up. Jeez, she was nervous. Because this meant more today than any other day before. They'd kissed, they'd had sex, but this was a request for the next step. She was about to ask Sophie out.

"Look, I... I'm sorry for Monday — and for what I said when I ran into you. I was stupid, and even more stupid to make you doubt me." She paused, wondering what face Sophie was making on the other end of the line. Was she rolling her eyes? She hoped not.

"You're the person who's got me through the most this past few weeks, and I've been too involved with myself to realise that. But I do now, I really do. So again, I'm sorry." She paused. "Can you forgive me enough to come over for dinner on Friday, so I can explain?"

There was silence on the other end of the line and Tanya swallowed down a hard lump of fear. If Sophie said no, so be it.

She'd crumble, she'd cry, and it might take her a lifetime to get over it.

But so be it.

The ball was in her court.

"Okay, dinner on Friday and I'll hear you out," Sophie said.

She was cool, calm — the opposite of Tanya.

"Great," Tanya replied. She would have liked a little more enthusiasm, but she guessed she was getting what she deserved.

"Text me what time you want me — and do you need me for Delilah this week? I saw her out with that other dog walker this week, you know. That's called cheating."

Tanya grimaced: she'd told the dog walker not to go near the river, but she guessed the options were limited around here. "I was desperate and I knew I'd pissed you off. But if you're offering, yes please. Can you do mornings and afternoons, tomorrow and Friday?"

"Sure," she said.

"Great," Tanya replied. "And Sophie?"

"Yeah?"

"I can't wait for Friday."

Chapter Forty-Four

As Sophie walked into Tanya's flat to collect Delilah on Friday morning, memories of the night they'd shared flooded her vision. Her body swirled with endorphins, and she wriggled as her clit stood to attention. Her body knew what it wanted, even if her mind was still in limbo.

Were they going to work things out later? Or were Tanya's hang-ups going to put paid to anything else? She knew what she hoped, but she had no idea of what the outcome might be.

Unaffected by Sophie's turmoil, Delilah was sitting, an aloof look on her face, with a chewed blue shoe at her feet. While she seemed to have taken the move well, the dog was having a few issues being left home alone during the day.

However, with Sophie looking in on her more often than she was charging for, she was acclimatising, and this was the first chewing incident Sophie had encountered. She walked across the lounge as Delilah jumped up at her, and she got down to her level.

"What you doing? Are you hungry? Eating Tanya's

shoes as an afternoon snack?" She glanced at the chewed heels and smiled: she didn't have heels in her wardrobe, but Tanya did. If you put them together on paper, they should never work. Sophie knew they could, but whether they'd get the chance was another thing.

"Shall we take you out, before you eat any more of Tanya's shoes? Take you to the café where Jess might have a treat for you?" Sophie didn't wait for an answer — she just clipped Delilah's lead to her collar and closed the door behind her.

Outside, the weather gods were playing blackjack again: sunshine or rain? Stick or twist? Sophie hoped for the sun that was clawing its way out from behind a cloud.

She quickened her step, heading towards the river: Jess wasn't there and the café was closed, but luckily, she had treats in her pocket. The café was opening tomorrow, and Sophie had been on-board for a few days already, helping out with last-minute preparations.

As they got to the waterfront, she clocked two dogs walking towards her: the grouchy Barney who liked to snarl, and a boxer she hadn't seen before. Sophie knew she had to take care with Delilah: she was a sociable dog, but she was still getting used to her new surroundings.

She tugged Delilah's lead towards the river, to steer her away from the two dogs, but then realised that Barney was walking his owner, Susan, rather than vice versa. It wasn't the first time she'd seen it happen, either, and now Barney was barrelling towards them at quite a clip. Sophie's heart began to race as the excitable dog drew near, Susan red in the face behind him, alarm painted across her features.

Barney began to bark menacingly, circling Delilah and Sophie, his lead wrapping around them, Susan helpless to stop it.

"Barney!" cried Sophie. "Stop, Barney!" Sophie tried to grab hold of Delilah, but she was too tangled and now wasn't quite sure which lead was Delilah and which was Barney. "Susan, can you do something? Get a grip of Barney?"

At her feet, Delilah was snarling, bewildered just like everyone else. She was jumping up at Sophie, then at Barney, while Susan eventually managed to calm Barney down, and began unwinding his lead from Sophie.

"So sorry, but he's just being playful. You know what he's like," she said, ruffling Barney's soft grey and white fur. "He just forgets how big he is sometimes, don't you, boy?"

"You need to walk him more. He's got too much energy."

"I have tried, but there aren't many dog walkers who'll take him," she said, out of breath as she finally got all of her lead back, with Barney still straining on it. "I don't suppose you'd be interested?"

Sophie glanced down at Barney, now bearing his teeth. She shook her head. "Not right now, I'm fully booked," she lied.

Delilah began barking again, squaring up to Barney — it was time to go before this got ugly. Sophie pulled Delilah's lead. "See you soon, Susan."

But just as the words were out of her mouth, Delilah leapt up at Barney, putting a paw in his face, and Barney reacted by lunging forward and sinking his teeth into Delilah.

Delilah let out a piercing howl, trying to wriggle away from Barney; she managed it, but he went back and got her ear the second time. It was all over in a second, yet it seemed to last forever, leaving Delilah wailing on the pavement.

Then Susan was shouting, as was Sophie, and the boxer ran over to see what all the fuss was.

Delilah was still barking like crazy, and when she shook her head, blood sprayed like machine-gun fire across the pavement, all over Sophie, hitting Barney and Susan, too.

"Fucking hell!" Sophie said, bending down and picking up Delilah, who was quivering. Blood was pooling on her fur, and Sophie could see where Barney's teeth had connected. "Get your crazy dog away from us!" she shouted at Susan.

Susan said something, but Sophie didn't hear it. Instead, she began to run with Delilah in her arms, getting as far away from the scene as possible. The world jogged up and down violently as she did, and when she passed the café, Jess was there, just opening the door. Sophie veered right and came to a screeching halt in front of her.

When Jess saw the state of her, her face fell. "What the fuck?" she began, giving Sophie a once over. "What's happened? Why do you look like you've just been shot? You haven't been shot, have you?"

Delilah's blood was seeping into her top at an alarming rate.

Sophie shook her head. "No, it's Delilah's blood, she was attacked by another dog. Have you got your van with you?"

Jess nodded.

"Can you take us to the vet? I don't think it's as bad as it looks, but I want to be safe rather than sorry." Sophie paused, picturing Tanya's beautiful face in her mind. Delilah was whimpering in her arms, and she juggled her, kissing the top of her head.

"Of course I can," Jess said, locking the café door again and already walking towards the car park under the building, with Sophie following. "Does Tanya know?"

Sophie shook her head. "It only just happened. I'll let her know when we get to the vet. I just want to make sure Delilah's okay, because Tanya's had enough death and bad news in her life recently, hasn't she?"

Chapter Forty-Five

"I'm sure she'll be fine," Alice said, as the black cab crawled through the Friday afternoon traffic. "She said just a few stitches, so try not to worry."

But Tanya wasn't listening. If anything had happened to Delilah, she'd never forgive herself. And if anything had happened to Sophie — well, it didn't bear thinking about. Sophie and Delilah were rapidly becoming Tanya's world, which was why her heart was beating so fast in her chest. Please let them both be okay.

She'd been having a coffee with Alice near her office when she'd got the call. Alice had spent the afternoon shopping, but when she saw the terror on Tanya's face, she'd insisted on jumping into the cab with her, and now her four shopping bags were sitting on the floor of the cab in front of them.

When they pulled up outside the vet's surgery 25 minutes later, Tanya stuffed two £20 notes through the tiny window that linked them to the driver, not even waiting for the change.

She ran up the path to the surgery, reaching out her

hand to pull open the door. What was she going to find on the other side? She braced herself mentally and physically. If the worst had happened, she was going to have to tell the whole world she'd failed in the one task her gran had left to her.

If the worst did happen, she didn't know how she was going to cope.

She tugged on the door handle, but it wouldn't move. What the hell? She tried again, but the door wasn't budging. Tanya bent over, hands on thighs, tears threatening. "For fuck's sake!" she said, unravelling on the spot.

"Hey," Alice said from behind her, dropping her shopping bags and pushing the door open.

Push not pull: it got Tanya every time. "Thank you," she said, shooting Alice a grateful look, before running in and scanning the waiting room.

Her eyes landed on Sophie, her top covered in blood, and the blood drained from Tanya's face. Why was Sophie's top covered in blood? What the hell had happened today?

"Oh my god, are you okay?" Tanya said, rushing over to Sophie, who stood up. Tanya took her in her arms and held her tight. "Is Delilah okay?" she asked, holding Sophie at arm's length. "Why do you look like you've been shot?"

Sophie shook her head, a tiny smile on her lips, her blue eyes streaked with red. "I haven't been shot, it's Delilah's blood," Sophie said, looking behind her. "And hi again, Alice."

Alice gave Sophie a smile. "Hi," she said. "I was in the area."

But Tanya wasn't listening — why was there so much of Delilah's blood all over Sophie? Her heart sped up to 100mph as she imagined the state of her dog. Her gran's dog, one she couldn't even keep her safe for a few weeks. Shit, what was her mum going to say? What about Alan? Fucking hell, please let Delilah be okay.

But Sophie shook her head, imploring Tanya with her eyes. "Delilah's okay, don't worry — I think Barney nicked a vein in her ear when he bit her, and the blood just didn't seem to stop. Jess said the same when she saw me, but I haven't been shot, honest."

"So Delilah's not critical? She's going to pull through?" Tanya held her breath, putting a hold on all the emails and letters she'd been writing in her head.

Sophie nodded. "She's fine — just a couple of stitches in her ear. I couldn't get hold of you at first, so she's been in there a while. The vet gave her a little anaethestic, but she's come round now and should be out any minute."

"Oh thank goodness," Tanya said, before taking Sophie in fully. "And you're okay? No injuries?" She took Sophie's hands and held them both out to the sides to get a good look at her.

Sophie shook her head again. "No, Barney only had eyes for Delilah."

"He's a bloody menace, that dog."

"It's not his fault," Sophie replied. "I don't think Susan's got a handle on him, yet."

"That's for sure," Tanya replied, blowing out a long breath. When she held out her hand, it was shaking. "I'm just so relieved you're both okay. I've been conjuring up all sorts of ideas in my head, and none of them have been pretty. If the outcome is you and Delilah are both fairly unharmed, then none of what I've been thinking has come true. Which, after all the drama of the past few weeks would be a result."

Seeing Tanya's shaking hand, Sophie took it in her own and kissed it. Tanya's knees buckled, her defences falling just as quick, too. She almost collapsed into the nearest seat, and Sophie sat next to her, holding her gaze, a smile on her face.

"To tell you the truth, Delilah was standing up for herself. She smacked Barney in the face after he'd terrorised us." Sophie began to giggle as she retold the story, wiping her eyes as she did. "For a little dog, she's kinda feisty — she made me proud."

Sophie's giggle was infectious, and Tanya soon joined in, all the emotion bubbling out in a flurry of laughs. The whole waiting room was suddenly lighter, like a blast of pure oxygen had been pumped in.

Alice leaned over, patting Tanya's leg. "You see, I told you Delilah could look after herself — she's your gran's dog, after all."

Tanya hiccupped at that. "She is," she said. "So it was

more Delilah making trouble than Barney?" Tanya asked Sophie, hiccupping again. She took another deep breath, but that only made it worse.

She pulled away from Sophie, reaching in her bag to find a tissue, but Sophie was one step ahead of her, pressing a clean tissue into her hand. Tanya took it gratefully, a blur of emotions swallowing her as she laughed, cried and hiccupped anew.

"I'm sorry," she said, shaking her head. "It's just, I was fearing the worst. I couldn't face going home and telling my parents and Alan that Delilah had died. It'd be too much. And how could I tell Gran, too?"

Fresh tears spilt down her cheeks, and Sophie took her in her arms. "You've been through quite a lot in the past month, haven't you?" Sophie whispered, kissing Tanya on the cheek.

A familiar barking broke the moment, and when Tanya looked up, Delilah was trotting over to her, tail wagging. She had a plastic cone jutting out from her collar, but otherwise, she looked just as she had when Tanya left her this morning.

Tanya got down on her knees and hugged her, looking upwards when a pair of black leather shoes came into view. The vet was a woman around their age, and she had a broad smile on her face.

"Delilah should be fine, just a couple of stitches to seal up the wounds — but it wasn't a bad injury, just a lot of blood, as Sophie knows." She smiled at Sophie as Tanya stood up. "We'll leave the collar on till the stitches heal."

"So anything I need to know about looking after her?" Tanya asked.

The vet shook her head. "I'd say, just carry on as normal, but avoid that dog if you can, just in case she has a bad reaction over the next few weeks. Just keep up your normal routine so Delilah doesn't have time to dwell on this. She should be fine, but she might be a little nervous around larger dogs, maybe a little more defensive. But other than that, there should be no lasting damage. Just keep her quiet today and make sure she drinks water."

"Thanks so much," Tanya said, relief sweeping through her. "We'll take good care of her from here on in," she added, realising too late she'd used the plural pronoun. But when she glanced over at Sophie, she was nodding right back, her eyes still swollen.

"We will," Sophie said. "She's going to be the most fussed-over dog in south east London."

Tanya picked Delilah up and hugged her: she hoped Delilah knew how loved she was. She grinned over at Sophie, and then glanced at Alice.

"You coming back with us or are you taking your spoils home?" Tanya asked.

Alice pursed her lips. "I'll come back with you and go home from there. Jake's out tonight, so no rush."

"Let's go home, then," Tanya said, taking Sophie's hand in hers.

Chapter Forty-Six

Awhile later, Sophie knocked on Tanya's door, freshly showered and changed, now totally blood-free. She was wearing her ripped jeans and a sky blue top that really brought out her eyes, and in turn brought Tanya up short.

"You look beautiful," she said, pressing her lips to Sophie's and feeling it everywhere. She inhaled her scent, which was quickly becoming one of her favourites; Tanya wanted to press her face to Sophie's neck, but she held back for now.

"So do you," Sophie said, as they pulled slowly apart.

Sophie kicked off her shoes and Tanya led her out to where Delilah was sitting in her now usual position at the edge of the glass balcony, watching the world from up high. Tanya had been amazed at the length of time Delilah could sit there, but she was tickled she'd found her favourite place in her flat already.

"Hello you," Sophie said, getting down to pet her. "How's the cone of shame?"

"She doesn't seem too upset yet," Tanya replied.

"Give her time," Sophie smiled.

On the balcony table was a bottle of Bollinger in a bucket of ice, two glasses by its side.

Sophie gave Tanya an appreciative look. "Wow, you're pushing the boat out today," she said. "Let's not tell our friends, shall we?"

"Is Alice still downstairs?"

Sophie nodded. "She is, and Rachel is showing her all her favourite cookbooks. They could be there for days."

Tanya grinned. "I knew they'd get on — Alice is mad about food, always trying new recipes." She paused. "So Alice is not even coming up to say hi?"

Sophie shook her head. "There were lots of shared looks when I suggested that," she said. "I think they both know we might need a little time to ourselves. They were talking about going down the pub in half an hour when I left." Sophie raised one eyebrow. "I say, if they knock, we ignore it."

Tanya laughed. "I couldn't agree more," she said. "I bought the champagne to celebrate my house move, but this seems like as good an excuse as any to open it, doesn't it?"

Sophie nodded. "Absolutely."

They sat down, the sky above a perfect pastel painting of pinks and blues, with wispy white clouds. The sun wasn't due to set for another hour at 8pm, but it was getting lower in the sky and turning a golden, burnt yellow already.

"Also, I wanted to say thanks for helping out with Delilah this week, and apologise for, well, me." Tanya popped the cork and poured the champagne, offering a glass to Sophie, who took it. "I'd like to explain, if you'll let me."

"I'm listening," Sophie said, taking a sip of her drink, her eyes never leaving Tanya. "What happened in Sturby? And why did things change after we slept together? I'm hoping it was nothing to do with me."

Tanya shook her head, reaching out for Sophie's hand and kissing it. "You've been dragged into it, but this is all me, nothing to do with you." Then she smiled. "I mean, you're involved... am I making sense yet?"

Sophie laughed. "I'm hoping you will any minute."

Tanya gave a big sigh. "I'll cut to the chase. When I was home my mum had a go at me — it's a skillset of hers she's honed over the years." Tanya took another swig of booze to boost her courage. It worked.

"She told me I was just like her, that I didn't let people in and that I was judgemental. And she questioned why I'd never been able to hold down a steady relationship. And that cut me to the core, you know?"

Sophie nodded her head. "I can imagine it would."

Tanya's nerves bristled as she continued. This was the moment where Tanya could be brave, lay it all out.

"And the thing is, there's an element of truth in what she said. I've only had one long-term relationship, and I've been single for nearly two years. And yes, I can get casual sex, but it's not what I want anymore." She glanced up at Sophie, her heart hammering in her chest.

"I want something more, something real. And then you arrived in my life, and you're about as real as it gets." She paused. "What we had for one night was electric and intense. And what we shared in Sturby was incredible, too. I knew that when we came home, and I knew that after we kissed. But then my mum's words kept playing in my head, my dreams kept coming and I started to worry whether my mum was right, whether I was just like her, difficult to love, destined to go through life alone."

Sophie frowned at that. "But your mum's not alone."

Tanya gave her a rueful laugh. "She might as well be. She exists in her own world and my dad jumps to her tune." Tanya fixed Sophie with her gaze, shaking her head. "That's not what I want and it's not what I want to put on anyone else. I want an honest-to-goodness *real* relationship, filled with ups and downs, shared triumphs and mistakes, but most of all, a relationship overflowing with messy, stupid love.

"And that's what I hope we might have the start of, unless I've fucked it up by freaking out that I was my mother. I'm not, by the way." Tanya breathed out, the last sentence coming out in a jumble. "Did any of that make sense?"

Sophie nodded her head slowly. "It does, and messy, stupid love is something I can get wholly behind."

Tanya hardly heard the words over her heartbeat, but she nodded all the same.

"But it makes me mad you just didn't tell me what you were thinking," Sophie added. "You just mumbled something about a dream, and I've been walking around all week thinking what happened in Sturby, in the lift and on Sunday *was* just a dream. You went radio silent, and you have to know what that did to me."

Tanya closed her eyes hearing that, her soaring hope suddenly juddering in mid-flight. But when she reopened them, Sophie's gaze was gentle, loving.

"Of course I do. I've been a total arse, and I haven't let you in — just like my mum predicted," Tanya said.

Thunder filled her ears as she thought about what she'd done and whether or not it was rectifiable. Had she mucked this up for good? Could Sophie forgive her? She sat forward, taking Sophie's hand in hers and staring deep into her eyes.

"Can you give me another chance? If you do, I promise not to freak out again." Tanya paused. "Or at least if I do, I promise to share it with you and talk about it. Is that enough?"

Sophie stared at her for a few seconds before she answered. "Before I tell you that, you have to hear my side."

Tanya nodded, her insides churning with doubt. Was Sophie about to drop a hammer blow on her hopes? "Go ahead," she replied.

* * *

"You've got your inner demons, and I've got mine. Mine stem from my mum, too, but for very different reasons —

she walked out and it made me doubt relationships and their validity. How can you trust people so much and then they desert you? I saw the devastation she left and vowed to protect myself from that ever happening to me."

But what she hadn't realised at the time was that in protecting herself, she was also shutting herself down from really living. Over the years, protection was wearing very thin as a core life value.

"And I've been pretty successful at it," Sophie added. "I've had relationships, but I keep people at arm's length — and I've never been in love." She paused, letting that revelation sink in. When she said it out loud, it sounded stark, angular. It sounded like she was the unlovable one, not Tanya.

Tanya duly widened her eyes in surprise. "But you're so warm and genuine. You seem far more sorted than me." She paused. "You've really never been in love?"

Sophie shook her head, avoiding Tanya's gaze. "Nope," she said. "But a few years ago I decided this was no way to live, so I've been trying to undo the damage, to open myself up. I wanted to give a relationship a try, but I was scared — scared of getting hurt."

"And I was scared of hurting you — we're a right pair, aren't we?"

Sophie laughed at that. "Turns out we are," she replied. "The last woman I had a thing with before you, she had a girlfriend and I never knew. So I was going to take some time off women after that.

"But then you appeared and blew my plans out of the water. No matter that you were rude, there was something about you. And we kept bumping into each other, and it seemed like destiny — at least that's what Rachel reckoned."

"I always liked Rachel, did I mention?" Tanya said, smiling.

"She's on your side," Sophie replied. "And what we shared in Sturby — I felt a shift. And then we kissed and you didn't call. And then we had sex and you freaked out." Sophie paused. "You can see how I thought this was a repeating pattern, can't you? That people running out on relationships is normal."

"I never knew," Tanya replied.

"Why would you?" Sophie said. "My point is, I do want to give this a go. I think there's something here — a whole lot of something here." Sophie stared at Tanya then, wanting so much to close the gap between them, but not quite knowing how to do it.

"I feel it here," Sophie said, pointing at her head. "I feel it here," she added, pointing to her chest. "And I feel it here," she finished, putting a hand between her legs, feeling a jolt of desire underneath it as she did so. The heat she had for Tanya was so intense, she was sure she was burning up. "If I'm honest, I feel it everywhere."

Tanya's chest was heaving up and down at that revelation, and she went to say something, but stopped.

"What were you going to say?" Sophie asked.

"I'm still trying to catch my breath and drag my eyes away from your hand," Tanya said, staring down at Sophie's fingers, still splayed between her legs.

Sophie smiled, but didn't move her hand.

"But I need to know you won't run away again."

"Cross my heart," Tanya replied, dragging her index finger across her chest once, twice.

"I'm holding you to that, Tanya Grant," Sophie said, a smile working its way from her mouth to her eyes.

Tanya reflected it right back. "How can I argue with a girl called London?" She paused, draining her champagne and then getting up, pulling Sophie up with her.

When Tanya pressed her lips to Sophie's, all bets were off.

Sophie was lost in Tanya, and there was no coming back.

"Are we done talking now?" Tanya stared deep into Sophie's eyes.

Sophie nodded, guided by her body, every square inch of which was screaming to be touched. "I think we're done," she replied, her voice sketchy. "I'm ready for some of that messy, stupid love you were talking about."

Chapter Forty-Seven

Sophie guided Tanya towards her oval dining table, running her hand over the smooth wood, her blood surging as she backed up to its edge. She'd been having lewd thoughts about this table and what they could do on it ever since she'd seen it — and hadn't they wasted enough time talking already?

As she slipped her hand into Tanya's, Sophie hoped this was the start of their real chapter, no more false starts. She took off her glasses, then her top, before spreading her legs, grabbing Tanya's belt loops and pulling her between them.

Tanya said nothing, her face flushed, her breathing sketchy.

"So, how messy are we talking?" Sophie asked, her voice gravelly.

Tanya backed her right up onto her wooden table, pressing her body to hers. "Super-messy," she said, cupping Sophie's right breast and squeezing gently. "You writhing beneath me, and me fucking-you-like-there's-no-tomorrow messy."

Sophie's insides collapsed, wetness pooling in her.

"You can talk the talk," she said, smiling, pulling Tanya's mouth to her. She bit her lip, before trailing her tongue along it, then sliding it into Tanya's mouth. She let it swirl in Tanya's mouth just long enough before pulling back, staring into her eyes, knowing the power they had.

"But can you walk the walk?" With that, Sophie pushed Tanya back with one hand, reaching around and unclipping her bra in one practised move. She threw it aside, holding Tanya in place with her actions.

Then Sophie leaned back on the table, both arms behind her, and shook her hair like a Hollywood starlet.

Tanya gaped, then stripped off her top, too.

* * *

Tanya pressed herself to Sophie, wanting to feel her skin next to hers, to finally touch her.

Their kisses were frantic now, a blur of teeth and tongues.

Sophie groaned into Tanya's mouth, raking her short nails down Tanya's back.

Tanya shuddered. Everything about this felt messy and delicious.

Just like Sophie.

Just like them.

Tanya knew she had so much to make up for, but the making up started right here, right now.

She placed hot, wet kisses all down Sophie's neck,

onto her breasts, her nipples. Then her hands worked nimbly to undo Sophie's jeans, pulling at her belt, before standing her up and getting her naked.

Tanya took a moment to appreciate that, before pushing her down on the table gently, Sophie's pupils blown wide open, her chest rising and falling with speed.

Tanya knew why. She understood completely because she was feeling it, too. *Right there*, just like Sophie had said. In her head, in her heart and deep inside her. And then, the need to be deep inside Sophie was overwhelming.

Tanya's fingers skated across Sophie's silky thighs, warm and inviting.

Sophie shuddered.

Tanya leaned over and pressed a kiss to Sophie's lips, at the same time running a finger through her slick juices.

Sophie bucked her hips and crushed her lips to Tanya, groaning into her mouth, breathing heavily. She thrust against Tanya's fingers, and Tanya slipped first one, then two into her, and Sophie stilled as she did, before sitting up, her face contorted, fixing Tanya with her gorgeous green stare.

"Please fuck me," she said as she rocked her hips, mouth open, blonde hair ruffled, just like when Tanya first met her. But they'd come such a long way since then, since that fateful meeting. And now, their future was in Tanya's hands. Or rather, Tanya's hand was in her future.

Sophie slung an arm around Tanya's neck, wrapping her legs around her hips as she threw back her head once more.

Tanya didn't need another invitation, curling another finger into Sophie, her heart rising and falling with every thrust of her hand, with every kiss to her lips.

And as she made love to her, everything else fell away; everything but Sophie. How she felt, how she tasted and how much she meant to Tanya. She loved this woman with everything she was, and that thought made Tanya open her eyes. When she did, Sophie was picture perfect, eyes closed, features blissed out, sinking into the moment.

Tanya could feel Sophie pulsing against her, she knew she was close. Tanya was close, too, and Sophie hadn't even touched her. She didn't like to think what would happen when she did.

When Tanya hit Sophie's sweet spot again and again, she stilled, every muscle tensed, and then she came in a rush of sounds, her fingers raking her shoulders, Sophie clinging on as she rode out wave after wave of orgasm.

Bliss slid down Tanya as she watched Sophie come: she didn't think she'd ever felt so in tune with a lover, so right. She knew then she never planned to let Sophie go: this was for real, finally.

As Sophie got back on an even keel, she wrapped both arms around her, slumping on her shoulder. Her breath was hot in Tanya's ear, Sophie's smile denting her skin.

"You think the neighbours saw any of that?" Sophie asked, pulling her head up, her blue eyes flecked with lust.

"I guess we'll find out at the next block meeting," Tanya replied, pulling back and kissing her lips.

"Shall we give them a little more to talk about?" Sophie asked, reaching down and undoing Tanya's belt. She watched as Tanya stepped out of her jeans, and when she put her hand between Tanya's legs, Tanya's eyes grew darker.

"Yes please," Tanya replied, pushing Sophie back on the table, before climbing up onto her knees and moving on top of her.

As Tanya parted her legs, Sophie slipped her fingers into her wetness, groaning as she did. "Fuck, you're so wet," she said.

All rational thought flew from Tanya as she ground down onto Sophie's hand, throwing her head back at the same time. "It's what you do to me," she replied, on her knees, ignoring the pain, as Sophie fucked her.

It didn't take long for her to come: she was too hyped from what had gone before. And when she did, she cried out, wondering if it was possible to feel any better than this, any more in love with the woman beneath her? She didn't think so.

When she was done, Tanya fell onto Sophie, their naked bodies melded as one. She kissed Sophie's neck, then cracked open an eyelid as their faces met.

"You want to go somewhere a bit more comfortable and private to carry this on?" Sophie asked, her fingers still inside Tanya.

"Does it mean you taking your fingers away?" Tanya asked, her insides still pulsing, a buzzing in her brain.

"Just for a few seconds," Sophie laughed.

"No more than 30 and you've got a deal."

Chapter Forty-Eight

Sophie woke up the next morning tired, but oh-so satisfied. She and Tanya had been up half the night showing the other what they'd been missing all week, and she was hoping for more of the same today. She yawned and rolled over… and Tanya wasn't there.

Oh no, please — had she freaked out again? If she had, Sophie wasn't sure she could take it.

Fear pooled in her stomach, and she put both hands to her head, frustration rising in her. She was in love with this woman, yet she was so stubborn. How was she going to change it?

Hang on, she was in love with her?

The bedroom door edged open, stopping Sophie's thoughts in their tracks. In walked Tanya, carrying a tray laden with coffee and croissants. Her long limbs were encased in tiny white shorts and a red T-shirt, her chestnut hair still stuck to the side of her face.

She looked gorgeous as always, and Sophie had never been more pleased to see her, relief flooding her body.

"Morning!" Tanya said, all white teeth and chirp,

putting the tray in the middle of the bed and sitting down. "You're awake — you were dead to the world when I got up ten minutes ago."

Sophie shook her head, all manner of emotions still ping-ponging inside it. "And you weren't here when I woke up. I was just sitting here wondering what to do to talk you round. Thank god you walked in when you did. You didn't freak out, did you?"

Tanya laughed, leaning over to kiss her.

When their lips connected, Sophie calmed down a little, revelling in how right it felt.

After a few seconds, Tanya pulled back, her smile broad. "You have some freckles on your nose. I only just noticed."

"You didn't answer the question," Sophie growled.

Tanya kissed her again. "When I woke up this morning, the only thing I thought was how beautiful you are and how lucky I am. That's it, nothing else."

"You sure?"

Tanya nodded, reaching out to push a bit of Sophie's hair behind her ear. "I'm sure. And you are beautiful."

Sophie blushed, happiness filling her to the brim. "I am not, you're insane."

"If that makes me insane, then I plead guilty." Tanya cast her gaze down to the tray, and Sophie followed her gaze. "Also, I forgot to give you something last night." She pointed to a white envelope, on the tray beside the raspberry jam.

Sophie raised an eyebrow. "I wouldn't say that."

Tanya grinned. "This is something a little different that I hope you'll like. Something I got as a way to show you how I feel."

Sophie sat up in the bed, her back leaning against Tanya's old-fashioned iron headboard, her brow furrowed. "This sounds serious. You haven't named a star after me, have you?"

Tanya laughed. "I haven't. Should I have?"

"No, those schemes are a licence to print money." She paused. "Have you adopted a polar bear in my name?"

Tanya handed Sophie the envelope. "I've got a list of things I need to do now, haven't I?"

"What is it?" Sophie asked, turning the envelope over in her hands.

"Open it and find out."

Sophie flicked her gaze up to Tanya, then reached over to get her glasses. She was pleased to feel Tanya's hand on her bum as she did so, so she stopped to kiss her lips as she got comfortable again.

She held the envelope in her hands, then ripped the top, pulling out what looked like some tickets. And when she focused properly, she saw they were two tickets to tonight's performance of Mamma Mia.

Sophie's breathing stalled as all the old feelings came flooding back to her of that fateful day. Her dad's incomprehension; her brother's defiance; her confusion and misery. All of them trying to work out how and if they could get her mum back. But the plain answer was they couldn't. She knew now it wasn't her fault.

Now Tanya was telling her it was time to let go and move on. It was time to put the past to bed and grasp her future — a future that definitely involved this delicious woman crouched on the bed beside her, a worried look on her face.

Nobody had ever done anything like this for her before. Tanya had stepped into a breach Sophie didn't even realise was there, and she'd never felt more loved and cared for in her entire life.

"I can't believe you bought these," Sophie said. She put a hand to her face, swallowing down in an attempt to stop her emotions spilling out of her. She knew it wasn't going to work even before she felt the wetness sliding down her cheeks.

"Don't cry," Tanya said. "I didn't buy them to make you sad!" She put a hand on Sophie's arm as her warm, generous gaze swept over her. "I bought them to make you happy, so you can move on. It's all part of the stupid, messy love contract."

"There's a contract?" Sophie said, wiping her eyes and sniffing.

"That's my next envelope," Tanya said with a grin, grabbing a tissue and handing it to Sophie.

Sophie blew her nose and wiped her eyes before replying. "I'm not sad, I'm happy," she said. "I always wanted to see this show."

"I hope so, because we're going tonight. So if you were lying, let me know and I'll rush out and buy you a star."

Sophie shook her head, still staring at the tickets and gulping down her emotions. "This is one of the most special things anyone has ever done for me, and that's the honest truth," she said. "It's so thoughtful." She put a hand out and touched the side of Tanya's face, and Tanya leaned into her touch.

"You're worth it," she said.

"You're so corny sometimes." But right at that moment, Sophie loved corny. She could have drowned in a vat of it.

"You bring it out in me," Tanya replied, smiling.

Sophie looked Tanya in the eye, before leaning forward and kissing her. And when she did, she remembered what she'd just realised, because it was lighting up her very core. Something she had to share with Tanya right this moment.

She pulled back from the kiss, smiling as Tanya's eyes followed her lips, both of them breathless. "Remember what I said last night? That I'd never been in love?"

Tanya nodded, still seemingly transfixed by their kiss.

"It's not quite true. I'd never been in love until I met you." Sophie paused, steadying her nerve before she said the words. She was a tightrope walker going out onto the centre of the rope for the first time, arms out either side of her, no safety net.

"You're my first love, Tanya," she said, drawing

Tanya's hand to her lips. "I'm in love with you." And as soon as she said the words, Sophie knew that even if she did fall, Tanya was her safety net — she didn't need anything else.

Tanya's pupils grew darker, and a shy smiled crept onto her face. "You're in love with me?" she said, her words studded with disbelief.

Sophie nodded, her heart pulsing as it never had before. That's because she'd never had Tanya-flavoured love pumping through her veins — but she did now, and it tasted divine.

"That's good, because I'm in love with you, too," Tanya replied, kissing Sophie's hand.

Sophie released a breath she felt like she'd been holding for days. "Oh, thank god for that. I don't know what I'd have done if you hadn't said it back."

"You doubted I loved you?" Tanya said, kissing Sophie's lips.

Sophie gave a groan as Tanya's tongue skated along her bottom lip. When they came up for air, it took a moment for her to pick up her train of thought. "I don't doubt it now," Sophie replied.

And just at that moment, Delilah woke up in her basket at the end of the bed, her tiny feet padding onto the laminate floor. She barked, letting the pair know she wanted to get up on the bed.

Tanya grinned. "Great timing, Delilah," she said, reaching down and putting her on her lap. "We were just sharing a moment, but you had to get in on the act, didn't you?" She kissed the top of Delilah's head, before looking back at Sophie.

"I love your dog, too, by the way," Sophie added, leaning over and stroking Delilah's head.

"That's good, because we come as a package."

"It's a package I love," Sophie replied. Then she picked up the tickets again. "As for these — you really don't know what they mean." Sophie didn't know if Tanya appreciated the magnitude of her gesture, but Sophie did, 100 per cent.

"I do," Tanya replied. "They mean we're going to a show tonight."

Chapter Forty-Nine

Sophie kicked a stone on the pavement and squinted up into the azure blue sky. Today, London resembled the Mediterranean, but they weren't going to be around to see it. Rather, they were going to be in a car driving up to visit Tanya's gran's grave. After all the stories she'd heard, she was sad she'd only get to meet Tanya's favourite relative in death, not life.

She heard the clank of their flat block's main doors, and looked up to see Tanya chattering to Delilah as she walked her out, bag slung over her shoulder, her hair fluttering in the breeze.

Sophie's heart pulsed: she was still stopped daily by Tanya's beauty, inside and out.

When Tanya caught her gaze, she gave her a broad smile. "Don't judge me for talking to my dog," she said, giving Sophie a kiss as they drew level.

"You're talking to the woman who gets paid to talk to dogs, so no judgement here," Sophie replied. "It's your constant singing of Tom Jones to her I object to."

Tanya smiled, looking down at Delilah. "You love it, though, don't you, Delilah?"

Delilah ignored her completely.

"She's so rude — you should have your manners talk with my dog," Tanya said, a grin on her face.

Sophie raised an eyebrow at her. "I'll wait till her owner's fully trained first. Dogs take on the traits of their owners, surely you know that by now?" She poked Tanya in the ribs when she said it.

"Ha ha," Tanya replied. "The words to that song are brutal, though — I never realised," she added, opening the car door and putting Delilah inside. "Did you know Delilah is about a man killing his wife?"

Tanya made a show of opening the passenger door to Sophie, bowing as she did. "Your carriage, my lady."

"I did know that," Sophie said, rolling her eyes at Tanya. "You're so polite, anyone ever tell you that?" she said, giving her girlfriend a grin.

Tanya shrugged. "Manners are very important," she said, swooping in for a kiss as Sophie got in the car, before giving her a wink.

"My dad used to play Delilah when we were little. I tried to sing it at a talent show in primary school once, but it was deemed unsuitable."

"I'm not surprised," Tanya replied, slamming her car door and settling herself in her seat.

"Remember when we did this drive only a short while ago?" Sophie cast her mind back, glancing at Tanya.

"I do," Tanya said, checking her mirror, then indicating to pull out onto the busy main road. "And I remember thinking then I was mad to take you anywhere near my home town, because nothing good ever came from visiting there. But it turned out I was wrong. My gran's from there and she was brilliant; Alan's from there and who doesn't love Alan?"

"Impossible not to," Sophie replied, putting on her seat belt belatedly. She was fond of Alan, and his spare bed would always hold a special place in her heart. "You're from there too, and I happen to think you're pretty cool."

"You do?" Tanya said, smiling at Sophie.

"I do," she replied. "Especially because you let me have control of the music while you drive."

"So long as there's no R&B."

"Thank you, Coldplay lover," Sophie replied. She switched on the radio and Abba's Waterloo was playing — but Sophie had no reaction other than to tap her foot.

Tanya glanced over, shooting out a hand to Sophie's arm. "Are we changing the station or are you cured of your Abba aversion? Did the show the other night work?"

Sophie smiled as she recalled the musical — it'd been bittersweet to finally see it, but she was so glad she had, especially with Tanya by her side. Because after her mother, Tanya was quickly becoming one of the most important women in her life.

"It sorta worked," Sophie said. "I think I'll still always duck Mamma Mia, but we can leave this on. If for no other reason than I know how happy Abba makes you." She smiled as Tanya sang along. "By the way, did you check the roads before we set out?"

"I did and they look miraculously clear. So let's not jinx it by talking about it too much, okay?"

Sophie nodded. "Goddit," she said. "What shall we talk about instead?"

"Anything but my mother," Tanya replied.

Sophie threw her hands up in the air. "There go all my conversational gambits."

* * *

The drive hadn't been too traffic-laden and the sky was almost the same colour as it had been in London, if you ignored the clouds — which Tanya was trying to do.

They arrived at the cemetery 20 minutes ahead of schedule, but Alan was already there, standing looking at his phone. Now Tanya knew he was gay, everything about him screamed gay — his stance, his jacket, his hair — whereas previously, he'd just been Alan.

She smiled as she realised how silly her thoughts were: he was still just Alan, but she was thrilled he was gay. It made everything they'd shared in life that little bit more special, even though she still wished she'd caught on earlier.

As they approached him, Tanya's hand firmly clasped with Sophie's, Alan looked up and a bright white smile lit up his face.

"My favourite Londoners," he said, holding out his

arms as Tanya walked into them: Alan was like a soft armrest for the soul. He then moved onto Sophie, before stooping to make a fuss of now cone-free Delilah, who jumped into his arms.

"Ready to see where Celia's lying, shouting at all the dead people around her?" Alan asked, motioning across the cemetery to a plot Tanya had last left open, with mounds of cold, brown earth piled up around it. She gulped, then nodded, feeling Sophie reach for her hand again.

And then there it was, her gran's final resting place, under a patchy blue sky in the middle of Sturby cemetery next to her husband, the granddad Tanya never really knew.

Her gran had been widowed young, and never remarried, although Alan had eluded to the fact she wasn't short of offers. However, she'd never quite got over the death of her husband, and had remained single till the day she died.

Sophie handed Tanya the white roses they'd bought on the way, her gran's favourite flowers. "So delicate, so pure," she'd always said. Tanya smiled when she saw the grave was already filled with two bunches of white roses, laying hers beside them.

"I see you've been here first," she said to Alan, as she stepped back from the gravestone.

But Alan shook his head. "Not me," he said, leaving the rest of the sentence unsaid.

Tanya took a few moments to fill in the blanks. "Mum?" she asked, her tone saying she barely believed that possible.

Alan nodded his head. "I keep coming, but every time, there are new flowers. There's nobody else who'd do that but Ann."

Tanya wasn't sure what to think about that, so she pushed it away. Instead, she focused on her gran's gravestone inscription, which read: 'The song may have ended, but the melody lingers on.'

"I still love that," Tanya said, pointing. "It's so Gran."

"Isn't it?" Alan said, smiling. "Every time I come, I'm a little sad — but then I see what Celia left us, and it makes me smile." He shrugged. "Death is a part of life, and life goes on, doesn't it?"

Tanya nodded: she of all people knew this. She might have lost her gran, and her parents for now, but the wheels still turned and new people popped up to fill their place. People like Sophie, Rachel, Jess and Lucy.

Sophie squeezed her hand, breaking her thoughts. "Do you want a moment alone before we go?"

Tanya sucked on her top lip, then nodded. "Do you mind?"

Sophie shook her head. "I'll take Delilah, and Alan will keep me company. You take your time." She kissed Tanya's cheek, and Alan squeezed her shoulder as he followed Sophie.

Left alone, Tanya bent down to arrange her flowers a little better, then rocked back on her haunches, staring at the gravestone. It didn't seem real that her lively, lovely gran was buried under the earth she was standing on, but she was. However, far from feeling glum, Tanya felt peace surge through her, along with the inevitable tears now she was alone.

"I miss you, Gran, I always will," she said, letting her tears stain her cheeks — she didn't try to stop them. "I miss seeing you and hugging you, I miss your smell, your smile. But I know you wouldn't want me to be sad, so I'm trying not to be." She paused, fishing in her pocket for a tissue and blowing her nose. Damn, tears created a lot of snot.

"Oh, and by the way, I'm still mad at you for not telling me about Alan! Although, yes, I know, I'm a terrible gay for not figuring it out myself." She smiled through her tears.

"I hope you like Sophie, and I want you to know that Delilah is safe — she's becoming a London dog, very cosmopolitan. She'll be demanding organic dog food soon, and I know what you would have said about that."

Tanya stood up, blowing her nose again. Then she stepped forward, the scent of fresh earth filling her nostrils, before kissing the tips of her fingers and pressing them to the headstone.

She couldn't stand here all day blathering to a lump of concrete — although a quick glance around told her there were plenty of other people doing just that, too.

How often did her mum stand exactly where she was, doing exactly what she was doing? Tanya pushed that thought to the back of her mind. Perhaps there was a heart beating under her brittle veneer, after all.

She took a deep breath and gave the grave a tiny wave. "Bye, Gran. I'll come back again soon. Although it looks like your flower stock is being taken care of."

Chapter Fifty

Tanya was quiet on the drive home, sitting in the passenger seat while Sophie took the wheel. In the back seat, Delilah's snores were permeating the car, which made Tanya smile.

"Funny how life changes so quickly, isn't it?" she said, almost as if to herself. "Who'd have thought I'd be a dog owner a few months ago?"

"Or that you'd have such a gorgeous girlfriend," Sophie added.

"That, too." Tanya paused. "A gorgeous, non-smoking girlfriend."

Sophie gave her a grin. "Six days and counting. I was worried for a while when you were playing silly buggers that I might turn into a chain-smoker, but I managed to turn it around."

Tanya smiled. "Sorry again."

Sophie stroked her leg as she glanced over at her. "I'm joking," she said. "And you know, I was thinking. Life's kinda settled a bit for you now, so you should have a party to celebrate — a belated flat-warming."

"I should?"

"You should. After all, this is a momentous time in your life, your new start. And you've got a couple of new additions you might not have expected — me and Delilah — but I hope we'll only add to your new beginning, not detract from it."

"I think you're making it just perfect."

"So what do you think? A party to celebrate your new chapter? Food, drink, people?"

"It sounds like a lot of work."

Sophie smiled. "It doesn't have to be. Just a few friends to celebrate your new beginning. I can invite mine, you can invite yours — they might all get on and we can create a lesbian supergroup."

Tanya let out a howl of laughter at that.

"Plus, I can help. Remember your new motto to let people help you?" Sophie was wagging a finger in her direction now, a grin on her face.

Tanya smiled at her. "I remember, yes, I'm not senile just yet."

"You are a few years older than me, so it's best to check these things," Sophie grinned. "In fact, I'll do a playlist, we can get some booze and Rachel can do the catering. All you have to do is show up and look pretty."

"And Rachel and Alice can swoon over each other again. Did you know they've been sending each other messages and recipes non-stop?"

"I live with Rachel — apart from work, Alice is her new

favourite topic. Shame she's straight and has a boyfriend — they'd be perfect for each other."

Tanya snorted. "That would be Alice's dream in another life," she said. "She took Jake to Rachel's restaurant the other night, you know — they loved it, especially the personal table visit from the chef."

"I heard," Sophie said, pumping the brakes as they hit some traffic.

"So this party — sounds like you've got it all worked out."

Sophie laughed. "It does, doesn't it? I'll invite everyone we know, and your job is to call Alan — he's the guest of honour. Okay?"

"Okay."

"I might even invite my dad so you can meet him."

Tanya's eyebrows both arched. "Jesus, I'm meeting the parents? This is getting serious."

Sophie gave her a wink. "It is, isn't it?"

* * *

The journey took four hours, and they made it back by 8pm, just in time to park their hire car and stroll back to their block of flats.

As they walked, wrapped in the still summer air, a strange feeling settled on Tanya. It took a few moments for her to recognise what it was, but when she did, she realised it was happiness. With Sophie and Delilah by her side, she had a new family to be a part of, and this was a family she saw lasting. She and Sophie had been in a relationship for nearly a month, and it was incredible.

Tanya was in love, no ifs or buts. It turned out, the simple act of allowing herself to be in love was enough to make it real. That, and the fact that Sophie was simply the best girlfriend in the world. She must be, to put up with her.

Sophie was more than Tanya had ever dared to dream.

They walked into their building, making sure Delilah didn't get crushed by the heavy door, and Tanya got her postbox key out.

"My favourite girls," Roger said, looking up from his desk.

Sophie beamed. "I thought tonight was your night off?"

Roger checked his watch. "The wife's picking me up in 15 minutes and we're going out for dinner."

"You have a lovely time — spoil her rotten," Sophie replied.

"I will — you have a lovely evening, too."

They walked over to the postboxes, Delilah's feet pattering on the waxed floor.

"You want me to check your mail?" Tanya asked.

Sophie shook her head. "Nah, it'll only be bills, I'll leave it for now." She paused, walking towards the lift and pressing the button.

Tanya grabbed a pile of four envelopes, put them in her bag, then turned, to where Sophie was already standing with Delilah in the lift, one finger holding the door.

"Come on, slow coach!" Sophie shouted, a look of mock-consternation on her face.

Tanya broke into a gentle jog, but just as she reached the lift door, her foot caught in the metal frame and she tripped forward, falling into Sophie and pressing her up against the back wall. The lift door slid shut behind them.

"Going up!" the announcer said, as Tanya gathered herself, head firmly planted on Sophie's shoulder, Delilah barking at their feet.

"Are you fucking kidding me?" Sophie asked, gently pushing Tanya away from her. "Is this your party piece?"

Tanya began to laugh as she peeled herself away from Sophie, planting a kiss on her lips as she did so. "When it comes to you, it seems like it might be, doesn't it?" she said. She couldn't quite believe she'd done it again, but put the two of them in this lift, and the script seemed to write itself.

Sophie shook her head, laughing now as Tanya bent down to pet Delilah. "Maybe we should make this a monthly thing, seeing as you seem so enamoured with it," Sophie said. "What do you think? Once a month you can fall on top of me in this lift and feel up my boobs."

Tanya pulled herself up straight, jaw open. "I wasn't feeling you up — I was saving myself."

"Who said I was complaining?" Sophie said with a smile. "I knew the moment you grabbed my boobs all those months ago that this could be the start of something. Even though you were terribly rude."

Tanya moved back into Sophie's space. She put one hand on her bum, pulling her close, their lips now inches apart. "And how are my manners now? Any improvement?" she asked, her heartbeat slamming in her chest as she smiled at her girlfriend close up.

"Marginal gains," Sophie replied, as the lift reached Tanya's floor. She pressed her lips to Tanya's, before breaking the kiss and stepping back, holding out her hand. "Let's just say, there's plenty of room for improvement, but we've got all the time in the world to work on it, haven't we?"

THE END

Want more from me? Sign up to join my VIP Readers' Group and get a FREE lesbian romance, **It Had To Be You!** *Claim your free book here: www.clarelydon.co.uk/it-had-to-be-you*

Also by Clare

London Romance Series
London Calling (Book 1)
This London Love (Book 2)
The London Of Us (Book 4)
London, Actually (Book 5)
Made In London (Book 6)

Other Novels
The Long Weekend
Nothing To Lose: A Lesbian Romance
Twice In A Lifetime
Once Upon A Princess
You're My Kind

All I Want Series
All I Want For Christmas (Book 1)
All I Want For Valentine's (Book 2)
All I Want For Spring (Book 3)
All I Want For Summer (Book 4)
All I Want For Autumn (Book 5)
All I Want Forever (Book 6)

Boxsets
All I Want Series Boxset, Books 1-3
All I Want Series Boxset, Books 4-6
All I Want Series Boxset, Books 1-6
London Romance Series Boxset, Books 1-3

A Note From Clare

I hope you enjoyed the story of Tanya and Sophie as much as I enjoyed writing it. Tanya was a bit of a baddie in *This London Love*, but I hope her back story explained some of her actions. I have a lot of time for Tanya! As I said in the acknowledgements, I am already writing a fourth London Romance novel, so keep an eye out for that this year.

If you have a moment, I'd also really appreciate an honest review on the site you bought it on. Reviews are hugely important as they encourage new readers to take a chance on me — if my book's got some reviews, they're far more likely to give me a try. So if you'd like more books from me, please take a moment to leave your thoughts. And it doesn't have to be a novel — even a few lines makes a difference and every review means so much!

If you fancy getting in touch, you can do so using one of the methods below — I'm most active on Twitter, Facebook or Instagram.

Twitter: @clarelydon

Facebook: www.facebook.com/clare.lydon

Instagram: @clarefic

Find out more and sign up for a free lesbian romance at: www.clarelydon.co.uk/it-had-to-be-you

Email: mail@clarelydon.co.uk

THANK YOU SO MUCH FOR READING!

Printed in Great Britain
by Amazon